"You are in a betting mood, aren't you?"

Ariel's heart jumped at his words. If he kissed her now she would be in trouble. "Isn't this what they call sexual harassment in the workplace?"

"Perhaps." His breath was seductively warm. "But I'm positive this will completely cross that line." He hooked his free arm behind her waist and slid her lower body tight against his.

They were alone. In his lair. If he didn't back off now, there would be no stopping his beast. So he ignored the dragon's demands and issued one of his own: "Why are you here, Ariel?"

Rather than answer she shook her head and got to the crux of the present matter. "Seducing me will gain you little."

He took his time trailing his gaze to where their bodies met. Returning his focus to her face, he smiled. "Who do you think you're fooling?"

Books by Denise Lynn

Harlequin Nocturne

Dragon's Curse #140

Harlequin Historical

Falcon's Desire #645
Falcon's Honor #744
Falcon's Love #761
Falcon's Heart #833
Commanded To His Bed #845
Bedded by Her Lord #874
Hallowe'en Husbands #917
  "Wedding at Warehaven"
Bedded by the Warrior #950
Pregnant by the Warrior #978

DENISE LYNN

Award-winning author Denise Lynn has been an avid reader of romance novels for many years. Between the pages of books she has traveled to lands and times filled with brave knights, courageous ladies and never-ending love. Now she can share with others her dream of telling tales of adventure and romance.

Denise lives with her real-life hero, Tom, and a slew of four-legged "kids" in northwestern Ohio, USA. Their two-legged son, Ken, serves in the USN. You can write to her at P.O. Box 17, Monclova, OH 43542, or visit her website, www.denise-lynn.com.

DRAGON'S CURSE

DENISE LYNN

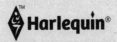

TORONTO NEW YORK LONDON
AMSTERDAM PARIS SYDNEY HAMBURG
STOCKHOLM ATHENS TOKYO MILAN MADRID
PRAGUE WARSAW BUDAPEST AUCKLAND

Recycling programs
for this product may
not exist in your area.

ISBN-13: 978-0-373-88550-3

DRAGON'S CURSE

Copyright © 2012 by Denise L. Koch

All rights reserved. Except for use in any review, the reproduction or utilization of this work in whole or in part in any form by any electronic, mechanical or other means, now known or hereafter invented, including xerography, photocopying and recording, or in any information storage or retrieval system, is forbidden without the written permission of the publisher, Harlequin Enterprises Limited, 225 Duncan Mill Road, Don Mills, Ontario M3B 3K9, Canada.

This is a work of fiction. Names, characters, places and incidents are either the product of the author's imagination or are used fictitiously, and any resemblance to actual persons, living or dead, business establishments, events or locales is entirely coincidental.

This edition published by arrangement with Harlequin Books S.A.

For questions and comments about the quality of this book please contact us at Customer_eCare@Harlequin.ca.

® and TM are trademarks of the publisher. Trademarks indicated with ® are registered in the United States Patent and Trademark Office, the Canadian Trade Marks Office and in other countries.

www.Harlequin.com

Printed in U.S.A.

Dear Reader,

I've missed you at the Lair during our long phase of renovation. Thanks for stopping by once again. A lot has happened since last we met—while Braeden and Alexia found and protected the emerald dragon pendant, and began translations of the family's ancient grimoire, there are more dragons to be found, more pages to bring to life....

And more secrets to share.

While you're here, keep an eye on Cam and Ariel—their "mating" dance is quite entertaining at times. It'll be interesting to see who can outfox whom.

Enjoy your stay, but beware, not just of the sharp swords, but of Ariel's stun gun. It's a highly charged weapon and she knows exactly how to use it—just ask Cam.

Take care,

Denise Lynn

For my sister, Cheryl—I freely bequeath to you all of Cam's magic, may it serve you well.
Much love, always.

Chapter 1

Mirabilus Keep—Isle of Mirabilus—Current Year

*D*ragons don't exist.

Ariel Johnson reassured herself of that simple fact for the hundredth time as she tossed the wire cutters back into the duffel bag.

It didn't matter that for all her childhood she'd dreamed of dragons. Those dreams had been nothing more than the wild imaginings of a child. In reality there were no dragons.

They just simply don't exist.

She slid a charged stun gun into the holster beneath her vest then shimmied through the hole she'd cut in the chain-link fence. Her watch vibrated against her wrist and she ducked, hiding her face in the ground. She would wait until the timed spotlight swept the area before quickly racing for the shed off the west wing of Mirabilus Castle.

Nine days ago, she'd stood at her younger brother Carl's hospital bed. She'd stared at his numerous injuries and the bullet wound. Guilt left her with one question at the forefront of her shocked mind—how could she have let this happen to him?

Even now, after she'd had several days to digest what had happened and why, her head still pounded with worry and she was sick to her stomach with the knowledge that it all could have been avoided.

And while mothering a nineteen-year-old was nearly impossible to do, especially when he no longer wanted a mother, she should have kept a closer eye on him— paid closer attention.

Since their parents' untimely deaths five years ago, Carl had become her responsibility. His welfare and safety were in her hands. Seeing him so helpless, so vulnerable, was tangible proof of her failure.

Ariel's watch vibrated again, startling her out of her painful misgivings. She ignored the throbbing of her head to rush across the darkened open space of ground and then ducked behind the far side of the shed to wait for another pass of the spotlight.

She wiped beads of sweat from her forehead. Her heart beat frantically with fear at what she was about to do. Her stomach churned harder than it had these last several days.

When their parents had died, Carl had just turned fourteen. He'd been frantic about their future in the way only a teenager could—dramatic and highly emotional. She'd promised over and over that they would be fine. She'd sworn to take care of him no matter what.

Through the years there'd been a few problems, but

nothing the two of them couldn't solve with a conversation over pizza.

During those talks, when night sometimes turned into day, they'd shared so many dreams and plans for their futures. After finishing college she was going to spend a few years working, gaining experience, and then open her own software company. Carl was going to use his inborn ability working with machines and electronics to open a repair shop next door to her. They were going to succeed together.

But dreams sometimes had a way of fading beyond reach. She had finished college with a degree in systems and landed a job as a project manager in a computer department at a local manufacturing plant.

Lately, however, she'd been so busy working—just trying to make ends meet, that she hadn't paid much attention to what Carl had been doing.

She'd soothed her guilt by telling herself that he'd graduated from high school and for the most part was capable of caring for himself.

She hadn't realized that he'd fallen in with the wrong group of people. Now, because of her inattention, his life was in grave danger.

There was no one else to blame—this was all her fault. No matter how many hours she'd had to work, or how adult he thought he'd become, she never should have let those Thursday-night pizza sessions lapse.

Upon learning about what had happened to Carl, she'd been, and still was, determined to do anything to make it all up to him. She'd quit her job to fulfill her responsibilities to her brother. Once this was over and Carl was safe, she'd find another one.

While she had never counted on risking her life for

him, she would. She had to—it meant saving his life and having the opportunity to make things right.

Ariel took a deep steadying breath, before moving to the front of the shed. She pressed the door latch, thankful that it was unlocked. Once inside, she reached out in the dark, located the shelving unit and pulled it away from the back wall.

Her hands shaking with fear and frustration, Ariel grazed the damp wall, feeling for a horizontal crack in the stone. Unable to locate the crack, she nearly cried from the overwhelming failure.

She paused for a moment to shake off the gathering coldness of doom. Fighting to regain a sense of purpose, Ariel straightened her spine and slowly inhaled a long, deep breath and then traced the width of the wall again. Finally, after the third pass, she detected the barely perceptible gap. Just as she'd been instructed, she followed the fissure with a fingertip until it made a ninety-degree bend.

Ariel traced the crack for two feet, pausing before she pressed her hand hard against the stone, to the left of the slight gap.

Her breath hitched with relief as the wall moved beneath her touch. The door swung slowly open. It scraped across the dirt floor and she paused, listening for any sign that someone had heard the sound.

She froze, barely breathing, certain she'd be discovered and hauled off to jail before she could complete her task.

When nothing but the steady lapping of water from the beach broke the silence of the night, she slipped through the narrow opening. Cold, damp, stale air brushed across her face. She held her breath and stepped into the corridor behind the hidden wall then flicked on her flashlight.

With a cursory glance at the inside of the movable wall, she made a mental note of the latch's location—she didn't want to fumble for it on her way out. After sliding the wall closed, Ariel followed the corridor, brushing spiderwebs aside with a shudder as she made her way deeper inside this hidden maze.

Carl had been forced to share what little information he knew about this secret room with his new employer, Jeremy Renalde—an extremely wealthy and powerful thief, from what Ariel could tell. Since Carl hadn't yet come out of his coma, the information about this chamber had been gained through a psychic.

At first, when Mr. Renalde had explained the process to her, she'd scoffed at the idea. She'd also scoffed at the idea of her breaking into Mirabilus. Yet here she was, looking for a puzzle box and jewelry, while staying on guard for dragons.

She didn't really believe in dragons. At least not the mythical, flying, fire-breathing kind. The beasts were nothing but folklore and dreams—an obsession she'd never been able to explain.

Her parents had indulged her when she'd been a small child by filling her bedroom with toys and posters of dragons. But when her fascination hadn't waned as she'd grown older, they'd insisted she set aside her childish fantasies and focus on things that truly existed.

It had been difficult, had felt as if she'd been cutting off a piece of herself, but to a point she had followed their orders. School, college, then work and Carl had left little time for feeding fantasies, and somewhere along the way her dreams of dragons had slipped into nothing more than childhood memories.

Mr. Renalde had only laughed at her disbelief. He had assured her that she would soon discover just how wrong her parents had been in their thinking.

So now, with less than sixty grueling hours of training, learning to use the stun gun, operate the one-person life raft and desperately trying not to scream as she jumped from a perfectly good helicopter into the water below, she had become a criminal.

The only thing that kept her from walking away was her certainty that Renalde would carry out his threat to kill Carl if she didn't bring him what he wanted. From the moment she had met the man, she'd been overwhelmed with a dire sense that he was more than a thief. She had little doubt that the man was a cold-blooded killer who would snuff out her brother's life without an ounce of remorse.

Finally, the corridor opened into a round chamber. She panned the room with the flashlight. Beneath layers of dust, more spiderwebs and grime were assorted containers, manuscript pages and maps littering every available space.

How was she supposed to find anything in this mess?

A breeze ruffled some of the papers on the small writing table in the middle of the chamber. Ariel froze and feared she was no longer alone. A sudden whoosh of sound sent her ducking behind a large wooden chest as she turned off the flashlight.

She chanced a quick glance around the chest. The hair on the back of her neck rose and her heart slammed against her rib cage. It was too dark to see anything, but she heard the heavy ruffling of what sounded like wings and the scraping of talons on the stone floor.

Had Mr. Renalde been correct about this, too? Did a mythical beast truly exist?

The urge to shine her flashlight on whatever had entered the chamber was strong, but the will to stay alive kept her from flipping the light on.

A chandelier overhead suddenly illuminated the room. She slapped a hand over her mouth to mute a gasp, as candles flickered to life and the shadow of a beast fell across the floor.

Wings folded against the long, sleek body before it turned in her direction. In that split second—before terror numbed her mind—she swore the beast smiled at her.

She'd laughed at Renalde when he'd warned her of the beast's existence. She'd fully expected to find some oversize lizard. That would have been frightening enough.

Ariel struggled desperately for breath against the hard beating of her heart. This was no lizard.

This…this…monster was not some frolicking imaginary friend that filled the dark, lonely hours of the night. It was not a dragon of her childhood dreams. Instead, with its great size, scales and lethal teeth, it was a creature right out of some late-night horror movie. One that usually killed the villagers before some reluctant warrior hero dispatched the brute.

But, there was no warrior hero at hand.

Ariel's shaking knees threatened to give out beneath her. She lunged from her squatting position to her hands and knees, quickly crawling backward—as fast and as far away from the beast as possible.

The pebbled, hard, dirt-packed floor bruised her knees and legs through the black military-style pants she wore. Her palms scraped across the floor, leaving trails of blood in their wake. Ignoring the self-imposed abuse, she scrambled to the far side of the chest.

Ariel silently cursed her trembling hands as she fumbled while trying to retrieve the stun gun from her holster. Unable to free the weapon, she swallowed a scream of desperation and closed her eyes.

Dragons don't exist, Ariel.

Her parents' words whispered in her mind. This wasn't happening. It was a dream. She tried to convince herself that when she opened her eyes, she would be back in London, sitting in a plush office. Better yet, she would be at home, still believing all was well and normal.

Hot, moist air brushed across her cheek, chasing away her last thread of hope.

Of all the gruesome deaths she could imagine, Ariel didn't want to die like this. She fell forward, her hands clasped together, facedown on the floor, begging, "Please. Please, don't kill me."

With her eyes still tightly closed, she heard the beast's scraping movement, then what sounded like the rustling of clothes and the metallic scratch of a zipper.

Confusion swirled into the fear. She raised her head and opened her eyes. Instead of a beast, she saw a man.

In that split second before cloth covered his muscular back, she swore she saw a glittering iridescent dragon etched along one shoulder blade that stretched before settling into place.

Frozen in place, Ariel blinked as the chamber was once again cloaked in darkness.

"You can come out."

His deep, raspy voice, an odd mixture of human and something not quite human, promised danger—and so much more.

"If I was going to kill you, I'd have done so by now."

Something in his tone beckoned her to trust him.

Ariel shook her head, fighting to ward off the increasing urge to obey his summons.

She couldn't permit herself to be that foolish. Not if she wanted to live. She *had* to live—her brother's life depended on her. Instead, she once again reached toward her holster, hoping this time she'd be able to free the charged weapon. Before she could even touch the stun gun, strong fingers clamped around her wrist.

Ariel shivered. The saying that life passed before one's eyes at the moment of death was true. It did—at a dizzying pace. Every mistake she'd made, each regret she carried close to her heart, flew through her mind in a flash.

As she drew in what would certainly be her last breath, the man—the creature—the changeling pulled her to her feet. They were surrounded by a darkness so black she couldn't see the end of her nose, but she sensed his nearness.

The sensual warmth of his body next to hers meant he was far too close. The feel of his breath against her cheek made her fear he'd consume her in a blaze of fire.

But instead of breathing out fire, he inhaled slowly, as if taking in her scent. His lips brushed her temple, making her heart thud even harder—faster, as he suggested, "You might want to run before I change my mind."

Ariel clutched the flashlight to her chest, realizing in that moment that he had released her wrist. Without a second thought, she turned and in the dark, raced blindly down the corridor. She bounced off the damp walls, but didn't slow her pace until she reached the door.

His deep, husky laugh followed her. It seemed to

rush against her ears as she fumbled with the latch and jerked the wall open wide enough to squeeze through.

Once outside, oblivious of the spotlight, Ariel kept running until she reached the hole she'd cut into the fence, then she dived through the opening to the other side. Renalde would have to find someone else to come back to Mirabilus, or devise a different plan.

Now that she knew dragons did indeed exist and they in no way resembled anything from her nearly forgotten dreams, there wasn't enough money in the world to convince her to return. She'd have to find another way to save her brother.

Cameron Drake stood outside the shed watching the woman's frantic escape. Anyone would be terrified to come face-to-face with a dragon. But more than fear had laced this woman's emotions.

He'd also sensed her flare of unwanted lust. To his chagrin, his beast had also sensed the brief spark of desire—with undivided interest.

An interest so strong and intense that even when he'd changed back into a human it had lingered warmly in his veins. An occurrence so out of character that he hadn't taken enough time to delve completely into the woman's mind. He'd only barely touched her thoughts.

She was here looking for a box and a piece of jewelry. Although he had no clue what kind of box or what jewelry. The one thing he was certain of was that she'd been sent by someone she greatly feared and that she felt compelled to do as she was told.

Which probably explained why he hadn't sensed any experience at thievery. This experience had been new to her, and not one she enjoyed.

So, who had sent her and how had they frightened

her into doing their bidding? More important, how had they, or she, known about the secret workroom?

There was one solitary answer that suited each question—*the Learned*. His inner beast rumbled, tearing his attention away from the woman and suddenly on alert.

The dread growing in the pit of Cam's stomach made him worry that his concerns had been valid all along—his brother and sister-in-law hadn't killed Nathan.

The wizard was still alive. Still intent on destroying the Drakes. And still intent on harnessing the magic they possessed to boost his own. The combined powers would make Nathan the Hierophant—the supreme ruler. With the ability to command everything living or dead, his reign of terror would be unstoppable.

"Mr. Drake, when did you arrive?"

"Hello, Albert. I got here just a few minutes ago." Cam turned toward the approaching caretaker. From the man's limp and slow gait, it was obvious the time for Mr. Brightworthe to retire was near. "You shouldn't be out here. It's too cold and damp."

"Could have something to do with living on an island."

"Possibly." Stating the obvious is what endeared the man to the family. The handyman-caretaker at Dragon's Lair, the family's nearly completed resort in east Tennessee, was of the same ilk.

Albert stopped next to Cameron and peered toward the fence. "Another one?"

"Looks that way." Mirabilus Castle had been broken into multiple times over the past few months. Nothing had been stolen. Property had been damaged, people killed in the attempts and yet another would-be thief was in a coma. "Except she was more interested in the workroom behind the shed than the castle."

"From the way she's moving, I'd say she came in contact with a beast."

"Maybe."

Only one other person besides Brightworthe knew about Cam's beast. And she was dead.

As close as he was to his twin brother, Cam was fairly certain Braeden had guessed that there was something else to Cam's abilities, but so far had said nothing.

Their younger brother, Sean, was too much of a skeptic when it came to magical powers and wizardry. And thankfully, Cam had successfully dodged their aunt Dani's attention.

"Should I send someone after her?"

"No." Cam shook his head at the caretaker's question. "She didn't take anything."

He swept the shoreline with an unblinking stare one last time before turning toward Mirabilus Castle. "Besides, I have a feeling she'll be back."

Ariel stared down at her brother. Carl looked so fragile and pale against the white sheets. Thankfully, he appeared to be resting peacefully.

She reached out to stroke the chestnut hair, so like her own, from his forehead. Before her fingers could make contact, the overhead lights clicked off and strong arms grabbed her from behind.

Ariel frantically fought against the steel-like grip pinning her against a rock-hard chest, but the man ignored her struggles. Easily holding her with one arm, he slapped his free hand over her mouth, cutting off her screams.

Against her ear, he said, "Mr. Renalde thinks you might have changed your mind about finishing the job."

The blood in her veins froze at the all-too-familiar voice. While Renalde's thug was frightening in the daylight, at night, alone in the dark, he was terrifying.

She'd seen what this man could do. When she'd returned from Mirabilus yesterday, she'd marched into Renalde's office to inform him that she was finished with dragons, boxes and pendants. She'd do anything else to save her brother, but she couldn't go back to that island.

Renalde hadn't seemed upset at all. Why hadn't she seen his easy manner as a clue something was dreadfully wrong?

He'd invited her to stay for lunch. A private lunch consisting not of food, but of a live demonstration of how many bones in the human body could be broken, one by one, before the victim died.

And now Renalde's cold-blooded killer had her pinned and helpless. Completely at his mercy, Ariel wasn't certain if she should pray for her life, or for a quick death.

The ceiling light clicked back on. Renalde closed and locked the door while asking, "Tell me, Ms. Johnson, are you very afraid?"

She nodded as much as the hand still clamped over her mouth would allow.

"Good." Renalde approached Carl's bed, motioning to his thug to release her.

He leaned over Carl. "Oh, my, my, Ms. Johnson. Have you ever seen anyone so defenseless or vulnerable?"

What had been fear, then terror, now turned into

abject horror. It sucked the breath from her chest and stripped away her ability to think.

Renalde straightened. He brushed the back of one knuckle lightly down Carl's cheek while pinning her with a demonic smile. "Since you seemed a little hesitant about going to Dragon's Lair, I feel it necessary to repeat myself."

She stared at him, still unable to fully believe this was nothing more than a prolonged nightmare.

"You are quite fond of young Carl."

Ariel could only nod.

"So am I. But I won't repeat myself again, Ms. Johnson. You *will* go to Dragon's Lair and you *will* do as you're told."

When she remained silent, he said, "While you are well aware that Bennett here—" Renalde nodded toward his thug, before he continued "—rather likes causing pain and suffering—" He paused, then frowning, added, "He also has a tender streak at times and is quite partial to sparing agony when allowed. Being the sensitive soul he is, on occasion he takes great pains to end lives as quickly as possible."

"I'll go." Ariel swallowed hard, trying to keep her breakfast in her stomach. "Just don't hurt my brother."

Renalde stepped away from Carl's bedside and headed toward the door, with his thug right behind. "Be in my office tomorrow morning. We'll go over the details then." He paused with his hand on the doorknob. "Oh, if you so much as think about calling the police, you'll need to make a second call to the mortuary for young Carl."

Ariel nodded her understanding. She couldn't call the police. What would she tell them? That if she didn't commit robbery and risk dying at the talons of a dragon, her brother would be killed? How many months would it take to find an officer who would believe that explanation? By then it'd be too late to save Carl.

The only thing she could do was pray that the dragon living at Mirabilus was the only one in existence.

Jeremy Renalde flicked an imaginary speck of dust from the sleeve of his custom-tailored suit coat. He glanced at the clock on his father's desk and fought back a snarl of impatience, knowing the old man kept him waiting on purpose.

Much pleasure could be gained from making his sire pay for the obvious slight. But pleasure was such a short-lived emotion. What he stood to gain would last an eternity—if he could keep his mind focused on the end goal. Jeremy settled back into the upholstered chair, making himself comfortable.

He couldn't permit himself to forget what had happened to his brothers. Their impatience and lack of attention to detail had cost them their lives. When they'd lost their focus and thought to defy their father, he'd killed them.

Jeremy had watched as their sire slowly sucked the life and power from each of them. He'd watched—and he'd learned.

The door to the office swung open, permitting his father to limp slowly into the room. Jeremy waited silently as the injured wizard eased himself into the leather chair behind the desk. He knew better than to offer assistance. The boot-licking servant who'd tried to do so yesterday was now permanently resting in a pine box six feet beneath the ground.

Jeremy thought he'd cater to his father's ego instead.

"You keep improving at this rate and I'll be headed home soon."

"You'll leave here when I say you can. Not before."

"Of course not. I'm simply relieved to see you're finally starting to heal."

His father slammed a shaking fist on the desk. "Blatherskite. You'd have been more relieved if that beast had burned me to a crisp."

There was no reason to lie. The old man would see right through any attempt. So, Jeremy said, "That would have been a terrible waste of power."

Nathan the Learned tipped his head forward to hide his smile. This youngest son of his would make him proud yet. Perhaps, between the two of them, they would finally be able to defeat the Drakes.

Until recently, the battle had always been between him and Drake wizards or near wizards. But now, just as his wife of so many centuries ago had foretold, a beast had come into play. Since this dragon wasn't born of the Dragon Lord's loins, as she'd vowed, he didn't place too much faith in her curse.

He had made the right decision in calling Jeremy home after the ordeal with the dragon that had carted him away from Dragon's Lair. Even though the beast's talons had caused him much bodily harm, Nathan hadn't requested his son's presence because of his physical condition.

The scars would eventually fade. The crushed bones of his ribs and spine were already repairing themselves nicely. He might not be able to fully restore the damaged muscles now, but the lingering pain would serve to remind him of the prize. Once he defeated his enemy, pain and walking like a broken crab would be a small price to pay.

Besides, Nathan knew that when he obtained supreme control as the Hierophant, fixing his physical body completely would be possible. For now, he was satisfied to be alive and to have his son at his side.

Jeremy was unknown to the Drakes. He would be able to move freely in places Nathan could no longer go. At this moment, he was useful.

Not for one second did Nathan believe he could let his guard down around Jeremy. After all, the boy was his flesh and blood, and he'd been trained to grab power at every opportunity. The day would come when father and son dueled for total control.

But this wasn't the day.

He looked up at his son and smiled. "True. It would have been a crime had my power faded into the air, wasted in such a manner."

Jeremy sat up straighter. "I didn't mean it like that."

"Yes, you did." Nathan brushed off his son's insincere objection before he opened a desk drawer to pull out a folder before handing it to Jeremy. "This is the list of books and websites Ms. Johnson needs to read and study before going to Dragon's Lair."

His son frowned. "Why don't I just gift her with the information?"

"Because the Drakes would sense even the slightest magic. They live and breathe magic, they'd recognize it inside her in a heartbeat."

Nathan tamped down the urge to shiver. Even the newest Drake, the Dragon Lord's wife, Alexia, had quickly learned to use magic. She'd been the one to give life to the emerald dragon pendant, creating the beast that had attacked him.

She would pay. They would all pay. Every last one of them would die slowly and as they gasped their final breath, they would feel the power seep from their body, into his. They would be fully aware of what he gained from the act.

Their deaths and the draining of their powers would provide him with the ultimate pleasure. Nathan gripped the arm of his chair, permitting his body to shiver with anticipation.

"And if she doesn't get the position?"

Nathan dragged his focus back to his son. To his amazement, Jeremy's eyes shimmered with the heat of desire. Apparently, he hoped Ms. Johnson failed.

To quell the younger man's passion, Nathan shook his head. "I fear your pleasure will have to wait. Just as mine does. I have no doubt about her ability to gain the position."

"We can't be certain of that. So, if she doesn't?"

Nearly depleted of energy, Nathan leaned his arms on the desktop. He needed to return to his chamber and cast himself into another healing sleep. But first, he had to make certain Jeremy would not thwart his plans simply because he desired the woman—or the moment of her death.

It was imperative that he regain possession of Aelthed's prison—the puzzle box. Otherwise, the ancient wizard might find a way to escape.

And since he would never be able to read the grimoire, he had no interest in that particular textbook of magic. However, he wanted that accursed emerald dragon pendant. The one that had come to life and put him in this condition.

He stared hard at his son and crooked an index finger, as if beckoning him forward. The movement caught Jeremy off guard. He leaned closer, permitting Nathan to wrap an unseen hand around the young man's neck.

"If Ms. Johnson fails to gain the position, you will fail to breathe."

Jeremy's eyes blazed with rage. Nathan squeezed harder, chasing away the anger until fear and obedience filtered into his son's bulging gaze.

"Do you understand me, my dearest child?"

His son nodded and as soon as Nathan released his grasp, Jeremy and the folder vanished.

Nathan rose slowly. Before whisking himself from the office, he turned to touch each of the dragon statues on the credenza behind him.

"Fear not, soon we will possess what's owed to us."

Chapter 2

Dragon's Lair, East Tennessee

Cameron Drake leaned farther back in his chair. With his feet propped up on the mahogany desk and the bright sunshine streaming through the floor-to-ceiling window warming him, he gave up his argument against dozing.

Glad to be home after a month-long absence, he was nevertheless disgruntled that the woman hadn't returned to Mirabilus. He'd scoured the workroom, trying to find anything that might resemble a box or piece of jewelry. Unfortunately, his search had turned up nothing.

Whatever she was looking for was either still there—somewhere on the grounds—or had never been there to begin with.

Which is why he'd waited for her to return. He needed to know exactly what she had been searching for, and he wanted to be absolutely certain she'd been sent by the Learneds before filling the rest of his family in on the details.

If he simply announced that Nathan hadn't died, his brother and sister-in-law wouldn't believe him. They were positive their magical dragon had killed the wizard.

The beast they'd conjured had flown away with the wizard in tow, and returned empty-handed, save a wooden cube it had dropped at Alexia's feet.

No matter how gruesome it might have been for the others, he wished the beast had killed the wizard right before their eyes. At least then there would be no doubt of the family's safety. As it was now, too much of Braeden's certainty was based on assumption. It seemed as if only he was doubtful of their success.

Cam stretched his neck and rolled his shoulders, hoping to ease some of the tension. It had been a long flight home from Mirabilus, even on the family's private jet.

Since his aunt had decided to return to the Lair with him, his preferred method of travel would have been problematic. He wasn't ready to let Danielle Drake know about his beast.

It wasn't that she'd be horrified—far from it. She'd probably be thrilled. And then she would want to closely study him under her mental magnifying glass. Putting it in a vernacular his younger brother, Sean, would employ—that would just suck.

Someday he'd have to work on explaining his extra ability to his family. But for right now, soaking up the sunshine was of greater importance.

"Cam." Sean's voice cut into the quiet.

With a groan, Cameron slid his legs off the desk then tapped the intercom button on the phone. "What do you want?"

"Your two o'clock is pulling up in the driveway."

Cam glanced out the window. A nondescript white panel van came to a stop in the circular entrance. But the woman who jumped out of the driver's side was anything but drab.

Her dark hair barely brushed the top of her shoulders. The navy blue suit fit her curves like a glove. Jacket just the right length, skirt hit just above the knee. The black, low-heeled pumps shined as if they'd just been taken out of the shoe box.

Her job application had raised his suspicions, which were now confirmed by her too-perfect textbook appearance. He'd already interviewed nearly fifty people for various management positions and not one of them had been dressed for Wall Street. Apparently, whoever instructed her on professional dress had used an outdated manual.

While he wasn't surprised to see she sported a white blouse beneath the jacket, he had expected some sort of faux tie—in red or maybe black. But not even a scarf covered the flesh beneath the open buttons of her blouse. His lips quirked at the flagrant display of rebellion against her mentor.

At his lengthy silence, Sean asked, "You want me to take it?"

Cam stared harder at the woman. She was somehow familiar, but from this distance, without the benefit of scent, he couldn't discern why, or from where. He shook his head and finally answered his brother, "No, I've got it. Have Jennie send her in."

Certain their new receptionist would point the woman in the right direction, Cam pulled a folder out of his top desk drawer.

Cam had interviewed a dozen candidates for this position before his trip to Mirabilus. Ariel Johnson was the first of three who were scheduled for this week.

She claimed to be a professional gardener. Her references all checked out—too well, in Cam's opinion. But unless the woman had a thing for cloying aftershave, the person who'd handled her application had been a man.

Innate curiosity had been the only reason he'd arranged an interview. Too much had happened at Mirabilus of late for him not to be suspicious of every little thing. He wanted to see if she was up to something.

While it could be possible that he was wrong, he doubted it. According to her application, she was single, which, of course, didn't necessarily mean she lived alone. Still, her references were too glowing—too over the top to be believed.

A knock at his door interrupted his thoughts. He closed the folder, then crossed toward the door.

Cam paused and took a deep breath. As he opened the door her scent wafted through his senses. Familiar smells raced through him, bringing a memory of fear and shock laced with denied lust to the fore.

He narrowed his eyes. She was familiar all right. This was the woman who'd been in the chamber at Mirabilus. She'd run like a frightened rabbit when he'd given her the chance.

And now she came willingly to the Lair?

In the guise of an overdressed and overqualified gardener?

She didn't flinch under his unwavering stare. Instead, she returned his look and smiled.

Smiled.

Whatever she was up to involved either a touch of insanity, or more bravado than any six mortals possessed.

If she *was* mortal. But he sensed nothing other-worldly, or magic.

"Mr. Drake?"

The soft, steady tone of her voice wisped against his ears before flitting across his mind. Discovering what she was up to suddenly seemed more than just a lark, it had become a priority.

He'd been unable to protect his wife. A tragedy that he would not permit to happen again. If this woman worked for the Learneds, she was a danger to his family. And he would do everything, sacrifice anything, to ensure their safety. But first he had to be sure of her involvement.

Cam eased the scowl from his face and held the door open, motioning toward his desk. "Ms. Johnson, thank you for coming. Please, have a seat."

She walked by him, insisting, "Ariel, please."

Ariel. He rolled his eyes, doubting if she'd prove to be an angel of healing, or new beginnings, as her name implied. He kept the thought to himself. Instead, he sat down behind his desk, facing her across the distance.

Ariel's stomach did a roller-coaster nosedive when he looked at her. He was…striking…to say the least. Not overtly gorgeous in a model's way. The strands of silver shimmering at the temples of his dark, sandy-blond hair lent an air of authority, certainty—as if he'd been around and knew exactly what he was doing.

She wondered if that air carried over into his personal life. A warmth slid over her cheeks at the outrageous thought.

Ariel closed her eyes. *What was she doing?* She was supposed to be here for a job interview, not checking out the would-be boss.

Yet, when she opened her eyes again, her gaze fastened instantly on his mouth and a full lower lip that was designed for kissing her senseless.

To hide the heat now flaring from her cheeks to her chest, she glanced around the room.

She'd been in homes less extravagant than this office—her home for one. From the thick midnight-blue carpet that looked more like velvet than floor covering, to the artwork hanging on the walls. Oils that appeared to be of such good quality that she wondered if they were originals. The ornate wooden frames alone were probably worth more than all her possessions added together.

Slowly turning her attention back to Mr. Drake, her gaze fell on a statue in the corner—an amethyst dragon. Her breathing hitched. The room swam around her. She swore she could feel the beast's warm breath rush across her cheek.

Like being outside in the midst of a gathering lightning storm, her skin tingled from the discharged energy. The fine hairs on the back of her neck rose in anticipation of being struck by a bolt of lightning.

She'd dreamed of nothing except dragons since the night she'd broken into Mirabilus. Nightmares that had her bolting awake with a scream on her lips and dreams that had left her strangely wanting.

To keep from racing out of his office and away from Dragon's Lair, she stared at Mr. Drake, trying to focus her thoughts on something other than the terror clawing at her chest.

His brilliant blue eyes caught and held her attention. Mesmerized by his gaze, she relaxed as a languid warmth flooded her veins, chasing away the fear. The flush of embarrassment mingled with desire caused her to quickly glance away.

Wasn't she already in enough danger? She didn't need to add more.

Cam studied her closely. For the most part, she held his gaze, glancing away now and then to look around the room. But for a second or two he'd seen her blush before looking away to hide the telltale flush.

He sensed immediately what had occupied her mind to cause such a reaction. He didn't need to delve into her thoughts. Even beneath the floral-based perfume she wore, he could smell the change in her chemistry. The flood of pheromones into the air acted like a mating call.

A call that threatened to prod his beast from self-imposed slumber. His stomach tightened in response. Cam swallowed, reining in his own rising desires.

He focused instead on the would-be criminal seated across the desk. Most humans were incapable of producing a chemical reaction intentionally. Was she one of the few who could control another person's response to her? Did she realize the danger inherent in playing with inhuman beasts?

Unable to detect that level of subterfuge lurking in her depths, he doubted if she had any control over her desires. And while he did sense an ulterior motive for being here, he wasn't able to sense any acknowledgment of who—or what—he was.

How could she? She hadn't seen him in human form—he'd doused the lights before she could have caught anything more than the briefest glimpse. And there was no way she'd recognize his voice. He'd spoken only a few words, right after shifting from a dragon. His tone would have still held the lingering rumble of the beast. It would be unrecognizable to her.

So, this interview was either a huge coincidence, or she'd been sent here.

Cam didn't believe in coincidences.

He leaned back in his chair. "Tell me, Ariel, why gardening?"

"I've always had a green thumb." Her wandering attention once again landed on the amethyst dragon in the corner of his office. For the briefest second, she froze, then quickly turned back to Cam. "I like working with my hands and living things."

The slight tremor in her voice and the tangy scent of fear filling the room alerted him to the fact that he hadn't been wrong—her presence here was no coincidence. The woman was lying to his face. She didn't want this position. She just wanted inside the Lair— most likely to find the items she couldn't locate in the workroom.

What was so important about that box and jewelry that she'd come here? There was a significance to those items that he didn't yet know—but he would.

If his suspicions were right, and she was working with the Learneds, he couldn't risk slipping into her conscious mind for answers. Not yet. Not until he knew for certain who she really was and her connection to Nathan.

The Learneds would easily be able to detect his lingering presence in her thoughts. He didn't want them to have any warning that he knew they were once again plotting his family's deaths. It was imperative that he catch them unaware.

It took less than the space of one heartbeat for him to make the decision to offer her the job. Having her at the Lair under surveillance would be safer for him and his family.

However, it took a few more heartbeats to calm the now fully awakened beast. His heightened senses, along with her uncontrolled flare of lust, had alerted the dragon sleeping inside him. And for some odd reason, the beast found Ms. Johnson—enticing.

The last thing he needed was to be drawn to a woman who worked with their enemy. Although, he was well aware that logic held little sway when it came to his darker desires.

Cam tapped the folder that was still open on his desk. "I see here that you did the greenery for the convention center in—" He leaned forward, acting as if he needed to look up the name of the town and inhaled her scent slowly.

While he wouldn't risk intruding on her thoughts, there was no hesitation to use his other—more than human—senses.

The smells of soap and floral shampoo did little to hide her nervousness. While her scent of fear was as tangy as a freshly peeled lemon, beneath it lay something far from bitter. He frowned to hide his surprise.

Her nervousness hadn't caught him off guard, but the still-lingering exotic spiced aroma of desire did. Whether Ms. Johnson was ready to admit it to herself or not, she was attracted to him on a basic level. Even though the attraction might be dangerous to both of them, it could also prove useful in the future.

Cam leaned back against his chair and finished his sentence. "Detroit...Michigan."

"Yes." She nodded. "They were pleased with my work."

Pleased? He'd been amazed that the letter of recommendation from them hadn't suggested Ms. Johnson be ordained. "I gathered that much from their letter."

She blushed and looked down at her lap. "They were a little…overwhelming with their praise, weren't they?"

"That depends." Cam asked, "Is it true?"

Ariel hated lying. She seemed to be getting better at it of late, but she still hated it. In this case, as in so many cases the past few weeks, there really wasn't any other choice. "Most of it's true. The manager and I were friends, so he embellished a bit."

From the way her pulse raced against her neck, Cam doubted if anything in the letter was true. It was more likely that the letter, the friend and her employment history were nothing more than complete fabrications.

"Actually, I think there is a request for sainthood in here somewhere." Cameron Drake closed the folder and slid it into his desk drawer. "Why don't you just tell me why you want this job and what your ideas are for the resort."

Ariel wanted to scream that she didn't want the job. Renalde had given her no choice. He'd sent in her application, résumé and references. All produced at his expense. It was only after the appointment was set when she'd been made aware of what had taken place and given copies of the paperwork to memorize.

Even knowing that the family who owned Mirabilus also owned this resort, she had to proceed as ordered, praying that she didn't run into any dragons other than the pendant Renalde wanted. Ariel glanced back at the amethyst beast in the corner and hoped there were none that lived and breathed here.

Running into one mythical beast at Mirabilus had been enough for her. She had no desire to ever repeat the experience.

She took a breath, folded her hands in her lap and

looked at Mr. Drake. She needed to convince him she was the right person for this position.

"I'll be the first to admit that I've never tackled a project this size before. But it seemed too much an interesting challenge to refuse." Her well-practiced speech rolled easily from her lips. When in truth, she could kill what was supposed to be an indestructible ivy plant in ten days—tops. What she knew about gardening and landscaping had been learned in the past couple weeks—from between the pages of books, websites and countless gardening shows on cable.

"So, you like challenges?"

No. She liked it when things were predictable. She was a project manager with a background in systems. Schedules, flowcharts and to-do lists were more up her alley. She preferred to know what was going to happen from one minute to the next. Ariel nodded. "Yes, I love them."

"Have you given any thought to the outdoor maze?"

"Maze?" She frowned, trying not to panic. Nobody had mentioned a maze. "What maze?"

Mr. Drake stared at her, and for a second she wondered if she'd just blown the interview. Finally, his hard features eased and he shook his head. "Maybe we didn't mention the maze to the agency."

Ariel swallowed. He'd tried to set her up. Why? Had he guessed she was here under false pretenses? How? She was certain she hadn't given him any clues.

Mr. Renalde had warned her what would happen if she failed him this time. He had promised her that Carl's death would fade to nothing compared to her own.

She knew Mr. Drake was waiting for a response. She leaned forward, more to settle her rolling stomach than anything else. "If you did, they forgot to mention it to me. I would have remembered something so grand. It's an outdoor maze you said?"

To let him think she was visualizing the design, she closed her eyes. He didn't need to know she was mentally scrambling to remember what she had read. "Boxwood could be an excellent choice for the border. If the parent plants are of good stock, you could propagate your own replacement plants from cuttings."

When he remained silent, she continued, "Yew could be another option." She opened her eyes and shook her head. "No, that might not work. Do your guests bring their children or pets?"

"Why?"

"The plant is poisonous. Kids might be attracted to the berries." Ariel snapped her fingers. "I've got it. Thuja…white cedar would be perfect. It grows fast, stays green year round and has that holiday-evergreen scent."

He just kept looking at her, studying her. She wondered if he was waiting for her to make a mistake. Would he know if she did? She sat back in her chair. "Forgive my eagerness. I got carried away."

"No need to apologize." Mr. Drake rose. "It shows your interest." He came around his desk and took a seat in the chair next to her.

He was tall. She'd noticed that when he'd opened the door to his office. He moved with the fluid grace of an athlete. Very little effort seemed to go into his movements.

What she'd not noticed was the length of his legs, or the width of his chest and shoulders. He dwarfed the armchair. Yet, when he stretched his legs out before him, he appeared comfortable. She only wished she could be half as relaxed.

"Since you live in Ohio, would there be a problem with moving to Tennessee?" Cam wanted to keep her talking. Her nervousness increased with every passing minute.

"No, that wouldn't be a problem at all. There isn't anything to keep me from relocating."

A sudden movement from the ancient pun-sai dragon tree on the corner of his desk caught his attention. The blasted plant was slowly inching a branch toward Ms. Johnson. Silently, he ordered, *Knock it off.* The plant shivered and he got the distinct impression it was from laughter, not fear.

He drew his focus back to the interview. "Your family wouldn't mind?"

She stared at her clasped hands. "There's only my younger brother and we don't see each other much anymore."

Cam picked up a tremor in her voice, and despair wafted in the air around her when she mentioned her brother. So, he asked, "Does his job keep him away?"

Ariel shrugged. "More or less."

"What does he do for a living?"

She hesitated. Her gaze drifted to the dragon statue, then roamed the office before she finally answered, "He's an archeologist for a museum in England."

Her lie sizzled and nearly crackled in the air between them. Once again the dragon tree stretched toward her. Cam rose and went over to pick up the plant. He wanted to get it away from the woman before she saw what it was doing.

"Oh, my, what a lovely bonsai."

The pot in his hand trembled at the insult. Cam placed it on the window ledge. "It's a pun-sai tree. It needs a little more sun than this office provides. I keep thinking I need to move it outside."

He knew full well how much the plant detested the outdoors. As if it understood the warning, the branches gently stroked his wrist before settling back into place. Cam resisted the urge to roll his eyes at the sudden pet-like obedience.

While at the window, he glanced outside. Harold, the family's right-hand man, sometimes chauffeur, mechanic and occasional handyman, inspected Ms. Johnson's van. Apparently, he didn't like the looks of the vehicle, or he'd found something suspicious, because he kept shaking his head as he scanned the undercarriage with a mirror.

Cam turned around to face Ariel and returned to his chair alongside her. "I apologize. You said your brother was an archeologist?"

"Yes."

Again, negative energy from the lie sizzled in the air. "Which museum is he with?"

"It's a private one." She unlaced her fingers to brush an imaginary strand of stray hair from her forehead. "I forget the full name—Renalde something or another."

Renalde? Cam frowned. *Renalde?* Something about that name felt…wrong. *Renalde.* The letters rearranged themselves in his mind. *R-e-n-a-l-d-e…L-e-a-r-n-e-d.* A cold, sinking feeling hit his gut like a fist. Silently cursing, he resisted the sudden urge to murder the woman where she sat.

He'd been right. About everything. Nathan wasn't dead. And this woman worked for him. So that meant the jewelry she was looking for was most likely Alexia's dragon pendant. She could look all she wanted, she wasn't getting her hands on it.

He wasn't certain what the box she sought might be—unless it was that cube Alexia's dragon had found, and he wondered why she wasn't searching for the grimoire, too. Not that it mattered, because that was another item she would never acquire—Braeden and Alexia had the family's book of Druid secrets under guard at all times.

He knew what Nathan's stake was in getting his hands on the pendant, but what was in it for her?

She was relatively new on the scene. She wasn't a member of either family—not the Drakes, nor the Learneds. She possessed not even a trace of magic, so where did she fit in?

He retraced events of the past few months in his mind. During the last break-in at Mirabilus an intruder had been shot and taken to the hospital in a coma. The young man had miraculously disappeared before they could discover anything about him. A few weeks later Ariel had *visited* Mirabilus.

Without staring, he studied her. She couldn't be more than twenty-six. The man in the coma was young enough to be her brother. While the shapes of their faces were different—the young man's was more squared at the chin, where Ariel's was more of a heart shape—they both had slight builds and dark hair. *Was the missing patient and her brother one and the same?*

If so, was she completing his job? She would fail.

His beast laughed, taunting him with the fact that she'd already succeeded at one task. She was here—the woman had gained entrance into the Drakes' stronghold.

Cam leaned closer to her. He still sensed no magic, no hidden powers, which he knew meant little. His sister-in-law hadn't possessed any powers when she'd first come to the Lair, either. But she'd quickly gained them.

The one thing he did sense was that she wasn't here of her own volition. He'd recognized that same fleeting emotion at Mirabilus, too. He had the impression that she was being forced against her will. Since she didn't seem to possess any darkness in her soul, it was likely that the Learneds held something over her.

Ariel leaned back against the chair, her eyes wide. Cam sat up straighter. Obviously he'd intruded on her space. At the moment, though, he didn't care.

What he was about to do would be dangerous. This might be a chance to thwart Nathan once and for all. Cam knew that it could cost him and his family their lives.

But from the day he'd first discovered his ability to shape-shift into a dragon, he'd been driven to outwit, and destroy Nathan the Learned. He wasn't going to start running from danger now—not with so much at stake.

Cam stood up. "I'd like to thank you for coming."

Ariel rose. He wondered at the panic briefly crossing her features, but pushed his questions aside. There would be plenty of time to find the answers.

"When would you be able to start?"

"You're offering me the job?"

Her relief caught him off guard. Cam went back to his desk as an excuse to glance out the window. Harold was no longer in sight. "The salary you requested is reasonable. Your references checked out. And you have the experience. So, yes, I'm offering you the position." He shifted his gaze to her face. "When can you start?"

Ariel fought to hide her surprise. Mr. Renalde had

told her she'd get the position. He'd been right. How had he known?

She realized Mr. Drake was staring at her, waiting for an answer. "I need to find an apartment—"

"No need." He cut her off. "We have a wing specifically for employees. An apartment can be ready in the morning."

Is that what Renalde wanted? For her to be here 24/7? What did it matter? The man wanted her to get the job and she had. Why would he care about where she lived? And if he did, she could always manufacture an excuse for Mr. Drake about how she'd changed her mind and wanted to move elsewhere.

She nodded. "That would be wonderful. Thank you, Mr. Drake. I could start tomorrow if that fits your schedule."

"Good." He extended his hand. "My father was Mr. Drake. I'm Cameron or Cam."

Ariel shook his hand. She nearly melted from the warmth of his touch. If this was what a handshake did, what would a kiss do? Confused by the direction of her thoughts, she released his hand.

He walked with her to the door. "I'll let Jennie know you've accepted the position. She'll have a contract and other paperwork for you to fill out and sign."

His words rushed against the side of her face and Ariel's heart skipped. She frowned. Something about this man was vaguely familiar. Since it was unlikely she'd have forgotten someone who could set her senses reeling as easily as Cameron Drake, she was certain they'd never met.

She stared up at him as he opened the door and placed a hand on the small of her back. His sapphire eyes shimmered. The bitter taste of fear dried her mouth and the vision of a darkened ancient workroom flitted through her mind.

Ariel shook the absurd thought from her mind to say, "Thank you."

She headed out to the receptionist wondering if she'd made a more costly mistake by accepting the position. Failure would have brought death.

Would success be worse?

Chapter 3

Something wasn't right, but Ariel reached for the door of her van and refused to look back at Dragon's Lair.

It was more the odd feeling of a presence than it was a knowing. If her off-kilter intuition could be trusted, someone watched her. Who—or what? More important, she wondered, why?

She gasped and peered into the windows at the rear of the van. What if the beast from Mirabilus was here? What if there really was more than just the one dragon changeling she'd seen on the island? What if he…it… had followed her here?

No. Ariel sucked in a steadying breath to stop the what-ifs from multiplying. Her concern for her brother, guilt about lying to get this position and the sudden re-occurrence of her dreams were fueling her fear.

She gritted her teeth against the all-too-familiar feelings of fear—terror—uncertainty. They'd become a part of her life—a part she despised.

Her days had been quiet, some might even say dull, before Renalde had entered her life.

Since then her days had consisted of constant worry and fear, not knowing from one minute to the next if she or Carl would live long enough to return to their dull, boring lives.

Never again would she complain that nothing exciting ever happened to her. She'd seen *exciting,* had witnessed the unexplained and as far as she was concerned the world was better off not knowing about magic— real magic with its wizards and beasts—that truly did walk the earth.

She had to wonder if she would ever be able to forget the events of these past few weeks. Would she ever again fall asleep and have normal dreams instead of nightmares?

Would she ever be able to walk down the street without looking over her shoulder, afraid that any moment a dragon would suddenly appear to bring an end to her life?

Stop! Ariel pushed the thoughts from her mind. She refused to let her imagination get the best of her.

Hopefully giving the appearance of a calmness she didn't feel, she climbed into the van and drove away. Once there was enough distance between her and the Lair, she glanced into the rearview mirror.

Even with dazzling sunlight as a backdrop, Dragon's Lair looked ominous. The imposing towers flanking the resort gave it the appearance of a medieval stronghold. It seemed more a place to be feared rather than revered.

Danger lived here, lurking around every corner, waiting for unsuspecting prey.

She could think of countless other things she'd rather do than take a position at Dragon's Lair. The idea of moving here, living inside what could essentially be the proverbial belly of the beast, made her ill.

Only for her brother's sake had she accepted the position. Ariel knew she would have to get as close to Cameron Drake as possible. But how close?

She'd be living under his roof while working for him. Would that be close enough to satisfy Mr. Renalde?

You will get as close as it takes to find what I need.

Ariel cringed, shuddering at the cold, ominous tone of Renalde's warning buzzing in her head.

As close as it takes? Didn't he realize where that could lead?

If you have to sleep with the man, try to smile.

Obviously he knew exactly where it could lead.

The mental image of Mr. Drake's…Cameron's… naked long legs and broad chest stirred warmth into her veins. Ariel's cheeks flamed at the sudden vision of him looming over her, with those sapphire eyes mesmerizing her, holding her spellbound, as he came closer… then closer—

Renalde's sudden burst of laughter in her mind chased away the warmth.

What had she been thinking? Did Renalde possess the power to control her desires? She waited, but nothing—no one—answered her unspoken question. Apparently she was once again alone with her thoughts.

Ariel gripped the steering wheel tighter. She might have no choice but to succeed at the task she'd been ordered to perform, but nobody was going to tell her who to sleep with.

* * *

Something nudged the ancient wizard, dragging his soul from a prolonged slumber.

Aelthed studied his prison knowing that nothing tangible could have invaded his makeshift cell. That was one certainty about being trapped inside a wooden puzzle box—nothing, and nobody, could gain entry.

Another certainty was that he couldn't escape. He'd tried for well over eight hundred years. But the spell Nathan the Learned had used still held fast.

Only love would set him free. He'd interjected that little kink in Nathan's spell of his own accord. Unfortunately, he'd not specified whose love.

He thought that once the Dragon Lord of Mirabilus found his soul's mate that he'd finally be free. Since each generation of Dragon Lords had found their specific mate, apparently that wasn't the case.

So, what had pulled him from his deep meditation, his only form of escape?

A tendril of warmth circled around him, inviting him to pay attention. He pulled away, unwilling to get involved once again.

But like a demanding child who refused to be denied, the warmth urged him to focus on the race of emotions building outside the walls of his cube.

Fear, lies and distrust wafted strong. Still, he wondered why he needed to pay attention to such mortal emotions.

Hunger, desire and need sizzled in the air. Like a thunderbolt lacing the night sky, the emotions crackled around him with an intensity that would not be ignored.

Aelthed rose, a smile curved his lips. "So, another dragon has found his mate."

From the power and hunger pulsing beneath the desire, he could only surmise it was the changeling.

A frown wiped away his smile. Getting this dragon to acknowledge his feelings wouldn't be easy. The man had fallen in love before.

Unfortunately, because of an angry, frightened curse spoken centuries earlier, his beast hadn't been interested. Unless it could find another of his kind it was cursed to thirst for nothing more than Learned blood, the dragon would never know love.

Since another of his kind didn't exist, the man had fallen in love with a human woman. And when danger had threatened the man's beloved, the dragon had ignored the frantic call for help. An act that had ended with a woman's death and a man's horrified distrust.

Aelthed worried that a part of this changeling unknowingly despised his beast. That hatred had been the downfall of the other Drake changelings.

If the Drake dragon wanted to break the curse, to live or to ever experience the fulfillment offered by taking a mate, the changeling needed to embrace his inner dragon.

Aelthed paced his cell. There had to be a way to help. He paused, his eyes widening as he sensed something else on the wind.

Impossible.

But as he focused harder, a smile curved his lips. The impossible had happened. He didn't know how and could hardly fathom the event, but somewhere out there this dragon's true mate did indeed exist and she was close at hand.

How would he bring them together? He frowned again, then finally rolled his eyes at his own stupidity.

Once again hunkering down in a corner of his prison,

he traced symbols and letters in the air. A thin trail of smoke followed his fingertip before dissipating.

With a wide grin Aelthed wrote faster, knowing for certain that the smoke would reappear as ink on the pages of the Drake family's grimoire.

Cam had watched the van disappear down the mountain and still he stood before the window, staring at the vast expanse of mountains and sky.

Something about Ariel Johnson affected him on a level he couldn't quite define—a level that made him strangely uncomfortable.

Her looks were most definitely a part of his attraction—after all, what man wouldn't be drawn to a woman with killer curves and a brazenness that belied her no-nonsense appearance? No one who looked at her would guess that beneath the all-business guise lurked a criminal and a liar.

Ariel Johnson could probably fool a not-so-discerning investigator. If they didn't pay close attention, they might miss the way the flecks of green in her hazel eyes darkened when something unsettled her. The sudden quickening of the pulse along her pale throat might have gone unnoticed by another—but he had seen it.

And his wayward beast had heard the increased tempo of her heart, along with the rush of blood flowing through her veins, when she lied.

But his odd fascination went deeper than the physical. Neither he, nor his beast, should be so aware of this woman. Her scents of fear and desire shouldn't be so easily detectable.

But they were.

Pheromones that were uniquely Ariel Johnson still lingered in his suddenly cramped office. His gut tightened, making him painfully aware that not only was he attuned to her emotions, he wanted more.

He wanted to taste her lips, stroke the softness of her flesh, feel her move beneath him and hear her sigh of pleasure as it turned to cries of fulfillment.

Muscles played across his back involuntarily. The oddly shaped birthmark on his shoulder blade burned. Cam tore his attention from the view and his thoughts from Ms. Johnson with a curse.

What the hell was he thinking? She worked for the Learneds, making her as much an enemy as they. He couldn't let desire and need cloud his judgment this way.

He swung away from the window determined to rein in the growing hunger and came face-to-face with his twin.

Braeden stared hard at him, frowning when Cam erected a wall to protect his thoughts. "The interview didn't go well?"

"It went fine." Cam sat down behind his desk. Careful not to reveal too much about the interview or his unease, he said, "She starts tomorrow."

"She?"

"Ariel Johnson." He pushed her folder across the desk. "She's too dangerous to turn down."

Braeden sat in one of the chairs in front of Cam's desk. He shook his head while thumbing through the glowing references. "Dangerous? How so?" He tossed the folder back on the desk. "All I see are some overblown references."

"She's our latest would-be thief at the castle."

Braeden's eyebrows rose sharply. "And you didn't think it worth mentioning before?"

"I wanted to be certain."

"Why did you hire her if you knew she could prove dangerous?"

"I'm not sure." He paused, unwilling to divulge everything to his brother. "Something…" Cam shrugged. "I figured it would be safer if I could watch her here to see what she's up to."

"Watch her?" Braeden leaned forward and, holding Cam's gaze, he asked, "You sure there's nothing more? Maybe another reason you want her close?"

Uncertain how to answer that loaded question, Cam frowned. The only woman he'd ever wanted that close was gone. It was doubtful anyone could take her place.

"Your pause says more than you think. I've known for a long time that you blamed yourself for Carol's death." He leaned back into the chair. "I just never knew why."

Cam absently traced the handle of the letter opener on his desk. Dragons etched on the smooth surface mocked him.

Images of an unknown beast—part dragon, part gargoyle—swooping down from the sky to attack his wife as she looked out across a deep gorge, and Carol falling from the cliff's edge as he watched in shocked helplessness flashed through his mind. Had he been able to awaken his dragon, Carol would still be here and these cold knots of failure and fear wouldn't still be eating at him.

While he could live with the failure and the fear, what he could hardly bear at times was the guilt. Guilt because he'd stood there frozen with shock. Guilt and rage because his dragon hadn't cared enough to even blink at the threat of danger.

He forcibly shook off the memories and answered his brother, "It's my fault because I did nothing."

Instead of rehashing the argument they'd had countless times over this very topic, Braeden frowned. Finally he said, "Tell me about this Ariel Johnson."

"Not much to tell. She broke into the workroom at Mirabilus."

"And you're certain it was her?"

"Without a doubt. I saw her, but she…bolted when she saw me." It wasn't exactly a lie. She had bolted from the island once he'd released her.

"How does that explain why she's here?"

"I think she's related to the missing coma thief." He explained about Ariel's brother and the timing that made him believe the thief and brother were the same person.

Braeden nodded in agreement. "Who'd she say her brother worked for?"

"A Renalde." Cam waited for Braeden's response.

"Renalde." Braeden frowned before repeating, "Renalde. I can't think of anyone with that name."

Cam grabbed a piece of paper and a pen. Beneath the name Renalde, he wrote *Learned* and pushed the paper toward Braeden.

His brother stared at it a moment before he nearly growled. "Learned." He cursed. "Nathan. I wonder if he's still alive."

"I'm sure he is. And since I sense no magic swirling around Ariel, I'm certain either he, or a member of his clan, is personally controlling her."

"Probably someone else under Nathan's orders." Braeden crumpled the paper and tossed it into the garbage. "You can't go against them alone. I'll call off my trip."

Even though he disagreed, Cam wasn't going to argue. "Maybe, maybe not. Either way, I don't need

you here right now. You know they aren't going to attack tomorrow—they can't."

The spells surrounding the Lair were too powerful for the Learneds to break. If another wizard came
within sight of the property uninvited, every Drake
would instantly know and be ready for whatever danger presented itself.

When Braeden remained silent, Cam asked, "Ariel
was sent here for a reason, don't you think it wise to
discover it?"

His brother nodded. "Yes, but—"

"No." Cam stood up. "There are no *buts*. Your wife
is seven months along with twins. She and the babies
are your main concern. I can take care of things here."

When a look of indecision crossed Braeden's face,
Cam said, "Go. See to Alexia. Make sure she's safe.
She's more important than anything else, including the
Lair." To drive it home, he added, "Besides, I can con-
tact you at will if and when I need you."

The door to the office opened a crack. "Are you two
still in here?"

Braeden answered his wife with an obvious lie. "No,
I'm in our apartment packing."

He rose and looked at Cam a moment before saying, "You damn well better call if you need anything."

"I will. Go."

Cam waited for his brother to disappear before
turning to once again stare out the window. He'd call
Braeden only if he absolutely had to. While he didn't
expect any trouble he couldn't handle, a part of him
hoped that Ariel Johnson wouldn't prove too easy an
adversary.

Chapter 4

Pockets of dense fog kept Ariel alert on her drive back up to the Lair the next morning. Without warning, the road ahead would be obscured from view and then just as suddenly the fog would disappear.

She lessened her grip on the steering wheel of her van only when the Lair came into view. But tightened it again the moment she saw Cameron Drake standing by the studded double doors.

Ariel hadn't expected the man to welcome her personally. She felt oddly as if a dragon was bidding her welcome to his lair as he stirred the boiling cook pot.

She threw the van in Park, fighting to calm her overwrought nerves and overactive imagination. While she knew that danger resided here, she doubted if anyone, or anything, was actually waiting to use her as the prime ingredient for a stew.

Cameron opened her door. "Good morning. Have you had breakfast yet?"

Ariel couldn't help herself, she gasped at what she hoped was an innocent question.

His eyebrows rose briefly at her response. Before he could say anything, she quickly swung out of the van, stumbled and ended up against the solid plane of his chest.

Cameron grasped her shoulders. "Steady there."

The touch of his hand lingered, sending a frisson of awareness through her. When she glanced up to apologize, the vision of him lowering his mouth to hers sent a rush of blood to her head.

She swayed against him and swore she felt him gather her close before he stepped back, keeping a hand on her shoulder. "Are you all right?"

Ariel shook the strange imaginings from her mind. "Yes, fine, thanks. I just moved too fast, I guess."

"You need breakfast."

"No, not really." She shook her head as the thought of food made her stomach knot. "But some coffee would be wonderful."

"We've got plenty." Cam followed her to the rear of the van. "Let me help with your things, then I'll show you where we hide the java."

When he grabbed her old battered briefcase, she held her breath, praying the latches didn't decide now would be a good time to give out.

She choked back a sigh of relief when he handed her the satchel intact. The last thing she needed was to have her new boss see all her notes and research on basic gardening. She feared this game of charades would be up before they played the first round.

"Morning, Ms. Johnson."

Ariel turned to see an elderly white-haired man approach pushing a baggage cart.

"Good morning…"

"Harold." Cam supplied the name, adding, "Harold is the lifeline that holds this place together."

The older man snorted. "Just the general maintenance man." He started unloading her suitcases. "I help out where I can."

Cameron piled the last bag onto the cart and shut the van's doors. "Watch him, Ariel, when he starts in with the modest act, he's out for something."

Harold chortled. "A day off would be nice."

"You had one last year."

"Oh, yes, I suppose an extra day off every hundred and fifty years is asking a bit much." Cameron frowned as the older man winked at her. "A bunch of slave drivers is what these Drakes are."

Ariel laughed at the man's joke, hoping the tremor of nervousness wasn't too apparent. "I'll keep that in mind, Harold."

"If there's anything you need, miss, you just holler and I'll see what I can do."

"Thank you, I'll do that. Please, call me Ariel."

She and Cameron followed Harold into the Lair. Once in the lobby, Jennie, the receptionist she'd met yesterday, called out, "Mr. Drake, a moment, please."

After Harold sauntered off with the baggage cart, Cameron excused himself, giving Ariel time to collect herself and to survey her surroundings. She'd noticed yesterday that the floor was planked wood made to look old with scuffs, knots and faded spots here and there.

Suits of chain mail and plate armor flanked the arched stone doorways. Shields and ancient weapons mounted on the walls, along with iron wall sconces, made the lobby look like a great hall in a medieval castle.

An appropriate setting for a place called Dragon's Lair, she guessed. Unfortunately, all her research on commercial gardening covered tropical-type gardens. She doubted if something like that would fit into this decor.

Now what would she do? Panic wormed its way into her head. If she couldn't come up with something, he'd realize she had no experience for this job whatsoever. The cold dread only increased when Cameron returned with an odd expression on his face.

"All the completed apartments in the employee wing are occupied."

The panic escalated. Where would she stay? Mr. Renalde had already told her that even though it would be impossible for him to communicate with her while she was on the Drakes' property, it was the perfect option. He wanted her close—and this would keep her as close to the Drakes as possible.

His being unable to communicate with her had seemed a blessing until he'd added that if she didn't check in with him at her appointed times, meaning she'd have to find excuses to leave the grounds, her brother's life would be forfeited.

What would Renalde do when he discovered she wasn't going to be living at the Lair?

Cameron's expression lighted. "No problem. For now, we'll put you in the family wing."

Ariel blinked. "Family wing?" Something about the idea of living so close to him and his family didn't seem right—or safe. "That isn't necessary."

"The fog settles in without warning. I won't have you driving up and down the mountain every day. There are plenty of rooms. We'll put you in a suite at the other end of the floor for your privacy."

She followed him to the far side of the lobby. A mural of a dragon battling with a knight covered the expanse of the wall. Were it not for the floor indicator above a barely perceptible seam in the mural, she wouldn't have realized there was an elevator behind the painting.

No matter how beautiful the painting, she couldn't help noticing that everywhere she looked, she saw dragons. Ariel shivered, wondering if this was an omen, or simply a manifestation of her worried mind.

The elevator doors whooshed closed behind them, increasing Ariel's feeling of unease. She moved to a far back corner, suddenly certain that moving to the Lair had been a very bad idea.

As Cameron turned toward her, his cell rang and he moved to the opposite corner to take the call.

His voice was too low, his one-word responses too brief for her to make any sense of his conversation, giving Ariel more time to ponder her situation.

Her knowledge of the Drakes was limited. The only information she had about them came from Mr. Renalde.

At first she'd thought the Drakes simply possessed items Renalde wanted—the dragon pendant and the puzzle box. But after meeting with him yesterday, Ariel realized he viewed them as something more than just a mark he wanted to rob. The Drakes were his enemy.

It wasn't so much what he said as the way he'd said it. When he'd given her his final orders, he'd half whispered something about making the Drakes suffer a very long and painful death.

What would she do if Renalde dropped the matter

of their deaths into her hands? Stealing was one thing. Murder was another story entirely.

The Drakes had done nothing to her, or Carl. They were her enemies only because they stood in the way of gaining the items she needed to give to Renalde. She wasn't going to be responsible for their deaths.

Besides, she couldn't. The mere thought of killing something or someone was so abhorrent that it wasn't even a consideration. That was something Renalde would have to do himself.

But he'd stated that he couldn't come onto the Drakes' property. She didn't know why, but she hoped that was true. Perhaps then he would never get the opportunity to do them physical harm while she was present.

Just as the elevator stopped and the doors parted, Cameron laughed.

The hairs on the back of Ariel's neck rose as she recognized the same deep laugh that had followed her escape from the chamber at Mirabilus. She stared at her new boss, clenching her hands into fists, trying to fight back the terror clawing at her chest, making it nearly impossible to breathe, let alone scream in fear.

Cameron clicked his cell off and then turned to Ariel. "I'll show you to your…" He paused, frowning. The woman was pale—far too pale. Her eyes were huge, her hands clenched as she mutely stared at him.

Even though the elevator had stopped and the doors were open, she seemed frozen to the back wall. "Ariel?"

He reached toward her, pulling his hand back when she jerked away from his touch.

He ignored the urge to dip into Ariel's thoughts, relying instead on her body language and what he could sense. The closer he got to her, the more she seemed to shrink into herself.

He'd obviously done something to frighten her. The sharp scent of pure fear swirled from her to fill the elevator and Cam frowned at the sharpness of the icy chill in the air surrounding them.

Standing in the elevator wasn't going to get them anywhere, so he reached a hand toward her. "Ariel?"

She jerked away with a gasp.

Determined to banish her terror and get to the bottom of the cause, Cam swept her from her feet and into his arms.

Ariel's eyes widened farther, she opened her mouth as if to scream and promptly passed out.

Cameron's emphatic curse brought his brother Sean into the hall. He looked at the woman in Cam's arms then said, "We really need to work on your method of picking up dates." Sarcasm dripped from his voice. "Don't you think the conversation's going to be a bit one-sided?"

"Shut up and open my door." Cam added, "The key is in my pocket."

Sean dug the key card from Cam's jacket pocket as they headed down the hall. Opening the door, he asked, "So, who's the unfortunate lady?"

"The new gardener." Before Sean could voice anything else, Cam kicked the door shut in his brother's face.

At a loss, Cam stood in the small foyer. *Now what?* If he took her to a bedroom and she woke up there, it was a safe bet she'd misconstrue his intentions.

His intentions? He wanted to laugh at the absurd thought. The woman was the Lair's gardener—not a romantic interest.

Although, it had been a while since he'd held a woman this close. Truth be told, he liked the feel of her in his arms. Her heart beating against his chest made him long to hold her even closer. How much better would it feel if she came into his arms willingly?

Cam shuddered. Where had that nonsense come from? He'd vowed to shun relationships after Carol's undeserved death. Since he couldn't guarantee their safety, he wasn't about to become involved with any woman—especially not this one. He crossed to the living room and laid Ariel on the sofa.

He straightened and stared down at her, wondering why he suddenly felt so empty. She was the enemy and an employee—a temporary one at that. Cam was certain that once he figured out why she was having to help the Learneds and confronted her, she'd be running back to her real boss as fast as she could.

But until then…he brushed an escaped curl from her face…until then he'd enjoy uncovering her secrets layer by layer.

Unable to resist the urge, Cam stroked her cheek with the back of his fingers. The softness of her skin was warm beneath his touch.

Even though he knew it would only create untold problems, he sat on the edge of the sofa. Something oddly comforting—almost inviting—washed over him.

He closed his eyes against the feelings making this woman—his enemy—seem somehow right, only to find himself taking flight in his mind.

His beast had taken control. As the mountains and streams fell away below him, a cool breeze rushed across his wings. His cares and mundane human concerns vanished as he reveled in the freedom of the air and warmth of the sun.

Just beyond the edge of his human awareness, Cam sensed that he wasn't alone—some other magical beast soared with him. Since he detected no danger, his defensive instincts remained dormant.

Never before had he sensed another of his kind. If any changelings besides him existed, they'd made it a point to hide from him.

Curious, he dipped a wing and craned his neck to look back. The air behind him was empty. He was as alone now as he'd ever been. Why had he thought it would ever be any different?

Heavy of heart and strangely ill at ease, he folded his wings snuggly against his body. Once again the air rushed past him, turning cold and damp as he descended into the shadows.

The touch of a hand resting lightly on top of his own jolted him back to reality. He looked from the hand, so small and pale compared to his, to Ariel.

Her eyes were still closed, but her features had relaxed. She appeared to be sleeping. If the seductive smile curving her lips was any indication, her dreams were more than just pleasant.

Did she dream about a lover from her past, or the present? Or, were her dreams giving her a glimpse into the future?

He shouldn't, Cam knew it would be an intrusion of the worst kind. But knowing that it would be the perfect way to discover her mission without detection, it was impossible to resist.

Like his aunt and Braeden, he could read minds. But the precise order of an active human mind, when perceived in more than quick snatches, tended to confuse and upset his beast.

However, he could leisurely take his time to see and

feel the dreams of other people. He had never been certain if it was him or his beast, but the unguarded, sometimes telling, and often frantic working of the dreamworld was within his reach.

Unwilling to miss an opportunity to gain insight and possible answers to his questions about Ariel and perhaps find a way to protect her against the Learneds, Cam shook off his hesitation and leaned forward.

Gently, so he didn't waken her, he cupped Ariel's cheeks between his hands. An electrified tremor, like a bolt of lightning, raced up his arms.

Undaunted by the brief shock, he closed his eyes and slipped unobtrusively into her dream.

Chapter 5

At first Cam wasn't certain where Ariel's dream had taken him. The surroundings caught him off guard. He hadn't been prepared to walk into a nightmare, not from the sensual look on her face. While it wasn't unusual to find that he'd walked into some night-terror dimension, he'd expected to find her in a social setting flirting with an unattached man.

Another glance told him this wasn't a nightmare. Instead, clear blue skies surrounded them. Cool, crisp air rushed by him as if he was flying. He looked down at mountains, valleys and streams below.

Again, not too unusual, as flying without the aid of mechanical devices, or wings, was another common dream device for humans. However, this seemed…different…somehow.

The look on her face was an expression of pure unadulterated bliss. Feelings he could understand completely. The freedom of being airborne, without restraints or limitations, was an addicting habit—one he had no intention of breaking.

But he sensed a deeper emotion of sharing, of oneness within her. As if she was enjoying this journey with someone she dearly loved.

Is this what it would feel like to share joy with someone? The feeling had become so foreign to him, a longing he'd forgotten he'd ever experienced. It was more than just a warmth, more than a welcoming comfort.

Jealousy licked at him. It teased him for no reason other than he'd intruded where he didn't belong. Cam reminded himself that this wasn't his experience. Any emotion he felt was nothing more than an extension of her dreams.

He set aside the unnatural emotions and looked around for her partner. Careful to keep his distance, Cam circled around her, finding nothing until overhead a dark shape came into view.

He slowed, falling behind her to watch as she soared higher. Ariel flew closer to the shadow. Cam held his breath. *Would she be welcomed or attacked?* But the beast paid little attention to her. Instead, it turned its focus toward Cam.

Fascinated by the odd situation, Cam paused. Never before had an object in a dream—human or otherwise—noticed him, let alone focused so much anger in his direction.

Normally his presence in a dream went unnoted. Not a participant, he was nothing more than an observer—invisible to those in the dream. But this time, pure, white-hot rage threatened to burn him. The shadowy beast circled. Then, with wings angled back for speed, head held low and blazing stare pinned solely on its target, it dived toward him.

Sun glinted off the dragon's body. Iridescent scales sparkled in the light. Sapphire eyes glimmered with deadly intent.

Cam cursed with the realization that fighting this beast was impossible. Ariel was in control of this dream, not him. The outcome to any confrontation would rest solely in her hands. A dangerous prospect for someone not considered a friend.

Battling this particular dragon would be foolish. Worse, it would literally be suicide since the beast was him.

There were tales that stated if you died in a dream, you died in life, too. Cam didn't believe that, but he wasn't immortal and had no desire to put the myth to a test.

More confused than he'd been before stepping into this dream, Cam pulled free.

He rose and moved away from the sofa—away from Ariel. He'd taken care to make certain she hadn't seen his face in human form at Mirabilus. She had no magical powers—of that he was certain. He and his family would have known the second she'd crossed onto the Lair's property if she did. So, she couldn't possibly know that he was the dragon changeling she'd seen in the ancient workroom.

She hadn't seen him in dragon form long enough to have conjured such an accurate replica in her dream. Besides, what miniscule view she'd had would have been distorted by her terror.

And that beast *had* terrified her. Cam had recognized the scent of fear, and heard the rush of blood flowing through her veins preparing her for flight.

So it made no sense that she would now dream of the beast that frightened her so.

Cam crossed the room to stand before the glass sliding doors. Thick fog obscured what had earlier been a panoramic view of the mist-dotted mountains and cloudless sky.

His mood mimicked the atmosphere. The interested curiosity that he'd woken up with was now leery trepidation.

Something had frightened Ariel in the elevator enough to make her pass out. And something had her dreaming of him in dragon form—even if she didn't realize it was him.

He'd known that hiring Ariel could prove a mistake—he hadn't been wrong. She'd been here less than an hour and already his questions, not to mention his unease, were growing. This hadn't been his intent. He was supposed to be uncovering answers.

A bloodcurdling scream tore his attention away from his concerns.

Cam spun around to see Ariel struggling with something on the sofa. She screamed again, kicking and pushing at the air as if trying to push something away.

"Ariel." Cam returned to her side. "Wake up." He touched her shoulder, dodging her flailing fists.

His initial attempts to awaken her were having no effect, so he grasped her shoulders to shake her. "Ariel, it's a dream, wake up."

She opened her eyes and stared at him a second before pulling free of his hold to bolt from the sofa.

Ariel scrambled away. She needed to escape, needed to find a way to shake off the nightmare still haunting her. It had been one thing to dream of a dragon. But it had been another thing entirely to dream of turning into one herself. The thought terrified her and made her suddenly afraid for her sanity.

She choked on a strangled breath, desperately needing air. It felt as if the walls were closing around her, making it hard to breathe, impossible to think.

She thought she'd recognized his laugh in the elevator as the one from the dragon-man at Mirabilus. But now, she wasn't sure. She wasn't sure of anything.

Cameron Drake stood between her and the door. So she spun around and fumbled with the lock on the sliding doors. Unable to force her trembling fingers to cooperate, she bit back a cry of frustration.

"Ariel." His voice was soft, deep, as he approached.

She wasn't about to be fooled by the soothing tone. Holding out a hand to ward him off, she nearly begged, "Please, stay away."

Her quivering words did nothing more than make him slow his approach. She swallowed hard, then ordered more firmly, "Stop. Stay away."

To her relief he stopped halfway across the room. He held his hands out with his palms up. "I'm not going to hurt you."

Ariel laughed weakly then batted at the door handle. "I need air."

Cameron merely moved his hand to the left slightly. The lock clicked and the door slid open. It was all she could do not to scream before stepping out onto the fog-shrouded balcony.

Ariel leaned against the railing, hanging on for dear life as her head spun. She dragged in deep gulps of breath, praying the cool damp air would help clear her mind.

"I won't hurt you," Cameron repeated from not more than four feet behind her.

She crowded closer to the railing, unable—unwilling—to admit her true fear. Instead, she whispered, "I know."

His sigh echoed into the fog. "Tell me what happened."

That was the last thing she had any intention of doing. She shook her head and said, "You people aren't...normal."

"That depends on how you define normal."

At least he hadn't lied and denied her claim outright. "What are you?"

"A man."

The certainty of his answer provided a measure of relief. But the tone of his answer warned her that he wasn't going to tell her anything. She didn't need him to supply information. While he wasn't a dragon, she was already well aware that he was like Renalde. Both men possessed some otherworldly power that made them far from normal.

It made them dangerous.

The danger Renalde presented was obvious. But the danger from Cameron Drake was more insidious—he threatened not her life, but her sanity and that part of her she'd hidden away for what seemed an eternity—her heart.

And from the dire longing throbbing deep in her chest, it was quite probable that he could also threaten her very soul.

She needed to keep her distance from this man. Ariel could not risk her brother's life. Not even for a man who could prove to be her other half.

She forced herself to turn around and face Cam. "I gather this isn't my apartment."

"No, it's mine." A devilish smile curved his full lips. "But you're welcome to stay here if you'd like."

His offer wasn't serious, but it would serve him right if she accepted. Unable to find the nerve to do so, Ariel ignored his teasing response. "If someone could show me to my room, I'll take my leave."

"Just like that?" One eyebrow hiked briefly into an arch. "You pass out in my arms, have a nightmare on my sofa and I get no explanation?"

How was she supposed to explain her reaction to his laughter in the elevator when doing so would only incriminate her as a thief?

There were times when a lie was the appropriate response. As far as she was concerned, this was one of those times.

Ariel shrugged. "Drop in blood sugar from not eating breakfast, I guess."

His narrowed gaze let her know he didn't believe her. But unless he could prove otherwise, she wasn't changing her story.

"That might explain the passing out. But what about the nightmare?"

The temptation to use the same excuse was strong. Unfortunately, she had no idea if it was plausible or not.

"I don't know—" Ariel paused, making it up as she went along. "—passing out…unfamiliar surroundings." She shivered from the cool damp air. "Strange, creepy atmosphere."

The woman was lying. Other than calling her on it, there was little he could do.

Ariel had already realized he was different from normal men, so he couldn't grill her about the dragon in her dream. Doing so would only prod her into asking questions he didn't want to answer.

He wasn't about to admit that he was the dragon changeling she'd seen at Mirabilus until she confessed to being the thief. And if he read her hesitation and expressions right, she had formed the same plan.

So, for now, it was a stalemate. Not that it mattered. In the end he would prove the victor.

Cam waved toward the entry door. "I'll show you to your apartment."

Ariel followed him out into the hallway. He explained. "There're two apartments in each hallway. I'm in thirteen-three." He handed her a key card as he led her around the corner. "You'll be in thirteen-five."

"Thirteen? I thought it was bad luck to have a thirteenth floor?"

Cam laughed. "If you believe luck exists, it might be bad."

"I take it you don't?"

"Believe in luck? No. But I realize others do, so none of the suites on this floor are available for guests."

He nodded at an archway as they walked by it. "The middle area through there is a common kitchen, bar and entertainment center." Remembering her earlier request, he added, "And there's always a pot of coffee on. Help yourself."

"Thank you."

He stopped in front of her door. "I'll leave you to get unpacked and settled in."

Ariel opened the door, turned around and leaned against the jamb. "I need to apologize."

"For what?"

She looked at the floor. "This was an awful way to start my first day on the job."

Her words were barely above a whisper. Cam moved closer to lean against the other side of the doorway. The warmth stealing over him at their nearness caught him off guard.

Urges to protect her and to claim this woman as his warred deep in his gut. He understood the second urge—Ariel Johnson was a desirable woman. Her sultry scent and luscious form made for a seductive package.

What he didn't understand was his urge to protect her. She wasn't like him and she wasn't his to protect. Besides, he sensed no danger close at hand. No threat— seen or unseen—lurked around the corners. The only explanation he could find for the urge was her tone of contrition and her weak, vulnerable stance.

Cam took her hands in his. "It's Saturday. Your first day isn't until Monday."

She stared at their joined hands, jumping slightly as he stroked his thumb across the top. He heard the rush of blood through her veins and felt her pulse quicken against his palms.

"Still, I've made a horrible first impression."

His slumbering dragon rumbled awake, coming to life at the tremor of her voice. The beast wanted to comfort her, wanted her to look up so he could gaze into her eyes.

Gently coaxing her closer, Cam brushed off her concern. "No, you haven't." When she stood mere inches from him, he lowered his head. "Your first impression happened yesterday and it was fine."

Ariel turned her face up toward his. "But—"

He stopped her words with his lips a hairbreadth from hers. "No buts."

"I..."

Cam held back a groan as her breath washed across his lips. He wanted to kiss her, to taste her. The burning mark on his shoulder blade and the clawing beast in his chest wanted more.

Just a kiss. That's all he wanted. It was all he'd take. He quelled his rebellious beast with a sharp, silent *No*.

This time the dragon listened. Cam knew he'd not be so lucky in the future. But at least now he'd be permitted to touch, to taste the woman leaning against his chest.

She parted her lips, granting him the taste he'd wanted. Her hesitantly returned kiss tasted of fruit—sweet, yet not cloying.

Cam gathered her closer, savoring the feel of her in his embrace and the taste of her on his lips.

Beneath the floral perfume she'd used, he once again caught the exotic aroma of spices—frankincense, myrrh, cinnamon, clove—a magical combination that blended perfectly, creating her unique pheromones.

This scent, belonging only to Ariel, branded an imprint onto his conscious.

She sighed, relaxing against him, offering herself without reservation. Her easy surrender chipped at his willpower, making it nearly impossible to keep a rein on his desires and wants.

Before his dragon took over, Cam regretfully broke their kiss.

Ariel stepped back and looked away. "I…I don't normally…"

Cam realized by her flushed cheek and stammering that she was embarrassed. Guilty for causing her discomfort, he pulled her back against his chest. "Don't."

Against his shirt she mumbled, "This isn't appropriate, you're my boss."

He brushed his chin across the top of her head. "Right, I'm the boss. You have to do as I say."

She shook with laughter. "We just met, this is insane."

He didn't disagree. The need to touch her, to hold

her close was insane. The only logical reason for doing so was that unbridled lust drove him to take a kiss, and lust was still urging him to take more. "Perhaps." He released her. "Unpack. Settle in. Meet me in the lobby at two and I'll show you around the Lair."

Ariel nodded, then walked into her apartment without another word.

Aelthed held his shaking stomach and fell into the corner of his prison cackling with glee. So far this Drake twin, this dragon changeling of Mirabilus, had made grave errors.

First, he'd promised his sister-by-marriage that while she was away, he'd guard her possessions—the emerald dragon pendant was now locked in a safe in the twin's office, along with the grimoire.

But unbeknownst to him, he along with everyone else seemed to have lost track of the old wooden puzzle cube—the one Aelthed called home. The changeling should have locked the cube away, too, instead of leaving it unattended on a bookshelf in his brother's apartment.

A fortunate mistake for Aelthed, it allowed him to hear and envision what was happening. More fortunately, since he was of the dragon line, they'd been unable to detect his weak magic as he'd practiced until he was able to levitate his cube, unseen, to the basement. To his relief, it seemed that his powers, which had been waning through the years, were now increasing.

Another error had been the changeling's interest in Ariel Johnson.

Enemy or not, this woman was the dragon's mate. Of that Aelthed was certain. It hummed in the air, vibrating through the Lair. There would be no way around that simple fact for the changeling.

Whether his human form eventually fell in love with the woman or not made little difference. His beast would never let the female go. It would kill her first.

One thing he needed to do was to arm the changeling with knowledge of the ancient curse. Somehow he had to get the grimoire into the woman's hands.

Chapter 6

Ariel clutched the Lair's map in her hand, making certain she wouldn't lose the thing. Even with her guided tour, she knew that she'd never find her way around the resort again without the map.

Cam plucked the key card from her hand. "Let me." He unlocked and opened the door to her apartment, then to her consternation followed her inside.

"You found everything to your satisfaction?"

She quickly scanned the lush surroundings. "With this apartment?" When he nodded, she said, "No. It's too much. I don't live like this."

He seemed surprised by her honest answer. "Like what? With a roof over your head?"

She ignored his comment and swung her arm toward the living room. "Suede-covered furniture isn't exactly made for those of us less than graceful with a full glass of soda. From the smell and feel, I'm guessing it's genuine suede, not something manufactured in a factory."

He shrugged. "It's just furniture."

Ariel glared at him. "But it's not *my* furniture."

She'd be a nervous wreck worrying that she might damage someone else's property. Completely absurd, considering she was here to steal someone else's property to begin with.

Cam glanced up at the ceiling before asking, "So, what would you prefer?"

"I'd prefer to move into the employee wing."

"Since Danielle will be helping with the plans for the maze, it's easier having you here for now. Besides, the available suites are full." Frowning, he ran a hand through the back of his hair. "If it's that big a deal, we can have the furniture changed. What kind do you want?"

Ariel didn't buy his reasoning about keeping her in proximity. So, she wondered, why was it so important? Did he suspect she'd been the thief? As far as she knew, she hadn't given herself away.

Knowing he waited for an answer, she replied, "Something practical like duck, denim or a heavyweight broadcloth. Something sturdy that I can scrub if I need to."

The temperature in the apartment dropped dramatically. Ariel shivered from the icy chill. A swift breeze whooshed through, whipping Ariel's hair in her face.

"What the—" Cam's harsh curse drowned out her question.

She dragged her fingers through her hair, raking it out of her eyes. Heart racing, she looked at Cameron, then followed his stare toward the furniture they'd been discussing.

Instead of the buff-colored suede, the pieces were now covered in off-white denim.

The temperature instantly returned to normal, but it did little to warm the frigid terror assaulting her.

Ariel clamped her open mouth shut and gritted her teeth as she backed toward the door.

Without turning around, Cam ordered, "Stay there and don't faint."

She froze at the anger evident in his tone. He was enraged with *her?* For what? Before she could get her tongue unstuck from the roof of her mouth to ask, Cam swung around to face her.

"Who are you?"

"Ar-Ariel John-Johnson," she stuttered. "You think I did that?" The idea would be laughable at any other time, or in any place other than the Lair.

"I know I didn't." He came closer. Rage darkened his eyes until they glittered like uncut gems. "There isn't any sign of another wizard."

"A what?" Ariel ignored his earlier command and headed for the door. Earlier he'd only admitted to being a man and nothing more. But she knew there was something different about Cameron Drake. She'd thought he was gifted with psychic abilities. Possible insanity hadn't entered her mind.

Too leery to take her stare off Cameron, she searched blindly with her hand behind her for the door handle. Unable to locate it immediately, she fought back her rising panic and tried again. When her fumbling hand finally touched metal, she held on to it like a lifeline.

Cameron hitched a brow. She thought she was leaving? He silently locked the door against her escape.

"Sit down."

Her eyes widened further and she shook her head.

"You aren't leaving here."

"You can't stop me."

Ariel spun around and tugged on the door.

He crossed his arms against his chest and watched her frantically struggle, pounding her fists against the solid slab of wood to no avail.

"Stop it. You're only going to hurt yourself."

When she ignored him, Cam went to pull her away from the door. He stopped behind her and put a hand on her shoulder.

Ariel screamed and jerked away from his touch. "Get away from me!"

She hadn't been lying—she hadn't changed the furniture. From the wide-eyed, unblinking stare on her near-colorless face, he could tell she was terrified.

Of him.

The woman was mortal. Cam was fairly certain that outside of the dragon changeling she'd barely seen at Mirabilus, she'd had little prior contact with magic.

Even so, she was working for the Learneds; if they hadn't used magic around her yet, they eventually would. Just as they would use her to work their vile magic here at the Lair.

That knowledge made it difficult to have much sympathy for her fear now.

"Ariel, sit down." He made no move to approach her, but she still took off running down the hall toward the master bedroom.

The slamming of the door and loud click of the lock made him shake his head. She thought that would keep him out?

He'd almost decided to play along with the locked-door routine until he heard the sound of furniture being moved in the room. Cam had just headed down the hall toward the bedroom, when his cell phone vibrated.

He pulled the phone from his pocket and glanced at the screen before answering. "What do you want, Sean?"

"You need any help in there?"

Cam flipped the phone closed, cutting off his brother's nosy sarcasm and slid it back into his pocket. He waved a spell to temporarily soundproof the apartment.

If Sean heard them, it was certain that Danielle would, too. He wasn't about to let his aunt get involved in this matter.

The sound of something heavy scraping against the inside of the bedroom door drew him back to the task at hand. He didn't need any special power to know she was pushing one of the dressers against the door.

If the crashing noise of something breaking and her curse were any indication, she wasn't having much luck rearranging the furniture.

Cam knew he could walk away—just leave the apartment and by morning she'd probably be gone. It would be easier. Unfortunately, his beast disagreed.

The mere thought of letting her leave the Lair sent a wave of pain lacing through him. He closed his eyes and tried to breathe through what felt like an explosion in his head.

Perhaps letting her leave would be a mistake. The Learneds would only find another way into the Lair. They obviously weren't going to give up until either they or the Drakes ceased to exist. While it was true that Ariel Johnson was a threat—at least she was a known threat.

Relieved that the pain in his head eased to a dull throb, Cam stood outside the bedroom door. The sooner he dealt with this difficulty, the sooner he could try to deal with his dragon's misconception about Ariel.

He rapped his knuckles on the door. "Ariel, open the door."

"Go away."

"I'm not going anywhere. Open the door."

"I'll call the police."

That's just what they didn't need—attention from outside authorities. Short of patience, he gave up on the idea of reasoning with her and materialized in the bedroom. Before Ariel could react, he grabbed her and dropped her onto the bed.

As he'd expected, she fought him wildly. Either she'd had some training in self-defense, or she was frightened to death.

Between her clawing fingers and kicking legs, he had his hands full. When he dodged, preventing her nails from raking his face, she dug gouges down his forearms. She planted the hard heel of her shoe into his knee, then brought her leg back, aiming higher.

"No, you don't." Strengthened by his own anger, and his beast's rage at the pain inflicted from her kick, Cam flipped her over onto her stomach, pinned her wrists to the mattress and straddled her on the bed.

"Let me up."

Her breathless, panting order made him laugh. "I like you better where you are."

She screamed her outrage at his comment and tried to unsuccessfully buck him off her.

"Ariel, Ariel, you're wasting your energy." He leaned forward. "No one is hurting you. There's no danger threatening your life." He kept his tone gentle and even, hoping to calm her.

She ignored him and switched from bucking to trying to twist herself free. "Do you think I'm stupid? You'll talk nice and sweet until I'm relaxed and then—" Her voice broke.

He felt her body heave with a sob beneath him. "If that's intended to make me feel sorry for you, it won't work."

She went limp. "Please, don't hurt me. I'll do whatever you say."

Cam frowned. Exactly what did she think he was going to do? His stomach rolled. Quickly turning her over onto her back, he readjusted his hold on her wrists. "Look at me."

When she kept her eyes tightly closed, he bounced her wrists on the bed. "I said, look at me."

He could tell by her washed-out, hesitant gaze that she was terrified. Cam shook his head. "Listen to me. I have never harmed a woman in my life. You don't have to fear me." He leaned closer. "Nod if you understand me."

After she nodded, he loosened his hold. "If I release your arms, will you attack me again?"

"Not today."

Cam was certain her bravado was nothing more than a cover for her wariness. He released his hold on her wrists, but he remained straddled over her.

"What are you?" Her question was little more than a whisper.

He could tell her anything, or everything, and it wouldn't matter. When he left this room she wouldn't remember a thing. It would all seem as nothing more than a strange, disconcerting dream to her.

"I'm a wizard."

The pulse point in her neck pounded visibly. "A what?"

"Wizard."

"Like a witch?"

"Not exactly." Leave it to a mortal to confuse an element-based belief system with a wizard. But it would be hard to explain the differences in just a few minutes.

"I was born this way." He didn't add that it had taken a lifetime to learn how to safely use the powers he'd been born with. Or that no sooner had he mastered those powers than another one had come into existence.

"Is that how you changed the furniture?"

No, he hadn't, but he was fairly certain that she hadn't, either. Since the only other *presence* in the room at the time had been his dragon, it had probably been the beast's doing. It had never happened before, but the beast had never been attracted to a woman like this before, either, so it was impossible to know at this moment.

But he wasn't about to tell her any of that. So he lied, "Yes. Isn't that what you wanted?" He did need to discover who, or what, had cast a spell at the Lair without his knowledge—later.

"Well, yes. Sort of. I expected a couple moving men and a truck."

"Things at the Lair aren't always what we expect."

"Your family…are they like you?"

"No." It wasn't exactly a lie. None of them were changelings as far as he knew.

"What else can you do?"

He could almost see the gears in her mind spinning. She thought she was pumping him for information she could relay to the Learneds.

The idea of playing along was tempting. And he would—to a point. He needed her to relax, but not for the reason she'd thought. And he needed her to trust him. That was something that would take a little more than just magic.

Cameron silently ordered the furniture away from the door and back to their original places. The broken pieces of glass rearranged back into a lamp, before sailing up to its spot on the nightstand.

Her eyes widened, but her pulse remained steady. "You'd be handy on cleaning day."

He leaned in a little closer. "You have no idea how many things I'm handy with."

Ariel's heart fluttered at the seduction evident in his half-closed eyes and deep, gravelly voice. If she wasn't careful, she would find herself drawing him closer to kiss him—and maybe more.

She closed her eyes and shivered at the thought of his strong hands stroking her, caressing her body.

The warmth of his lips at the corner of her mouth made her shiver again. She gazed up at him, ignoring the self-satisfied smile curving his lips.

Cameron Drake wasn't some young inexperienced boy, he knew full well the effect he had on her. What was the point in denying it?

Gathering her courage, she slid a hand up his arm, coming to rest on his shoulder, then asked, "So, tell me some of the other things you're handy with."

Heat flooded her cheeks, but she held his gaze. Cameron's smile deepened. "*Tell* you?"

She stroked his neck, summoning up enough courage to finally say, "Show me."

With his hands planted on the bed alongside her head, he leaned down and pressed a light, teasing kiss against her cheek. "What would you like me to show you, Ariel?"

Of course, he wasn't going to make this easy. She

should have expected that. Too embarrassed to come right out and ask for exactly what she wanted, Ariel hedged, "Show me what you're handy with."

The lights in the bedroom flickered on and off.

She narrowed her eyes at his game. "Is that all?"

Cameron traced the seam of her lips with his tongue. Ariel gasped at the jolt of desire shooting down her spine. She threaded her fingers through his hair.

He easily pulled away and music filled the room.

Breathless with mounting frustration, she managed to ask, "Surely you can do better than that."

Cameron stretched out on top of her, supporting his weight on his forearms. This time there was nothing teasing about his kiss.

The heady caress of his mouth against hers, tasting, stroking, set fire racing through her veins. Ariel wrapped her arms around him, pulling him closer.

Already-heated lust flared hotter, taking away her ability to think clearly, or reason. She moaned against his lips and pulled the hem of his shirt free so she could stroke his back. And still it wasn't enough.

Something about this man brought all her desires and longings to the surface. He made her unbelievably hot and she doubted if anyone else but him would be able to douse the flames.

Cameron felt the heat of her desire as he stroked and caressed her skin. Any hotter and it would have burned his palm.

The scent of her lust was as intoxicating as a stiff double shot of scotch. He could easily lose control if he let his focus waver.

She was his enemy. As long as she worked for the Learneds that wouldn't change. What would change, however, was that if he possessed her, she would be easier for him to read, making it harder for her to hide things from him.

He still wouldn't be able to read her conscious mind any easier, or avoid detection by the Learneds. But he would be able to decipher any change—even the slightest shift in her body language, flicker of an eye or minute change in her scent.

The ability to sense those things instantly would make it easier for him to protect her if need be. He would know immediately if she was in danger and needed his help.

While using her in this manner might be considered underhanded by mortal human standards, he wasn't a normal human. When it came to his and his family's safety, Cam would do anything, including breaking any moral code, to protect them. And as long as Ariel was under his roof, her safety was his responsibility, too.

At least that's what he told himself. He knew in his soul that it went much deeper than that. His beast wanted—needed—to protect this woman.

He also knew that if he gave in to his urges, she would be a potential threat that he would desire every time she came near. A desire he'd be unable to easily quench. It would be hard not to hold her, or kiss her, but managing his lust would get easier with time. As long as he didn't permit his beast to lose control.

The risk was familiar—his human self had taken it before. And he'd always been able to easily rein in his dragon. It wouldn't be any different this time.

But already his beast had caught the scent of desire and was awakening. Cam breathed deeply, seeking to calm his lust. Even though Ariel would remember this only as a dream, Cam wanted it to be one she would look back on with longing—not loathing.

The mark on his shoulder blade throbbed. His beast roared, demanding to claim this woman as his own.

Without warning, an inviting warmth stole over him, rushing through his limbs to settle around his heart. His beast crooned, rumbling with anticipation.

Shocked, Cam cursed silently. Why now? Why this woman and not Carol? Like tongues of fire, pain and regret seeped through the warmth and flicked at his heart. This possession, this all-encompassing completion should have been shared with his wife, not his enemy.

His beast roared, demanding he set aside his memories, forget his hurt and accept what this woman offered.

No. He had to remain in control. But the beast beckoned him forward relentlessly. Cam shook with need. The wild desires within couldn't be unleashed. Letting them go would be disastrous in ways he could barely imagine at the moment.

Ariel moved beneath him. Before he could stop her, she drew her hands up his back, grazing his skin with the tips of her fingernails. Her touch across his birthmark sent shivers down his spine.

He knew the moment of indecision had passed. He needed to stop this now—or do something they might both regret later. Cameron pushed away with a strangled groan.

Cam rolled onto his side, taking Ariel with him. She snuggled against his chest with a frustrated sigh, making him wish for a second that what he was about to do wasn't necessary.

Holding her close, he brushed his cheek across her hair. He grabbed the corner of the quilt and pulled the edge over them. "It's been a long day, Ariel, go to sleep."

She tilted her head back to look up at him. "Are you staying?"

He dropped a kiss on the end of her nose. "For a while."

"I don't know if I can sleep." She sighed, then rested her cheek against his chest.

"Sure you can. Just think of something relaxing, like the warmth of the sun, the sound of waves lapping on a white beach."

He stroked lazy circles on her back and kept his voice low and steady. "Can you see it?"

"Almost."

"Can't you feel how warm the sun is? Not too hot, and there's a gentle breeze to keep you from getting too warm. The beach is empty except for one lone seagull."

"Mmm."

She was nearly asleep already. "There's a small stand of palm trees with a hammock strung between two of them. That's where you are now—swinging gently in a red-and-white-striped hammock."

"Nice." Her voice was barely audible.

"Yes, it is." He lowered his voice to a whisper. "The gentle sway of the hammock rocks you to sleep."

He knew that as long as he kept his tone low, soft and steady, he could recite civil code and she'd still be lulled into a dream dimension.

But if he wanted to control this dream, she had to follow his suggestions.

Still tracing circles on her back, he said, "The gull takes flight and you follow, flying higher and higher above the water. The crisp, clear air feels good against your skin. Your hair is streaming out behind you."

He paused to gauge her level of consciousness. Ariel's slow, steady pulse and even, light breathing let him know the time was near.

Cameron continued, waiting for the right moment

to step into her dream. "The sparkling water far below shimmers in different shades of blue and turquoise. It's so clear, you can see a coral reef. You fly lower to take a closer look and discover hundreds of brightly colored fish swimming around the reef."

She sighed in her sleep. Cam closed his eyes, pressed his lips against her head and joined her in her dream.

Ariel had followed his suggestions. In her dream he was beside her as they flew low over a coral reef.

Hands clasped, they circled the reef then headed back to the beach.

Once they landed, Cam scooped her up into his arms and carried her to the hammock. She sighed as he laid her crosswise at the edge of the striped fabric.

He cupped her cheek and leaned over her, whispering, "Ariel, close your eyes."

Her eyelids fluttered closed and he exhaled a soft, gentle breath against her lips. "This is nothing but a dream. Everything since the moment we arrived at your apartment door after the tour has been one glorious dream."

Her brow furrowed. "But…"

Cameron exhaled another warm breath against her mouth, willing her mind to accept his words as the truth. "Just a dream. One you can carry with you for as long as you desire."

"A dream?"

"Yes." He stroked his thumb across her cheek, then breathed into her once more. "Just a dream."

She rolled away, stretching lengthwise on the hammock. Cameron slowly backed off. A sound behind him caught his attention. The shuffle of heavy wings dragging across the sand came closer.

What the hell was his dragon doing here? Surely Ariel wasn't dreaming about the beast?

He pulled himself from the dream, needing to get out of her apartment before she woke up.

Once back in her bedroom, on the bed with her still in his arms, he marveled at the feel of hot tears on his chest. She was crying?

Ariel rolled over in her sleep and Cam gently extricated himself from the bed. He removed the sound-proofing spell and carefully checked the room to make sure everything was where it belonged before turning to leave.

He paused at the doorway to glance back at her. He ignored the tightening in his chest. She was his enemy, there was nothing either one of them could do to change that. What he had done was the best for both of them.

Cam gently closed the door behind him and walked into the living room. He spelled the suede furniture to return, making a note to remember to ask her about her preference later, then left her apartment.

Chapter 7

"Has she contacted you yet?"

Jeremy looked over the top of his morning newspaper and stared at his underling. The man swayed from one foot to the other.

Apparently he realized his mistake, because he avoided Jeremy's glare at his audacity.

Bennett shrugged as he backed toward the dining room door. "I was just curious."

Jeremy was tired of the constant questioning. His father questioned him nonstop and now this...minion decided to also? Did they both think he didn't know what he was doing?

"Curious?" Jeremy set his paper down. "Why? What difference could it possibly make to you?"

Bennett scratched his head. "Well, the boy—"

Jeremy lunged from his seat, shouting, "What have

you done?" If this moron killed that kid he'd have nothing to hold over Ms. Johnson.

"Nothing." Bennett raised his hands before his face as if to ward off whatever might come his way. "I did nothing, boss. The doc says—"

"The doctor?"

Nathan chose that moment to enter the formal dining room. Shuffling past Bennett, he pinned his son with a searching stare. "Something wrong?"

Even old and injured, his father's timing was impeccable. Jeremy fisted his hands at his sides. "Something is wrong with the Johnson boy."

"Wrong?" Nathan looked from one man to the other. "Someone needs to explain."

Again with the questioning? Jeremy waved toward Bennett. "He was just about to do that when you interrupted."

The elder wizard narrowed his glare. "Watch your attitude, boy."

Bennett's mouth opened and closed like a dying fish. His normally short patience strained, Jeremy ordered, "Tell us what happened."

Finally, the man stammered, "He…he…the machines… his heart."

Jeremy felt his eyes bulge as the pressure behind them increased. When this mission was done, he'd make it a point to put Bennett out of everyone's misery. "His heart what? Stopped?"

"Yes." When both wizards made a move toward him, the hired man added in a rush, "But they got it started again. The doc says he'll be fine. We just have to keep an eye on him."

Before Jeremy could respond, Nathan used his

powers to lift both men from the floor and slam them against the wall.

The old man's powers had been slowly returning, but Jeremy hadn't realized just how strong they'd become. He struggled uselessly against the magic keeping him pinned to the wall.

His father stood beneath them and shoved the end of his cane into Bennett's stomach. "Listen to me well, oaf. If anything happens to that boy, you will beg for death."

Nathan pulled his cane away, letting Bennett crash to the floor. The man crawled quickly for the door.

Once they were alone, Jeremy held his breath, fearful of what his sire might do to him. His father stared up at him, saying nothing until beads of sweat dripped from the end of Jeremy's nose.

"What am I going to do with you, child?"

"I've done nothing wrong." His father had always treated him like a rebellious teenager. Right now, that's how he felt. But he was no longer a teenager and he knew full well that rebellion would gain him only death.

"Do you not understand how important it is that we succeed this time?"

Jeremy swallowed. "Sir, I'll keep a closer watch on the boy myself."

"Yes, you will." Nathan tapped the cane repeatedly against his palm. "And you'll make certain he survives for as long as we need him."

"Yes, sir." Jeremy nodded, but he knew his father wasn't finished, so he said nothing further. But he silently hoped that he would be able to heal whatever damage his father inflicted.

Nathan raised his cane. "Next time perhaps you'll remember not to be so careless with the captive."

Jeremy closed his eyes as the cane swung toward him.

* * *

Cam watched from his office window as Ariel took the keys from Harold, then jumped into her van and left.

A few minutes later, his office phone rang. The call came from Harold's extension. Picking up the receiver, he asked, "Did she say where she was going?"

"Just into town. But she dropped her cell in the lobby. I thought you might want to take it to her, just in case she needs it."

There were moments when having a longtime employee who could make magic happen without any powers was a blessing. Cam didn't doubt for a minute that Harold had lifted Ariel's phone without her knowledge.

"I'll be right down. Get the car ready."

"Which one? Did you want me to drive?"

Taking the limo into town was always a hassle. It attracted unwanted attention. "No, I'll take the sedan." At least the black Mercury was inconspicuous.

He hung up the phone and untangled a pun-sai limb from his sapphire-studded cuff link. "Right. Good catch."

While the car might be inconspicuous, his suit wouldn't be. This was a mountain tourist town and as far as he was aware, there weren't any professional conventions going on right now. Walking around in a suit would be out of place amongst the shoppers and vacationing hikers.

He switched into jeans and a button-down shirt, and traded his dress shoes for a pair of trail boots, then headed to the garage.

Taking the keys and Ariel's cell from Harold, he commented, "You should have talked her into one of the smaller cars instead of that van she drives."

"I tried. I offered her the coupé, but she acted like it was a poisonous snake."

Cam rolled his eyes. Of course she wouldn't take Braeden's Phantom. The car would make anyone queasy if they'd never driven a higher-end vehicle before, especially if it wasn't theirs. "Next time insist she take the Jeep."

Driving down the twisting, turning mountain road, he wondered what had taken her so long. Ariel had been at the Lair five days now and she hadn't left to contact the Learneds until now.

He knew that's what she was doing. It was the only thing that made sense. They couldn't contact her at the Lair because of the security at the resort and they certainly weren't going to send her there without having her report back to them.

She wouldn't be sightseeing or shopping. Ariel didn't seem the type to cut out of work to do something like that her first week on the job. She'd wait until after hours, or the weekend.

Cam drove around the last curve and hit the straightaway into town. Thankfully, since it was the middle of the day and midweek, there weren't too many tourists milling about and the hikers were still in the forest. It made it easier to drive and check the parking lots for her van at the same time without hitting anyone.

He spotted her pulling into the garage at the other end of town. Cam drove across the road into a motel entrance that had a through way with a parking lot on the other end.

He took his time parking the car and walked toward the garage. There were too many scents in town and he needed the extra time to weed out the aromas of cinnamon-roasted nuts, grilled sausages and the ever-present chocolate from the fudge shops.

Coaxing his dragon to help, he quickly zeroed in on her location. Ariel stood at the entrance to the garage looking up and down the sidewalks—searching for a public phone perhaps?

Cam wished her luck. Public phones were nearly extinct in this town.

Or, was she looking for her contact? He studied the area and detected no magic, nothing out of the ordinary. He positioned himself behind an ornate light post, using the hanging planter to hide his face, and waited to see where she went.

Ariel wanted to scream. How could she have lost her cell phone? She could have sworn she'd put it in her purse before leaving her apartment, because she'd had to go back inside to grab it off the nightstand.

And of course there wasn't a phone booth in sight. But luckily there was a bar on the opposite corner. Surely they'd have a phone.

Standing at the crosswalk, waiting for the light to change, she had the strangest feeling of being watched. Ariel looked around. Even though she didn't see anyone suspicious, the feeling didn't go away.

Guilt. That's all it was. What else could it be?

Ariel glanced at her watch. Thirty minutes was all she had left. If she didn't call Renalde by then, everything she'd done so far would have been for nothing— Carl would be killed.

The light turned green. She melted into a group of women tourists who were pointing at the bar and talking about getting lunch. She didn't know if there really was safety in numbers or not, but joining the group made the tingle at the base of her neck lessen.

Ariel followed them into the bar and headed for the hostess while the group veered off into the gift shop.

The hostess looked around Ariel. "Just one?"

"Actually none. I just need a phone."

"I can bring one to your table."

She didn't have time to run around looking for a pay phone, so she'd nab a bite to eat. "That'll be fine as long as I can get the phone right away."

"I'll grab one on the way through."

True to her word, the hostess retrieved a wireless handset from the bartender and led Ariel to a booth in the back corner. "It's quieter back here."

As soon as the woman left, Ariel punched in Renalde's number. After seven rings her heart slammed into her stomach. She checked her watch again. There was still twenty minutes to spare.

Finally, after the tenth ring, she heard a click on the other end. "This had better be Ariel."

His voice was strained. He sounded as if he was in a great deal of pain. She didn't care enough to ask. "Yes, it's me."

"Why aren't you using your cell? Where are you?"

"I seem to have lost it, so I'm at a bar in town."

He made some sort of indistinguishable sound, then asked, "You are still staying at the Lair?"

"Yes, I am." As soon as she answered, Ariel swore that something unseen entered her head. She rubbed her temples trying to ease the strange feeling.

"Stop it."

She froze. Something—someone—*had* entered her mind.

"What have you found?"

His voice was coming from inside her head, not through the phone. Somehow Renalde was able to invade her mind even from a distance. At his huff of impatience, she answered, "I haven't found anything yet."

"Have you been trying?"

Why was he *asking* her? If he could slip into her mind, why couldn't he just find the answer himself? Why did she even have to bother coming to town?

Something closed around her throat. Ariel gasped for breath.

"Don't question me. Don't get smart with me. Both you and Carl are quite dispensable." The invisible hand around her throat tightened. "Do you understand me?"

Unable to talk, Ariel nodded. The hold disappeared.

"Now, my dear."

She made a face at his use of the word *dear,* but let him continue without comment.

"You have one week to call me back with the news that you know the location of both the pendant and cube, or that they are in your possession."

She didn't need to ask what would happen if she failed. "I'll try."

"You'll do more than just try."

Her ears buzzed and eyes watered as the room spun for a moment. Apparently, Renalde had made his exit from her mind. Even though she was getting used to the intrusion, this was all just way too strange for her. It was more like a nightmare than reality.

The idea of eating lunch made her ill. Her hands were shaking too much to even pick up her glass of water. When all of this was over, Carl had some serious explaining to do.

"Drink?"

Ariel closed her eyes. This is exactly what she didn't want—some guy trying to pick her up in the bar. She clicked off the phone and set it on the table without looking up. "No, thank you. I'm waiting for someone."

"Anyone I know?"

She groaned, recognizing Cameron's voice. Ariel glanced up at him. "Sorry, I thought you were some stranger trying to pick up women."

Now her heart really was in her stomach. She'd avoided Cameron Drake as much as she possibly could these past few days—ever since she'd started having extremely realistic dreams about him...and her. Ariel felt her cheeks burn just thinking about the dreams and tried to swallow past the dryness in her mouth.

Cam gritted his teeth against the tidal wave of her pheromones crashing against him. He knew exactly what thoughts had put the telltale flush on her cheeks. Unfortunately, so did his now-alert beast.

At least his spell had worked—she believed that what had happened in her apartment was nothing more than a dream. Apparently the scene on the beach was one that obviously haunted her.

Good. He hoped the dream kept her warm at night, because he would never make the mistake of getting too close to her again. It was too dangerous. He didn't know if next time he'd be able to resist the desire that flared so easily between them. And he didn't like the longing that still tortured him after denying the passion the last time.

Cam's chest tightened. His thoughts upset the dragon within. He didn't care—the last thing he wanted to do was risk making love to Ariel Johnson, regardless of what desires drove his demon to spit and snarl in protest. Besides, at this moment, his fantasies consisted of strangling her more than anything else.

He'd followed her into the bar and made certain the

hostess seated him close enough for him to overhear some of her conversation. Once the Learned had slipped into Ariel's mind, Cam had been unable to follow.

But her body's reactions—pounding heart, racing blood, tang of fear—had clued him in to the general idea of what was being said. He got the distinct impression that she was being threatened.

What did the Learneds have to hold against her that would make her live a lie and intentionally put another family—*his* family—in danger?

Cam once again offered her the glass he held. "It's just iced tea."

She took the glass from him, being extra careful not to let their fingers touch. "Thank you. Please, join me."

"I had every intention of doing so since you're on my clock." He slid onto the bench across from her.

"I didn't know I needed permission to leave for lunch."

"Permission? No, but some notice would have been nice, and leaving without your cell phone wasn't a wise move." He pulled it from his pocket and set it on the table. "And quit driving that van up and down the mountain."

"My van is perfectly safe."

"It's top-heavy, rear-wheel drive and most likely doesn't handle well."

She visibly bristled. Her eyes blazed and she tightened her lips. Ariel leaned forward. "I appreciate your concern, but you are not my father and I don't need a keeper." She shot him a hot, narrow-eyed glare, adding, "And I am *not* driving the car Harold recommended."

Cam stirred his tea, studying the ice cubes in an attempt not to laugh at her flash of outrage. "Harold was teasing you. There's a sedan or a Jeep that you're free to use."

She said nothing, but he didn't have to be a genius to know she resented being told what to do. "Look, Ariel, when those roads get the slightest bit wet, they're treacherous. I have no desire to explain your death to your brother."

"I know how to drive."

"I never said you didn't."

"That's what it sounded like to me."

Cam leaned back on the bench. "Awful defensive for such a small thing. Obviously something else is wrong, care to discuss it?"

She paled and stared down at the table. He was disappointed by her reaction. This would be no fun at all if she clammed up under stress.

He resisted the urge to reach across the table and cover her folded hands with his. Offering comfort over something this small wouldn't be to his benefit.

"Ariel, you may be offended, but I insist—" His cell phone vibrated against his chest. He pulled it out and frowned. Why was Alexia calling him?

He sent the call to voice mail and turned his focus back to Ariel. "I insist you take one of the smaller vehicles. They handle better, both are four-wheel drive, so you'll have better traction and control. There's less chance of—" He glanced down at his cell, then told her, "I have to take this, it's my sister-in-law."

Ariel nodded.

Cam flipped open the phone. "What do you need, Lexi?"

"Make sure the grimoire is safe, would you?" Alexia's voice whispered through his phone.

"Why wouldn't it be?" The family book of spells was locked securely in his office desk.

"Just check for me." Alexia sounded frantic.

"I'm not at the Lair."

"Can't you just pop back and check?"

"No. But Braeden can."

"No, he can't. He doesn't know."

Cam blinked at her whining tone. Something was obviously wrong. Alexia wasn't a whiner. "What's going on?"

"I don't know, that's why I need you to check. Something just feels wrong. I keep seeing the grimoire and it's not in your office."

The lock on his desk was spelled, so the book damn well better still be there. "Where is it then?"

"I don't know, some woman has it."

Cam glanced across the table at Ariel. "What does she look like?"

"I can't tell. It's like I'm seeing her through some foggy dream."

Certain she was seeing Ariel, he cursed to himself. "I'll be leaving here in a few minutes. I'll give you a call as soon as I get back there, okay?"

"Please, hurry."

"I will."

He put the phone back in his pocket. "Something's come up. We'll finish this conversation later."

"There's nothing to finish."

"I don't have time to argue, I need to get back to the Lair." He stood up and dropped some money on the table. "Have lunch on me."

Ariel grabbed the money and threw it at him. "I don't need your money."

Cam refused to get drawn into a petty argument with her. He left the money on the floor and walked away.

She had never felt like such a fool in her entire life. Ariel covered her burning face with her hands. She'd humiliated herself in public and acted like some spoiled brat.

The man was her employer, not her lover. What was wrong with her? Ever since breaking into Mirabilus, she'd been haunted by dreams, teased by cravings she didn't fully understand.

She'd lost count of the times she'd stood on the balcony of her suite letting the brisk wind whip about her while she watched the hawks soar, wishing all the while she could join them.

What bothered her was that it wasn't just a wish— it was more a need, a craving to let something deep inside her be free—something dark and wild that she didn't comprehend.

Ariel rubbed her forehead and breathed deeply. The sooner she found what Renalde wanted and got away from the Lair and Cameron, the better.

"Give me your keys."

She jumped at Cam's voice and uncovered her face to look up at him. His hair and shoulders were wet.

"It's raining. You aren't driving that van back to the Lair." He set his keys on the table. "The sedan is parked in the lot one block down and one street behind here." He handed her a prepaid parking-ticket stub. "It's a black Mercury."

"I still don't understand—"

He leaned down, his hands flat on the table, his face inches from hers. "My sister-in-law nearly died making that drive in the rain. Her unborn baby did die. I am not—I repeat *not*—pulling your dead body from that van."

She pulled her keys from her purse and handed them to him. "I'm sorry, I didn't…" Her words trailed off as he turned around and walked away again.

The waitress approached the table, stopping to retrieve the money from the floor. She started to place it on the table, but Ariel held up her hand. "No, keep it."

The young woman looked at the bill. Her eyes flew open wide. "But, ma'am, it's a hundred-dollar bill."

"It's yours."

"Thank you. Can I get you anything else?"

"No, just a bill for the drinks."

"Your boyfriend already paid for them."

"He's not my boyfriend." Ariel rubbed her temples. "He's my boss."

The waitress's eyebrows nearly disappeared behind her bangs. "I should be so lucky."

Lucky? Oh, yeah, that's what she was—lucky. Ariel felt, oh, so lucky.

The waitress put the empty glasses on her tray. "You have a wonderful day and thanks again."

"You, too." Ariel grabbed her purse and took off to find Cam's car. She needed to get back and do some more snooping. How she was going to find something as small as a pendant in a building the size of the Lair was beyond her understanding, but there really wasn't any other choice.

Besides, she couldn't spend the afternoon dallying here; she also needed to get back to her laptop to do some more gardening research.

There were some plants depending on her supposed expertise. She could only hope they didn't die before she could figure out what was wrong with them.

Chapter 8

Through a red haze of rage, Cam stared at the grimoire lying on the desk in Ariel's apartment office. How had she got it out of his desk? And why couldn't he pry it from the top of hers?

He'd tried to pick it up, repeatedly, then he'd resorted to spells. And still he'd had no success. It was as if the grimoire was permanently attached to her desk.

How?

There had been no indication that any magic had been performed at the Lair this last week. He hadn't so much as sensed his aunt casting charm spells, let alone something powerful enough to get past his locks—tangible or magical.

"What are you doing?"

He hadn't heard Ariel enter the apartment. Not that it mattered, it saved him from having to go and find her.

Without turning around, Cam asked, "How did you get past my spell?"

"Your what?"

Her little game of playing ignorant needed to stop. "Enough." He spun around. "No more."

She backed away from him. "I don't know what you're talking about."

"This." Cam pointed at the book on the table. "The grimoire. When did you steal it?"

Ariel leaned a little to look around him. "Steal it? I've never seen it before. What is it?"

If confronting her outright didn't work, what was it going to take to get her to admit what she was doing? "Right, Ariel, like you don't know what it is."

"No." She shook her head. "I don't."

It would be easier if he could believe her, but the proof of her lie was right there, seemingly glued to her desk. He took a breath, but it did nothing to cool his anger. Normally he was capable of controlling his emotions. But something about this woman shattered any semblance of self-control he—and his dragon—possessed.

"Knock it off. Your game is up. The proof is right there for anyone to see. You didn't even bother to try hiding it."

Knock it off? Cameron was acting as if he'd lost his ability to reason. "Look, I don't know how that book got there, but I sure as hell didn't put it there."

He advanced on her—there was no other word she could think of to describe his feral appearance or approach. He stalked her as if she was nothing more than helpless prey. The glittering eyes, tensed jaw and fisted hands as he loomed over her sent her adrenaline racing.

Ariel backed away, careful to keep a close eye on

him. She had to get out of here, otherwise she feared he'd completely lose control.

"Don't lie to me anymore. I know you work for the Learneds."

"Who?" Even though he had the name wrong, Ariel knew he was onto something. It didn't matter if he'd figured out that she worked for someone else or not. She wouldn't admit it—doing so would only assure Carl's death. "I work for you. Remember, I'm your gardener?"

Cameron lifted his arm and moved his hand as if he was writing something on an invisible blackboard, then made a motion to turn the imaginary board toward her. He said nothing, just glared at her.

Ariel held up her hands and shrugged. Was she supposed to do or see something? "What?"

"You can break a lock spell, but can't read?"

"Read what? There's nothing there to read."

He hadn't lost the ability to reason—he'd lost his mind altogether. She backed up another step and ran into a brick wall where there should have been nothing. Sick to her stomach, Ariel looked over her shoulder and saw exactly what was there—nothing. Yet when she pressed back with her body she hit a solid, albeit invisible, wall.

She looked back toward Cam and saw writing in the air. Fighting the urge to faint, she read and reread the two lines until she realized it was an anagram—Renalde followed by Learned.

Still, it didn't matter. Nothing did. Not the impending danger closing in on her, or what Cameron might know. The only thing that mattered was keeping Carl safe. And it was that single goal that gave her the strength to stiffen her spine and say, "Nice trick. You should host a magic show here at the Lair."

Quicker than she could blink, Cameron cleared the few steps separating them and clamped one large hand behind her neck.

As he shoved her toward the desk, Ariel swore he growled. Like some animal.

Yet, to her consternation, now that he touched her, she was no longer afraid of him. While his touch conveyed anger, it wasn't a cold icy touch of impending doom. His grasp around the back of her neck acted more like a solid anchor in what had quickly turned into an extremely bizarre argument.

Although, that fact made her wonder who had lost the ability to reason. Obviously, she had.

"Let me go." Her struggle proved useless and he pushed her down onto the chair behind the desk.

"Magic show? Trick? You come to the Lair to help the Learneds kill me and my family and then act like it's a game? Do you think this is fake?"

Before she could respond, he flicked a wrist, flashing his hand above the desk.

A movie with no screen—like the holograms from nearly any science-fiction show—appeared. She watched two families warring against each other through the centuries. From the Dark Ages to modern day she saw gruesome images of torture and death. The years flew past her eyes, one more brutal than the last.

Eventually the setting started to look more familiar. Ariel guessed she was now watching something from about the time her own parents were married. The cars and clothing were similar to those in her parents' photo albums.

A car with two smiling and laughing adults—Cam's parents, from his resemblance to the man—picked up speed and rammed into a giant tree. Ariel jumped back, but Cam held her firmly in place. She watched in horror as another man, one who looked like an older version of Renalde, laughed with apparent satisfaction, then took flight from a nearby tree limb to circle the now-burning car before flying away.

The next several years, a decade or two, zipped by uneventfully. She watched as three boys—two twins and a younger boy—grew up with a woman she recognized now as Danielle Drake.

But suddenly another car, one more modern being driven by a very pregnant woman about her own age, came into view. The dark night sky poured rain, rumbled with thunder and flashed with lightning.

It was apparent by the woman's tears and tight expression that she was very angry with someone—a husband or lover perhaps?

The woman's anger swiftly turned to fear and terror as a dragon repeatedly rushed the car from behind as if to attack. Ariel realized that the beast had no intention of attacking the vehicle. It sought only to frighten the woman into running the car off the slick mountain road.

This was not the dragon from her dreams, nor was it the one she'd seen at Mirabilus. She knew that by the vile, cruel face, dripping fangs and glowing-red eyes.

After it succeeded in running the car over the side of the mountain, the beast turned into a human. One that once again resembled Renalde. The man leaned over the edge of the road and cursed before disappearing.

Her view focused in on the car. Ariel saw the woman's life slipping away. To her shocked dismay, she also saw the woman's belly glow, sending a touch of color back into the unconscious woman's cheeks.

By the time help arrived, the woman lived, but the

babe she carried had somehow given so much of its own life for the mother that he couldn't be saved.

Behind her, Cam cursed softly. He sounded surprised, as if he had never known what had happened in that wrecked car. Without thinking, Ariel reached up and covered his hand with her own, offering what little comfort she could. A long moment passed before he pulled his hand away, saying, "That's Alexia, my twin brother's wife."

She nodded, then turned her attention back to the next set of images. Another woman, a dark-haired, blue-eyed beauty, stood laughing on top of a rock outcrop. The shadow of a winged beast attacking shrouded her in darkness.

Cam once again stretched out his hand. "No more."

Ariel stared at the now-empty space above the desk. From the thick pain lacing his voice, she could only assume that this had been *his* wife or lover. And that she, too, had died at the hands of Renalde or his family.

Ariel wanted to cry, to throw herself across the desk and sob in despair. If the Drakes with their apparent powers had been unable to defeat these monsters for centuries, she and her brother didn't stand a chance if she couldn't find the items Renalde wanted.

"Now do you understand?"

She nodded mutely. Oh, she understood, all right. She understood that like Renalde, Cam was more than just a mere human. She also understood that his family was at war with the family who held her brother.

"What are they after? What do you protect?" She had the gut-churning idea that she already knew the answer to both questions.

Cameron tapped the manuscript on the desk. "This, for one thing."

No one had ordered her to search for a book, so she felt safe asking, "Exactly what is a grimoire?"

"It's an ancient diary containing the family's spells and secrets."

She stared at the blank pages. "There's nothing there."

"No, there isn't. Not for you and me. But words and symbols appear for Braeden and Alexia."

"She's like…you?"

"Like me?"

Ariel didn't want to ask if his sister-in-law was…un-human…inhuman…not normal, too, so she reworded her thought. "Does she have powers?"

"Not until they were given to her."

"Given to her?"

"By the grimoire."

Ariel leaned back. She had no desire to change who or what she was.

Cameron laughed at her. "The book won't spell you. Not if you can't read it."

She wasn't taking any chances and moved farther away from the desk.

Without preamble, Cam said, "You work for my enemy."

Ariel remained mute. While he hadn't asked a question, if she agreed with him, he would expect—perhaps even force—information from her. Yet, if she denied his claim, he would know she lied. Then what would he do to her?

After he obtained the information he wanted, what then? Would she be tossed out of the Lair before she could find what she needed to save her brother?

"No." Cam leaned over her shoulder to whisper

against her ear. "Don't answer. It will be more entertaining to find out for myself."

Ariel shivered, uncertain if the sudden increase in her nervousness was caused from his implied threat, or from his nearness.

He stroked a finger down her neck. "And don't worry, you haven't lost your front as a gardener—yet. I intend to keep you close." His breath was hot against her flesh. "Very, very close."

"And since I can't move this—" he reached around her to jab at the edges of the book "—I'm closing down this apartment and sealing off the room. Your things have already been moved to another one."

"One has opened up?"

Cam smiled. Even though he knew she referred to an apartment in the employee wing, he deliberately chose to misunderstand. "Yes. One has."

She wouldn't like the apartment she was moving into, but he didn't care. The only thing that mattered to him was that while she was at the Lair, she never left his sight.

He pulled out the chair. "I'll show you to the apartment."

When they left her suite, he paused to turn back toward the room. After clearing the room of everything except the desk and the grimoire, Cam cast an ancient, powerful spell, one that only he could undo. The room was instantly sealed in a solid block of concrete.

The desk and book were protected from the concrete by a thin layer of pure energy. However, if anyone but him tried to break the spell, both items would disintegrate and the grimoire would be lost for all time.

He turned back to Ariel and placed his hand under

her elbow to lead her out of the apartment, down the hall and around the corner to his.

"Where are we going?"

Cam didn't answer until they were both inside his apartment. Then he released her elbow. Heading for the kitchen, he simply said, "Welcome home, roomie."

Chapter 9

"I am *not* staying here with you."

Cam poured two glasses of water, answering, "Want to make a bet on that?"

When she didn't respond, he went to the kitchen door. Ariel was still standing in the foyer. Her arms were crossed against her chest. The mutinous look on her face might have bode ill for another man, but he found it amusing. "Come in here. We need to talk."

"Go to—"

Before she could finish telling him where to go, he crooked a finger at her, moving her bodily to the kitchen against her will.

Her mouth fell open and she frantically tried to grab the doorknob as she floated by the coat closet.

He shrugged, warning, "You break that door, you'll fix it yourself."

When she *joined* him in the kitchen, he guided her to

a stool at the counter and handed her a glass of water. "Drink this."

She set the glass on the counter untouched.

Cam sighed. "You can be as obstinate as you want, but you aren't going to get your way in this, not if you want to stay at the Lair."

He leaned both hands on the countertop, effectively encircling her between his body and the counter.

With his mouth against her ear, he said, "Now that we're putting our cards on the table, why don't you tell me what your assignment is here?"

He didn't expect her to answer, but on the off chance she might suffer a sudden attack of honesty, he had to give it a shot.

"I can't."

She sounded so small, so defeated. Cam fought back a wave of sympathy. He'd already guessed that she'd been forced into this position, but there were always choices.

"What is he holding over you?"

She shook her head, refusing to answer.

"Ariel, I know you have little reason to believe me, but you can trust me. Whatever it is, I can protect you."

She wanted to laugh at the absurdity of his claim. But the sincerity she heard behind the words rang strong.

Ariel didn't want to feel anything for this man—least of all gratitude. She shoved back hard, breaking free of the prison he'd created with his arms.

"Protect me?" She rose and moved away from him. "I've seen how well your family has fared against Renalde's. Your parents, your sister-in-law's baby, and your own...wife...lover. The track record for you Drakes isn't stellar on the protection end."

Cam jerked as if she'd physically slapped him. The

half smile should have been a warning, but she hesitated a second too long.

He snagged one arm around her waist and deposited her on top of the counter. Ariel smacked at his arms, demanding, "Let me go."

"You're going to hurt yourself if you don't stop it." When she swung at him again, he grabbed her wrists. Pinning them against the kitchen wall over her head with one hand, he moved between her legs. "Tell me why you're here."

Rage and humiliation waged a war in her mind and heart. Renalde and his thug had mentally and physically threatened her and she'd been terrified.

But this man wasn't seeking to hurt her physically. He was manhandling her in a show of greater strength and that angered her more than frightened her. Never in her life had any man treated her this way.

And beneath the anger, that still-unfamiliar wildness inside her sprang to life beneath his demanding touch. It set her heart racing with anticipation. His closeness inflamed her senses, Ariel swore she could smell desire—exotically spiced, it called to her, bidding her to let go, to set reserve and common sense aside.

She'd wondered earlier if she'd lost her mind. She no longer wondered. Her lack of fear and unwarranted response to this situation confirmed her insanity.

Ariel mentally shook free from the lust-filled hold threatening to consume her and glared at him. "When did you realize Renalde was an anagram for Learned?"

"At your interview."

She relaxed a little against the wall. "If you haven't done anything to force the information from me so far, I have to wonder why." Cam's frown prompted her to add, "I don't think you can."

He leaned down and placed his lips nearly against hers. "You are in a betting mood, aren't you?"

Ariel's heart jumped. If he kissed her now she would be in trouble and she doubted she'd resist. Hoping to ward him off, she asked, "Isn't this what they call sexual harassment in the workplace?"

"Perhaps." His breath was warm against her lips— seductively warm. "But I'm positive this will completely cross that line." He hooked his free arm behind her waist and slid her lower body tight against his.

Ariel gasped at the heat of the contact, giving him the opportunity to capture her open mouth with his own.

Against all common sense and any rational thought she possessed, Ariel let the anger flow out of her body. She'd known this would happen if he kissed her. Heat and desire rushed through her. And while she despised her response, she couldn't find the will to demand he stop this assault on her senses.

A tiny part of her mind warned of the danger inherent in permitting a virtual stranger this much intimacy. They were alone. In his apartment.

Riskier yet, this man possessed powers she could barely imagine and he had her pinned helpless between a wall and his body. He could do anything he wanted.

His hand caressing her breast made her realize that she wouldn't stop him. Ariel moaned, pushing aside the insignificant worries.

Cam knew that if he didn't back off now, there would be no stopping him. Already his beast was screaming for more contact than this kiss and a touch through her shirt. By her ardent response he doubted she'd care.

He ignored the dragon's demands and tore his mouth from hers, staring down at her flushed face until she opened her eyes.

"Why are you here, Ariel?"

She shook her head. "Sorry, but seducing me will gain you nothing."

Her breathlessness gave little weight to her words. He took his time trailing his gaze from the spot above her head where he held her wrists, down to where their bodies met. Returning his focus to her face, he smiled. "Who do you think you're fooling?"

When she didn't respond, he stroked his thumb across her captured wrists. "I have you trapped and completely at my mercy. Yet, instead of being scared, you challenge me?"

Cam breathed deeply—a dangerous move considering the war being raged between his mind and beast. The sultry scent of desire confirmed his suspicions, and strengthened his desire. She was as hot as he.

Stroking her cheek with his free hand, he observed, "Judging by your enlarged pupils, flushed cheeks and parted lips, you're more turned on than afraid."

He expected her to look away out of embarrassment. And while a deeper flush spread across her cheeks and down her neck, she held his gaze without flinching.

"Did it take some kind of special power to come to that conclusion, or were you able to figure it out on your own?"

She was intentionally trying to anger him. What did she think to gain? And what would she do if he refused to play along?

Keeping his tone light, he answered, "A little of both."

Ariel narrowed her stare to a glittering glare. "You wasted your energy. It doesn't matter how much you coax me into wanting you, we are never satisfying that want."

When she presented him with a challenge, she went all out. How could he resist? Cam brushed his lips against the side of her neck, asking, "And why is that?"

She shivered beneath his teasing touch before answering. "For one thing, Mr. Drake," she drawled his name, making it sound like a curse. "You're my boss."

She tugged her arms and he released her wrists. Ariel looped her arms around his neck and played with his hair. "And I work for your enemy, remember?"

He traced the vein in her neck. The tremor in her voice took the sting out of her words as she threw his accusation back in his face.

Ariel tilted her head, giving him better access to the soft flesh beneath her ear. "Besides, I can't let lust rule my mind, can I?"

Cam realized with a start that he was enjoying this conversation. For the life of him, he couldn't pinpoint the moment his anger had changed to interest. When had the two forces battling inside him decided to unite?

Without breaking his attention to her neck, he shrugged. "I don't know, can you?"

"No. It wouldn't be wise."

He nipped at her earlobe. "I can fix your first problem."

Ariel twirled a lock of his hair before giving it a swift yank.

Cam chuckled at her retaliation, then told her, "You're fired, Ms. Johnson."

She slid her arms down and wrapped him in her embrace. "We signed a contract, Mr. Drake. I get a month to wrap up whatever project I'm working on and don't forget that severance package."

"You're here under false pretenses, so I'm fairly certain that contract isn't binding."

She countered, "And you've already admitted you knew about the false pretenses before you offered me the contract."

"I have more spendable money than you do. I could drag it out in court for years."

"True." Ariel ran her hands up his back. "But look at all the time you'd have to spend away from the Lair."

She trailed her fingertips along his shoulder blades, brushing across the dragon mark. The light contact whipped through him like a storm.

"You might have me there." He paused to take a steadying breath as she grazed his mark again. "How about we make a deal?"

"Depends."

"You tell me why you're here and I might let you keep your job."

Ariel laughed softly. "Nice try."

He lifted her in his arms. Heading for his bedroom, he said, "I guess I'll just have to try harder."

"You do that. But I'm not sleeping in your bed."

Cam did a one-eighty and headed for the guest bedroom. "Not a problem."

"There is one small, tiny problem."

He paused at the bedroom door. "And that is?"

"I'm not on the pill."

Cam froze. "You aren't on the pill?"

"No. I've had no reason to be. Don't tell me that you don't have any condoms?"

"No." He lowered her to her feet. "I've had no need for them."

Ariel leaned against the door and sighed. "Well, I guess you'll have to try harder some other time then, won't you?"

She didn't seem too upset by this predicament at

all. Suspicious, he narrowed his eyes. "You saved this little bit of information until just the right minute on purpose, didn't you?"

Ariel widened her eyes. "Me? A mere human female? You think I would try to outwit a…" She paused, frowning. "What exactly are you?"

Cam gritted his teeth. "I told you, a wizard."

She opened the bedroom door. "Well, *Mr. Wizard*—" she stepped inside the room "—I think this round goes to the girl."

He stared at the closed door a long minute before turning on his heel and leaving the apartment.

Ariel waited, with her ear pressed against the door, until she heard the entry door slam. Closing her eyes, she turned around with her back against the door, and slid to the floor before her trembling legs could buckle beneath her.

Of course she'd saved that information on purpose. He wasn't dealing with a complete idiot. Since he hadn't harmed her, she'd gambled that taking the chance of creating a child would be too much for him to risk.

It didn't happen often, but thankfully, this time she'd been right.

What would she do next time? She was certain there would be a next time. Cameron Drake wasn't going to give up this easily. And since it was nearly impossible not to respond to what his touch did to her, *next time* might turn out quite differently.

She needed to find that pendant and cube. Locating those cursed items and getting out of here was the only way she could save Carl and herself.

It wouldn't be easy, but to save her brother she would do anything, would sacrifice anything—including her self-respect and her heart.

Determined to find the strength of spirit required to bolster her wavering bravado, she rose, then strolled into the dressing room. Cameron had been right, all of her things had been moved.

Ariel walked back out into the bedroom and froze under the archway between the two rooms.

Impossible.

When the floor beneath her feet stopped heaving and her heart slowed enough for her to think, her first impulse was to turn around and run as fast and as far from the Lair as she could. Unfortunately, that option wasn't available.

She stepped hesitantly through the room, reminding herself to breathe as she approached the small writing desk.

Ariel stared down at the desk in disbelief. How did that book…that grimoire…get here? She reached out, then, remembering what Cam had said about the book giving his sister-in-law powers, pulled her arm back, fearing if she touched it something would happen to her, too.

The door to the apartment opened, then closed. She gasped and turned around quickly, hiding the book with her body. If Cameron saw it he would mistakenly assume she'd stolen it again.

Although how she would have gotten it out of a room-size block of concrete was beyond her comprehension. She would have had to use a jackhammer and that would have been a little loud for anyone to have missed. Not to mention the time involved in that process.

He opened the bedroom door, but stopped just outside the doorway. "Is everything here?"

Oh, yeah—everything and then some. "Yes."

Cam winged a handful of flat square packets onto the bed. "You should have a few of these in your purse."

She knew without looking that he hadn't tossed packets of sugar on her bed. They were condoms. It was done as a warning—he wasn't through with her yet.

Couldn't he have found a more insulting way to tell her?

The man obviously had gotten his own way far too often. Ariel looked from the packets to Cam. Returning his hard stare, she opened her mouth to give him a piece of her mind. But before she could say a word, something bumped her from behind.

Without breaking her stare, she reached back only to have her fingers brush against the book. It had slid to the edge of the desk. She pushed it back, trying not to shriek when it closed on her hand.

Cam frowned. She stepped forward to distract him, saying in a rush, "Gee, thanks. I've never had a boss give me such a personal gift before."

It was a lame response and had all the zing of a boiled noodle. But it drew his attention back to her and that's what she wanted.

"You don't sound very appreciative."

"Ha, ha, Mr. Drake." She waved toward the door. "If you don't mind…?"

"Sure." He came all the way into the room, closing the door behind him.

"That's *not* what I meant."

Cam was well aware she wanted him to leave. He wanted to know what she was trying so hard to hide behind her on the desk.

He sat on the bed. "I thought we might try…" Cam let his suggestion trail off and picked up a foil packet. He had to hand it to her, he'd gone out of his way to enrage her with the condoms, hoping she'd let something slip, but she'd yet to scream at him or resort to four-letter words.

"Get out of my room."

"It's my apartment."

"And I wouldn't be here if you hadn't forced me."

"That's your own fault. I can't have you running around the Lair casting spells and causing trouble, can I?"

"Spells?" She shook her head. "How many times do I have to tell you that I don't know any magic?"

"Right. The grimoire just appeared in your apartment on its own."

Her darting eyes and suddenly pale cheeks brought him to his feet. She backed up against the desk as he approached. "What are you hiding, Ariel?"

"Nothing. I just don't want you any closer." She pointed at the condoms. "Did you leave earlier to get those?"

"No." He'd left to blow off some steam. He hadn't thought about the packets until he'd returned to the apartment and realized she was still in the bedroom. He'd only materialized the condoms then.

Cam knew she was grasping at straws to distract him. Before she could stop him, he reached out, moved her aside and stared down at the empty desk.

"What were you hiding?"

Ariel stood beside him with her eyes closed.

"There's nothing there."

She opened her eyes and looked at the desk. "But—"

"But what?"

Ariel looked under the desk and through the drawers. "It was right there."

Cam studied her closely. Either she was a better actress than he thought, or she believed that she'd seen something on the desk—something she needed to hide from him.

"What was there?"

She stumbled to the bed and sat down, mumbling to herself, "There has to be another way."

"Another way for what?"

Ariel didn't answer. Instead, she wrapped her arms around her chest and rocked on the bed.

Cam paused. Whatever reason she had for doing the Learneds' bidding was obviously of great importance to her. If his earlier assumption was right—if the thief in the coma was her brother—that might be why he disappeared from the hospital.

And if he was being held by the Learneds, her fear of divulging any information was understandable. Not acceptable—he would discover what she was after one way or another—but he could understand her resistance.

Right now, in her current state, he wasn't going to get anything out of her. Cam touched her shoulder. "Are you all right?"

After she nodded, he said, "Get some rest. I'll wake you up later for dinner."

When Ariel didn't respond or move, Cam warned, "I'm not above using magic to force you. If you don't stretch out and at least pretend to take a nap, I'll take matters into my own hands."

She kicked off her shoes and climbed onto the bed. A strangled sniffle stopped him with his hand on the doorknob.

Cam swallowed a groan. He needed to get out of this room. Another sniffle made his stomach twist.

Cursing softly, he kicked off his own shoes, then slid onto the bed behind her and pulled her into his arms.

Ariel stiffened against his chest. "What—"

"Don't mistake this for surrender. It's not. I just can't stand to hear a woman cry."

"I'm not—"

"Yeah, right." He cut off her denial. "Go to sleep."

Chapter 10

Ariel yanked the half-dead rosebush from the loosened ground. She tossed it onto the growing pile before grabbing the shovel to dig around another bush.

"What are you doing?"

The act of swallowing a groan—or curse—every time Danielle Drake showed up to criticize was getting tedious. For whatever reason, the woman despised her—she'd been cold and critical from the moment they'd met. Ariel jabbed the shovel into the ground before turning to face the woman. "Digging out these bushes."

"Those are rosebushes." Indignation dripped from Danielle's voice.

No kidding? Roses? Who would have guessed? Unspoken sarcasm choked her. Ariel waved at the two young men helping her. "Why don't you two break for lunch. We can finish up afterward."

Once they were out of earshot, she explained as patiently as possible, "Mr. Drake told me to do whatever I wanted with the landscape. I'm replacing these hybrids with some old English and rugosa bushes."

"I picked those out myself."

The woman would have claimed she had even if she hadn't. "I'm sorry, Ms. Drake," Ariel marveled at the ease with which she lied of late. "I should have conferred with you first." The older woman's pursed lips softened. "I just thought the older-style roses would be a perfect fit for such a medieval-looking resort."

Danielle nodded toward the herb beds. "What are you doing over there?"

Even though she knew it'd be a waste of time, Ariel tried to ease the woman's concerns. "I talked to the chef and we won't be touching his cooking herbs. I'm just going to add a few for looks and scent. Some lavender, lemon balm and maybe some different-colored yarrows."

"What about mint?"

From reading the notes he'd left behind, she knew that the last gardener had refused to sow the invasive plant for fear it would cover the entire mountainside once it took root. "We'll plant some in pots up by the kitchen."

What exactly was Ms. Drake after? She hadn't come out here to discuss plants.

"Have you given any thought to the maze?"

Ariel rubbed her temples. This constant questioning of everything she did would have her screaming if this were a permanent position. Cam's aunt was a bear to work with.

She had already chased off a young woman who had been working with Sean on the computer system. A

Play the

Lucky Hearts

Game

and get...
2 FREE BOOKS *and*
FREE MYSTERY GIFTS...

YOURS TO KEEP!

HOW TO PLAY:

- Scratch off the gold area at the right. Then check the claim chart to see what we have for you— **2 FREE BOOKS** and **2 FREE GIFTS—ALL YOURS FOR FREE!**

- There's no catch. You're under no obligation to buy anything. We charge nothing—ZERO—for your first shipment. And you don't have to make any minimum number of purchases—not even one!

- We hope that after receiving your free books you'll want to remain a subscriber. But the choice is yours—to continue or cancel, anytime at all! So why not take us up on our invitation. You'll be glad you did!

2 FREE GIFTS

We can't tell you what they are… but we're sure you'll like them when you accept our No-Risk offer!

Visit us online at
www.ReaderService.com

Play the

Lucky Hearts Game

and get...
2 FREE BOOKS and
2 FREE MYSTERY GIFTS...
YOURS TO KEEP!

Yes! I have scratched off the gold card. Please send me my *2 FREE BOOKS* and *2 FREE MYSTERY GIFTS* (gifts are worth about $10). I understand that I am under no obligation to purchase any books as explained on the back of this card.

Scratch Here!

237/337 HDL FS7J

FIRST NAME	LAST NAME

ADDRESS

APT.#	CITY

STATE/PROV.   ZIP/POSTAL CODE

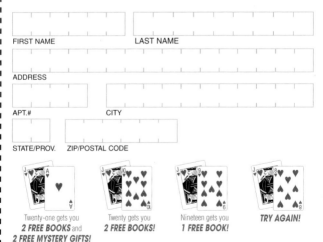

Twenty-one gets you
2 FREE BOOKS and
2 FREE MYSTERY GIFTS!

Twenty gets you
2 FREE BOOKS!

Nineteen gets you
1 FREE BOOK!

TRY AGAIN!

© 2012 HARLEQUIN ENTERPRISES LIMITED. Printed in the U.S.A.

▼ DETACH AND MAIL CARD TODAY! ▼

HPAR-LH4-07/12

The Reader Service—Here's how it works:

Accepting your 2 free books and 2 free gifts (gifts valued at approximately $10.00) places you under no obligation to buy anything. You may keep the books and gifts and return the shipping statement marked "cancel". If you do not cancel, about a month later we'll send you 4 additional books and bill you just $21.42 in the U.S. or $23.46 in Canada. That is a savings of at least 21% off the cover price of all 4 books! It's quite a bargain! Shipping and handling is just 50¢ per book in the U.S. and 75¢ per book in Canada.* You may cancel at any time, but if you choose to continue, every month we'll send you 4 more books, which you may either purchase at the discount price or return to us and cancel your subscription.

*Terms and prices subject to change without notice. Prices do not include applicable taxes. Sales tax applicable in N.Y. Canadian residents will be charged applicable taxes. Offer not valid in Quebec. All orders subject to credit approval. Credit or debit balances in a customer's account(s) may be offset by any other outstanding balance owed by or to the customer. Please allow 4 to 6 weeks for delivery. Offer available while quantities last.

▲ If offer card is missing write to: The Reader Service, P.O. Box 1867, Buffalo, NY 14240-1867 or visit www.ReaderService.com ▲

BUSINESS REPLY MAIL
FIRST-CLASS MAIL PERMIT NO. 717 BUFFALO, NY

POSTAGE WILL BE PAID BY ADDRESSEE

THE READER SERVICE
PO BOX 1867
BUFFALO NY 14240-9952

NO POSTAGE
NECESSARY
IF MAILED
IN THE
UNITED STATES

shame, really, considering the two made a cute couple and seemed to have hit it off.

"That's none of your business."

Ariel tensed at the realization that Danielle hadn't moved her lips. "Not you, too."

"Not me, too—what?" Ms. Drake's feigned look of innocence was laughable.

"You just put those words into my head."

"I don't know what you're talking about."

"Cam already told me that he isn't…normal. It's fairly obvious that you aren't, either, so there's no need to hide it."

Danielle squinted. "You should really wear a hat if you're going to be out in the sun this long."

It was apparent that Ms. Drake's sole purpose for coming to the garden was to pick a fight. If that's what the woman wanted, that's what she would get. "Is that what happened to you?"

"Why, you—"

Danielle drew back her arm as if she was going to throw something overhand. Ariel ducked and put up her hands to ward off whatever the woman was about to throw at her.

"Stop. Now." Cam glared at his aunt. "Don't you have anything else to do?"

"Not really," Danielle answered before she whipped what looked like a small ball of fire at Ariel.

She watched in shocked disbelief as the fiery ball bounced off an invisible shield, exploding into a shower of embers at her feet without hitting her.

Danielle Drake stomped past Cam, warning, "You can't protect her all the time."

Ariel lowered her arms. "Thank you."

He didn't move. Just asked, "For what?"

"For not letting me get burned alive, I suppose."

"I didn't do that."

"Your aunt certainly didn't. And if you didn't, who did?"

Cam surveyed the grounds. "There's no one else here except you."

Not again. He hadn't accused her of possessing magic since the evening he'd held her while she'd slept. That had been six days ago. She thought they'd gotten past the accusations. "How many times do I have to tell you—"

He raised a hand. "Save it, Ariel."

Before she could reply, he turned and left.

Once again she wanted to scream. Instead, she grabbed the shovel and attacked the rosebush with a vengeance.

Wasn't it enough that she'd broken the law and was now putting her life in danger to save her brother?

On top of that, she had to have dreams not just of flying as a dragon, but of her and Cameron together? Not just dreams, but ones so real, so erotic and hot that she woke up every morning in desperate need. And cold showers were a myth. They didn't help. Granted, the cold water cooled her skin, but it did nothing to cool the lust.

Now she had to deal with an insane woman who wanted to fry her to a crisp—and worse—one who could.

What really bothered her was that she wasn't terrified. Ariel knew she should be. Any rational person would fear so much for their safety that they would go out of their way to avoid Danielle Drake.

Of course, any rational person would have lost their wits by now. Hearing voices in one's head normally spelled trouble. And while it had terrified her at first, now it was merely irritating.

And this gut feeling that she could fly? If she was in the habit of taking pharmaceuticals maybe that would be a valid explanation. But the strongest med she swallowed was asprin.

This whole magic...wizard...thing wasn't possible. Yet, she'd just seen a ball of fire shoot from Ms. Drake's fingertips. And she'd seen a dragon turn into a man.

So, why wasn't she babbling incoherently in a corner somewhere? What was keeping her from running away in disbelief and terror?

And she knew something was helping her. She could feel it—could sense that something was lending her strength.

Certain she'd find no answers to the puzzles plaguing her, Ariel realized she was missing one of the few opportunities she had to do some more snooping before she talked with Renalde tomorrow.

She dropped the shovel and her gloves into the empty wheelbarrow and ducked into the Lair through the kitchen door.

The only places she hadn't checked for the pendant and cube were the family's private offices and the basement. There was no way she was going to get access to the offices while Cam was around. That would have to wait until she could figure out a way to get past his ever-watchful eyes.

The basement, however, was manageable. The entrance was located in a rear hall, away from the lobby and offices.

She'd discovered the door last night and had picked the lock this morning before heading out to the gardens. Hopefully, nobody had noticed and relocked it.

She stuck her head out of the dining room, making sure the hallway was empty before slipping toward the backside of the Lair.

Hearing voices, Ariel ducked through the basement door and held her breath. She waited until the people passed, then headed down the stairs.

The basement was gigantic. They could put ten full-size tennis courts down here and still have room to spare. Uncertain where to start, she chose the bar area. It seemed the most obvious place to hide something. Sort of that hidden-in-plain-sight concept someone like Cam might employ.

Unfortunately, after what seemed like hours later, she'd found nothing. Leaning on the counter, she scanned the basement.

Her attention fell on an old wooden chest against the far wall. Ariel shrugged, then headed toward it. "It's worth a shot."

The lid screeched open. The sound echoed in the nearly empty basement. She cringed and held her breath, coming to a dead stop. Certain nobody upstairs had heard the noise, she knelt and started emptying out the chest.

"How long do you plan on protecting the enemy?"

Cam glanced up from the accounts on his desk. "I'll protect her as long as she's here."

He took one look at his aunt's face, threw an invisible shield around his mind and leaned back in his chair. "What were you thinking?"

Danielle's tight face flushed with rage. "Someone needs to do something about that woman. And if you won't, I will."

"Burning her alive is not an option."

His aunt sat down and casually inspected her long, painted fingernails. "I don't see why not."

She was just trying to get him to lose his temper; it was, after all, an old trick they'd learned at her knee, so to speak. Get your opponent to drop their focus and you've gained the upper hand.

"There's that unlawful part of the idea that's going to be rather hard to explain away. And I'm sure the High Wizard can find better things to do than hold a trial and execution." Especially considering Braeden was the High Wizard.

Danielle sighed and shook her head. "Braeden would never condemn me."

"Depends on who speaks for Ariel."

"You wouldn't."

"If you killed her? Yes, I would."

His aunt stared at him a moment before frowning. "You're sleeping with her."

That was none of her business. "It doesn't matter if I am or not. What does matter is the law. And you are well aware that killing a powerless human with wizardry is punishable by lasting death."

Danielle Drake wasn't any different than anyone else of their kind. She wasn't about to risk not having her essence pass over into the next dimension at the time of her physical body's death.

The law had been on the records for over four hundred years. High council had enacted such a severe penalty because human deaths of the otherworldly nature drew too much attention to the clans.

For all their good intentions, too many humans weren't accepting of those who were different. To protect their dwindling numbers, the wizards who lived among the general populace kept their powers a secret.

"Sometimes laws need to be broken."

"So, you're declaring open season on humankind?"

Since they both knew she didn't have the power to make such a declaration, she ignored the question and stated, "That woman needs to go."

He wasn't arguing that point. Ariel did need to go—before he became too used to having her around. The past few days had been...different...almost pleasant. Her familiar scents and ever-changing moods had become a part of his day.

Still, he wanted to hear his aunt's reasoning. "Why does she need to go?"

"For one thing, she works for the Learneds."

"I know that." Cam flicked the pun-sai tree limb away from the computer keyboard on his desk. The plant flicked back and then started tapping keys, bringing a view from a security camera in the basement up on the screen. "I'd like to discover what she's after, what they have her doing."

"That's fairly obvious. She's here to see us killed. Doesn't that matter to you?"

What the hell was Ariel looking for in the basement? She had his and Braeden's swords and armor out of the chest.

Splitting his attention between his aunt and Ariel, he answered, "Of course it matters."

Ariel took his sword out of the scabbard and ran her fingertips along the dragons etched into the blade. The warmth of her touch trailed down his spine.

"If you won't let me deal with her, what do you plan on doing?"

Cam forced his wandering mind back to the conversation. "I'd like to have the advantage of knowing what the Learneds are up to this time."

With the help of Harold and Jennie, he thought he'd been keeping close enough tabs on Ariel. From the looks of things, he'd been mistaken.

Cam froze when Ariel looked directly at the camera and frowned. Did she realize she was being watched? He flinched when she carelessly dropped the swords back into the chest.

"Did you hear me?" Dani's screech jolted his attention away from Ariel and the monitor.

"What?"

"I said I'm calling Braeden."

"For what?"

"You seem unable to deal with this woman. Maybe he'll do what's necessary."

Cam leaned forward. "Aunt Dani, I love you dearly, but your threats get rather tiring at times. Feel free to call Braeden. And I'll make certain he finds out about your little stunt in the garden."

Danielle rose. To his relief, she turned and walked out of his office without another word.

Ariel lifted her hair from her neck and sighed as a breeze rushed across her warm skin. She paused a moment to enjoy the coolness before going inside.

Now that the rose beds were bare and she'd sent her helpers packing for the night, the only thing she wanted to do was to slip into a nice hot bubble bath.

If she had any luck whatsoever, Cameron would still be working. She wanted to unwind in the tub without any interruptions.

She unlocked the door and stepped into the dark silence of an empty apartment with a relieved whoosh of breath. Ariel hurried to her room intent on getting into a tub of bubbles behind a locked bathroom door before Cam arrived.

A cautious glance toward the desk made her groan. That cursed book was still there.

Every morning she woke up hoping it would be gone. And every morning it silently mocked her from the top of the desk.

It didn't matter where she tried to stash the thing at night—in a drawer, closet, or under the bed—when the sun rose it was back on the desk. The only difference was that it was open to a different page each day.

What appeared as rough sketches of half-formed images and symbols in the sun's light were highly detailed and vibrantly colored by the end of the day. Either way—draft or completed—made little difference since she didn't look at the pages long enough to decipher what was unveiled. The chance of being given any type of magical powers wasn't one she wanted to risk.

The only saving grace with this particular insanity was that the book remained invisible to everyone except her.

"Done for the day?"

She jumped at Cam's question. Without having to hide the book this time, she turned around. "I didn't hear you come in."

He walked into her bedroom. "I asked if you were done for the day." His calm, even tone was in complete contrast with his angry expression.

"According to the clock I am." She glanced with longing toward the bathroom. Her bubbles would have to wait. "Unless there's something else I should be doing."

"You could explain what you were doing in the basement."

"Just being nosy." She'd had her fill of confrontation today and was determined to keep this conversation light. Besides, it wasn't as if she'd found anything that she needed to lie about. "Wasn't that obvious?"

"Nosy?"

Ariel chose another word. "Curious."

"Curious about what was behind a locked door?" Two steps brought him closer. "When you picked the lock, didn't a part of your mind warn you not to go down into the dark?"

"There was a light switch." She cringed, wishing that just once she would employ her brain before giving her mouth free rein.

Another step brought him against her. "What were you looking for, Ariel?"

His calm, steady tone chafed. It was the same tone her mother had used whenever she or Carl were being unreasonable. She was no longer a child and Cameron Drake most certainly wasn't her mother.

The pulse throbbing against his neck caught her attention. While he might be trying to keep his words even and steady, his heartbeat told another story.

Ariel reached up and ran a fingertip across the not-so-steady pulsing. Cam grasped her wrist. "Don't."

She tugged her arm free. "I wasn't looking for anything in particular. You were watching, I saw the light on the security camera, so you know exactly what I found—nothing."

He lifted a lock of her hair. She shivered as his knuckles brushed against her neck. Cam leaned closer. "Yes, I know what you found."

Ariel held her breath, fighting the unexpected flash of terror beating against her mind. She knew that voice, recognized the darkly ominous tone.

No.

She pushed back the fear. It wasn't possible. Cameron was not the dragon changeling from Mirabilus. That creature had frightened her so much she was certain she'd have realized it before now. This unwarranted emotion was caused by nothing more than the heated rush of desire chipping away at her ability to think clearly.

Cameron continued, "What I want to know is what you were looking for in the first place."

Ariel closed her eyes against another rush of emotions turning the floor into waves beneath her feet. He was too close. His breath wafted too warmly across her ear.

She swayed briefly against his chest, before forcing her legs to hold her steady. "I wasn't looking for anything."

"You are such a liar, Ariel."

His breathless comment sounded more like an endearment whispered by a lover in the heat of the moment than an accusation by a mythical beast. She gazed up at him.

His shimmering gaze reflected the desire coursing through her. He might be angry with her for snooping and he might never trust her, but at this moment he wanted her.

She could feel his longing, sense his need. Ariel didn't question how she knew it, because she wanted—needed—him, too. Just being near him this past week had been maddening.

She didn't want to be here—not like this, as a spy and a thief. The Drakes were nothing to her except owners of the items that would spare her brother's life.

Once she found what she needed, she'd leave the Lair without looking back.

Except for Cameron.

It would be hard walking away from him. She'd been attracted to him from the moment she'd walked into his office. Ariel wasn't foolish enough to hold any illusions about their attraction. There was no budding relationship between them—it was purely physical.

She hadn't had time for dating. One-night stands didn't interest her. Acquaintances had called her a prude, but her friends had understood. Juggling the responsibilities of school, work and Carl were all she could handle. Adding the emotional complications that came with relationships and sex would tip the scales.

And now, a man had the ability to make her shiver with desire. It seemed as if she'd waited years for just this moment—for just this man.

When she had nothing to tell Renalde tomorrow, her time at the Lair might come to an end. Tonight could very well be the last chance she had to see if her dreams were right. Would making love with Cam be as erotic and fulfilling as her nightly visions had promised?

She leaned purposely against his chest. "Cam…" Uncertain how to ask for what she wanted, she let her plea trail off.

His heart pounded in unison with her own. He pulled her close to bury his face against her neck, and warned, "Don't offer more than you're willing to give."

Ariel knew that at this moment she would offer him everything—no matter the cost. She was drawn to him by a power she couldn't imagine let alone define.

Nothing could keep her from his arms. She craved his kisses, needed his touch too much to back away now.

She brushed her cheek across his. "I'm not."

Cam groaned. Her response broke the chains holding the dragon in check. He couldn't tell who wanted her more—him or the beast.

His hands shook with the effort required to coax the now-raging beast to be patient. Never, until meeting Ariel, had controlling the dragon been so difficult.

Each time he'd sensed her desire, breathed in the fragrance of her lust or heard her blood rushing with need, the threads of his restraint had frayed.

It wasn't that he cared for her—his heart wasn't involved, even if his lust-crazed beast momentarily thought otherwise. But he feared that if he relinquished control, gave the desire full rein, he could quite possibly come to care far too much.

Caring too much now would only make being alone once again more difficult. Because once this was over, she would leave—she would have no choice. And he would return to his solitary existence.

But there was tonight. They could share just one night and somehow he'd make the memory last a lifetime.

Cam took a deep breath, willing himself and his beast to go easy. They had all night. There was no need to rush.

With the blink of an eye, he set the scene. Soft, gentle music filtered in through the ceiling speakers. Candlelight replaced the glare of the lamps. Incense that mimicked her pheromones scented the air.

Still holding her close, he swayed, dancing slowly to the music. She followed his lead as if they had done this a thousand times in the past.

"This feels like a strange date." Ariel tipped her head back to ask, "No wine, or flowers?"

Did she think she was dealing with an amateur? He

spun her around the room, pausing next to a side table set with a white lace cloth, orange-hued roses and two full champagne flutes. Cam relaxed his embrace and handed her a glass.

A flash of disappointment raced across her face before she tasted the champagne. He cupped her cheek, stroking his thumb over the softness of her face. "What's wrong?"

"Impressive." Ariel's gaze roamed the bedroom before coming back to him. "How many times have you done this?"

"Never."

Her eyebrows arched above her shimmering gaze. "Never?"

He stroked her lower lip, smiling at the tremor his touch created. "No."

Ariel lowered her gaze and set her glass down. She touched the roses. "Orange?"

"The color symbolizes desire." Cam drew her back into his embrace and onto their makeshift dance floor. "Roses for a beautiful woman."

"I'm not beautiful."

"Stop it, Ariel." She was nervous. He'd expected that. But he had hoped the music and wine would help. Apparently not.

She glared up at him. "Stop what?"

"Stop thinking and questioning. Stop trying to find fault with every little thing. Stop worrying. Tomorrow will get here tomorrow, no matter what."

Still dancing slowly, he lowered his mouth to brush her lips, whispering, "Right now, just let it all go. Let yourself enjoy this moment."

She clung to his shoulders. "I don't think I know how."

"Like this." He covered her lips, kissing her, teasing her, coaxing her to relax, beckoning her to feel instead of think.

Chapter 11

Ariel leaned into his kiss with a sigh of surrender, giving up any pretense of control over her desires. She would follow where he led, submit to his will and worry about the consequences tomorrow.

She had waited her whole adult life for this moment—for just this touch, just this kiss—just this man. One with the ability to chase away her breath with a glance and steal her mind with a simple caress.

Why it had to be *this* man, one who was not quite human and more foe than friend, didn't matter. She didn't know how, or why, but some primal part of him spoke to the wildness in her. It whispered to her soul, seducing her with a promise of safety and completion.

At this moment, with his arms holding her, his lips warm and demanding on hers, she felt no fear, no trepidation, only want and need.

"Ariel." Her name was a heated whisper against her cheek. "Send me away, now."

"No." She slipped her hands beneath his shirt, marveling at the warmth of his flesh, and wanting to feel the heat of his skin against hers. "Stay."

Either he read her thoughts, or had the same desire, because before she could draw another breath they were on the bed—naked. Only partially surprised, she stared up at him. "Isn't that cheating?"

"Yes." Cam's husky answer and shimmering gaze sent a rush down her spine. He looked at her as if she was the only thing in his world.

His gentle, seeking caress as it trailed along her side conveyed the same message—no one else existed except the two of them.

Wizardry and cheating fell to the wayside. She ran a hand through his hair, tugging him closer, drawing his mouth back to hers. He gave in to her silent demand, kissing her until she moaned with need for more than just the feel of his lips.

Moments ago his caress had been gentle and seeking, but now his thoroughness left her gasping at the icy fire skittering along every nerve ending.

Every caress, each erotic kiss against her skin made her feel alive, nearly frantic with longing.

Other than in her dreams, she'd not realized it could be this—intoxicating. Her heart pounded, her body throbbed beneath his insistent onslaught.

The heat of his hands on her legs, stroking, teasing his way over her knee, up her thigh, made the muscles low in her belly clench.

Even though she knew it wasn't possible, Ariel's body responded as if his touch was familiar. She moved instinctively beneath him, anticipating his next caress, knowing what he wanted her to do.

She frowned. Her dreams had been vivid, but how had they been so realistic?

His lips following the path his hands had just taken chased her wonderings aside. When the bed seemed to spin beneath them it no longer mattered if this was their first time together or hundredth.

She wanted more than just the caress of his hands on her flesh, or the exquisite kiss at her core. She tugged on his hair, wanting him over her, filling her.

"Cam." Ariel's breath caught in her throat as the already intense throbbing quickened. She moaned, calling out his name again, "Cam, please."

Thankfully he didn't have to leave to get condoms, they were at hand. The mark on his shoulder blade throbbed. His beast roared, demanding to claim this woman as his own.

Again, he felt an inviting warmth steal over him, rushing through his limbs to settle around his heart. His beast crooned, rumbling with anticipation.

Shocked, Cam cursed silently. Why now? Why this woman and not Carol? This possession, this all-encompassing completion should have been shared with his wife, not with his enemy.

His beast roared, demanding he forget his hurt and accept what this woman offered.

No. He had to remain in control. The wild desires within couldn't be unleashed. It would be disastrous in ways he could barely imagine at the moment. But the beast beckoned him forward relentlessly.

Ariel moved beneath him. Before he could stop her, she drew her hands up his back, grazing his skin with the tips of her fingernails. Her touch once more across his birthmark sent shivers down his spine.

He couldn't hold back any longer and Cameron gave in with a strangled groan.

His control slipped, but to his relief, his dragon didn't ravage the woman as he'd feared. For the first time since he'd recognized the creature inside, they acted as one. Instead of being at odds with him, the beast let him remain in human form as they sought release.

He and Ariel moved together, their rhythms in tune as though this wasn't their first time together. The sound of his name on her lips was an aphrodisiac that nearly sent him over the edge.

Ariel's fingers grazed the mark on his shoulder blade, curling, pressing her nails into his flesh as she found her release.

Now the beast growled, pushed over the edge at the contact with the oversensitive birthmark. Cam gasped, his muscles straining against the urge to forget his human nature.

Before he fully realized what was happening, reality fell away in a dizzying rush. There was no bed beneath them, no confining walls surrounding them. Nothing but air and the wide-open sky served as a backdrop for two mating dragons.

No matter how hard he tried, Cam was unable to pull away from the near-brutal savagery of their dance. He closed his eyes, but in his mind saw his beast shake the smaller female into submission before folding his wings around her, holding her close.

Fingernails pressing into his shoulders and his name whispered as a breathless sigh shook him free. Spent, he dropped beside Ariel, pulling her roughly into his embrace, thankful that what he'd seen had not crossed the border between dream and reality.

Ariel's heart beat hard against his chest, nearly as hard and erratic as his own.

She trailed her fingertips up his spine and across his shoulder blades, breathlessly asking, "Was that man or wizard?"

He closed his eyes as she lightly brushed over the still-pulsing mark. "Neither. It was magic."

She sighed against his chest. "I'll agree with that."

He chuckled, leaning closer to kiss her. A shimmer of light cut through the darkness behind his closed eyelids. Reluctantly breaking their kiss, he glanced toward the light.

What the hell was going on here?

Speechless, he jerked free of Ariel's embrace and stared from her to the grimoire on her dresser.

The music came to an instant stop. A glaring overhead light replaced the soft flicker of the candles. Ariel shook off her daze and followed the direction of Cam's stare.

A glowing light shimmered around the book on her dresser. From the rigidity of his muscles and the even more rigid expression, she knew that he could see the grimoire.

She gasped, hoping he'd believe her feigned surprise. "Where did that come from?"

His brittle, humorless laugh evaporated her hope. "Why don't you tell me?"

"There isn't anything I can tell you." Just as there'd been a time for lying, perhaps this was a time for the truth—especially now when it was more believable to her than any fabrication she could concoct.

When he glared down at her, she rushed into her

explanation. "It just appeared when you forced me to move in here."

He turned away, sat on the edge of the bed and rubbed his temples. She could completely understand if his head was pounding—so was hers.

She touched his arm, trying to get him to turn around and look at her. "What do you want me to say? It was just here."

Cam jerked away from her touch. "And how long has it been—just here?"

"It's been here as long as I have." When he did turn to look at her, Ariel scooted away from the anger that seemed to glow from his eyes.

"Who helped you?"

"What?"

Cameron rose, grasped her arms to drag her from the bed, then tugged her toward the dresser. "This didn't get here on its own. The Learneds can't gain entrance into the Lair. So, who is helping you?"

He ran his gaze down her naked body. Before she could decipher his look, he waved their clothes back on and continued, "Even if you have any abilities, they can't possibly be strong enough to have broken the spell encasing this book."

Ariel frowned. "So, even if I was a—" she choked on the insanity of even saying the word "—wizard, I couldn't possibly be as strong, or magical, as you?"

"Since your powers of comprehension are still intact, tell me who's helping you."

She gritted her teeth. They'd just made love, but that obviously meant little. How dare he use that overly caustic tone of voice with her? She jerked free of his hold. "Who do you think you are?"

"Your boss."

Her *boss?* Even though his response stung, she dismissed it with a wave of her hand. "We both know how much truth there is in that. You act like you're the king of the wizards or something." She shook her head. "And I sound like an imbecile. Wizards. Kings."

"Close."

"To an imbecile?"

"King." He shrugged, before turning back toward the grimoire, saying, "More like the Dragon Lord spare."

Ariel didn't know who, or what, to stare at first—the man who just declared he was some sort of lord, or the book that was now glowing with a shocking red light.

She finally settled on Cam. "What are you—"

He raised a hand, cutting off her question. "Come here."

"No." Ariel backed out of his reach. She wasn't getting any closer to that book than she had to. In fact, she edged toward the door, intent on making her escape.

Cam looked over his shoulder and crooked a finger in her direction. She dug in her heels and grabbed for the bedpost, knowing it would do little good.

She closed her eyes as once again she levitated a fraction of an inch above the floor and floated to his side. The instant her feet hit the floor she opened her eyes, demanding, "Stop doing that."

"Listen to yourself."

"Listen to myself? Why? Are my words coming out funny?"

"Funny? No. Angry? Yes. Sarcastic? Most definitely."

"You should talk."

He draped an arm over her shoulder. "Shut up a minute, then listen."

Ariel swallowed, but clamped her lips together to

keep from shouting. A warmth stole over her. It slowly flowed from his arm into her, relaxing her, chasing away her anger. She glanced up at him. "What is going on?"

Surprised at her calmer tone of voice, she shook her head. "This doesn't make sense."

"No, it doesn't." He nodded toward the book. "But look."

The grimoire now glowed with a soft pink light. "How did you do that?"

"I didn't."

"Neither did I. I didn't sneak Renalde into the Lair, if that's what you think."

"You couldn't have. I would have known the instant he stepped on our property."

"So, what's making the book do that?"

"I think it's us."

Ariel leaned as far away from him as his hold would permit. "What do you mean 'us'? There is no 'us.'"

Cameron looked down at her. He cocked one eyebrow and shot her a half smile that made her stomach flip. "Oh, really?"

She swallowed and worked to unglue her tongue from the roof of her suddenly dry mouth. Finally composing herself enough to speak, she answered, "Really."

His soft chuckle set her heart skipping.

"Watch and see if this works like I think it will." Cam lowered his arm and gently pushed her away from the dresser. He crossed to the other side of the room.

Within a moment, his smile faded and her renewed anger grew. Ariel's spine stiffened, her stomach tightened. The throbbing in her temples returned as she clenched her jaw.

"When did you say the grimoire first appeared?"

She closed her eyes against the harshness of his voice. "The same day you made me move in here."

"Right."

"Are you calling me a liar?"

"It is something you seem to excel at. Where have you been hiding it?"

Ariel flinched at his accusation. "Nowhere. It's been right there this whole time. That's what I was trying to hide that first day."

"Is this what the Learneds sent you here to find? How much have you told them about the grimoire?"

"No." To her horror, her bottom lip started to tremble. She was tired of arguing with him, especially now. It took too much energy, leaving her drained. "I haven't...told them..." Ariel paused, determined to keep her voice from breaking. "I haven't told them anything."

Cam fought the urge to groan. Even though he'd rather be wrong in this, his guess was that she hadn't broken through his spell. Somehow, the grimoire had done it without help.

And for whatever reason, it was causing this false, overblown feeling of anger. His rage had been inexplicable, especially since the beast had remained calm and unconcerned, still soaking up the afterglow of sex.

If the shimmer of tears in Ariel's eyes and her trembling lip were any indication, her overwhelming emotions were being forced on her, too. He went toward her. "Come here."

"Just leave me alone." She backed away. "And don't even think about floating me over there."

"Fine, we'll do it the old-fashioned way." He cleared the distance between them in three long strides and pulled her into his arms.

Nearly dragging her along, Cam stopped in front of the dresser, whispering, "Now watch."

When he covered her lips briefly with his, Ariel relaxed and rested her cheek against his shoulder. "Now what?"

As much as he hated to admit it, he explained, "It's only a guess, but I think it's our turn."

"That makes about as much sense as anything else." She sighed, then asked, "Our turn for what?"

"The grimoire has a spell on it."

"I'm shocked."

He tightened his embrace in response to her sarcasm. "Braeden and Alexia had to work together to decipher the first part of the book."

"And?"

"As much as I hate to admit this, it seems it's our turn to translate more of it."

"Wasn't your sister-in-law given powers in the process?"

"Yes."

"No."

"No?" Cam leaned back to look down at her. "No, what?"

"No," she repeated, shaking her head. Ariel pulled out of his embrace. "I'm not game for this."

He should have known she'd be less than thrilled with that idea. From what he'd seen, humans fell into two categories—those who jumped at the chance to gain extraordinary powers and those who would rather swallow hot coals than change. Unfortunately, Ariel fell into the latter group.

"What makes you think you have a choice?"

She flashed him a wary gaze before turning to walk

away. Cam grabbed her hand to keep her from leaving the area around the grimoire. "Don't."

Ariel's shoulders slumped, but she turned back to face him. "I don't want to be like you."

"You won't be." Nobody could be like him.

She glanced toward the dresser. "I never should have touched it."

"Too late, the process has already started." He stood before the grimoire and ran a fingertip down a page half filled with images. A spark of interest shot into his beast. Cam felt it shake off the afterglow to shoot a curious stare at the book.

"What does it say?" Ariel joined him.

"It looks like a story of some sort." He tried unsuccessfully to turn back a page to see what came before.

Ariel sighed. "Let me." She gingerly reached out and to Cam's surprise, the pages easily turned beneath her touch.

"It likes you."

She spun around. "More than happy to leave."

He snatched her hand, drawing her back to his side. "Tell me what you know about the book."

"Not much. In the morning the page is blank, it fills in slowly all day long. No matter where I hide it, the damn thing ends up on the dresser or the desk by the time night falls."

It was all he could do not to laugh at the exasperation in her tone. "Does it just fill in one page a day?"

"So far, yes."

"Move it over to the desk."

"I don't want to do this."

Cam sat down at the small writing desk and nodded from the book to the desk. Her personal feelings about the grimoire, or the risks surrounding it, mattered little. Since the book had chosen her, she was going to help. It was just that simple.

He wasn't about to miss out on the chance to discover what the grimoire contained. He had to know if there was anything in there that could help him defeat the Learneds. This ancient clannish war had gone on too long; he wanted it to end.

When Ariel folded her arms in front of her and shook her head, he warned, "You can do this the easy way, or the hard way, but you are going to help."

"You can't force me."

"Don't tempt me, Ariel." He might not be able to control her mind and actions with his thoughts, but there were other ways.

When she remained immobile, he shrugged. "Okay." With a crook of his finger, she was at his side. Cam pulled her down across his lap. "You want to play?"

"No." She turned her face away from his. "I should be angry."

"I'm sure you will be later—as will I." He trailed a fingertip along the side of her neck. "Right now, though, it seems the grimoire has control of our emotions. At least while we're in this room."

Ariel thought the idea of anyone—or anything—having control over Cameron Drake was ludicrous. "And you're okay with that?"

"Are you implying I have control issues?"

"I'm not implying anything."

Cam laughed at her answer before following his stroking finger with his lips. She shivered beneath his touch. This was more than disconcerting, it was dangerous.

There was one sure way to stop him. Ariel leaned

over, grabbed the grimoire and set it on the desk. "There."

Just as she thought he would, Cam left off teasing her to stare intently at the book. She took his concentration as an opportunity to slip off his lap.

Before she could walk away, he hooked his fingers around her wrist to keep her close. He wasn't as distracted as she'd hoped.

"I'm not going to stand here all night." She jiggled her wrist.

Without turning away from the page, Cam nodded toward a chair that instantly materialized on his other side. He released her, suggesting, "Have a seat."

After she perched on the edge of the chair, he said, "It's a curse."

Ariel jumped up from the chair and stood behind Cam. "What's cursed?"

"I'm not sure." He ran a finger beneath the symbols and pictures. "This one here—" he tapped the first symbol "—is familiar. It shows that a curse was spoken. Since the symbol is ancient, I can only assume the curse was issued centuries ago."

"And this concerns us, how?" She didn't care about curses, or the grimoire, for that matter. Ariel just wanted to find the pendant and the cube and get out of the Lair before anything happened to Carl—or her.

Cam reached back and stroked her leg. "It concerns you because I need you here."

She closed her eyes. If he didn't stop with the touching and caressing, they'd be back on the bed naked and his precious book would be in the closet.

"And it concerns me," Cam continued, "because it seems to have been placed on Nathan the Learned along with certain members of the Drake family."

She ran her fingers through his hair, almost jealous of the silken softness. "Which members?"

"I'm not—" He tensed beneath her touch before rising.

"Cam?" She looked up at his furrowed brow and clenched jaw. "What's wrong?"

"Nothing." He headed for the door. "I forgot that I have an appointment."

"No. Wait. Tell me—" Before she could finish her sentence he was gone.

Ariel went back to stare down at the book. He had to have seen, or read, something that unsettled him. What?

She flipped the pages back and forth. The only thing she could make sense of, besides the symbol he'd pointed out a few minutes ago, was a brilliant picture of a sapphire dragon.

Ariel stepped back, confused. A sapphire dragon? Why would that upset him so?

Knowing she'd find no answers staring at the grimoire, she left the bedroom and stepped out onto the apartment's balcony.

She shivered as the cold night air brushed across her face. Hugging herself for warmth, Ariel stared up at the stars shimmering against the blackness of the sky.

It seemed darker here than at home. Bereft of the constant glow of city lights, stars appeared brighter... close enough to almost touch.

She breathed in deeply, savoring the scents of the forest...the freshness of evergreens and the musty yet earthy aroma of dirt. The air green and alive swelled her heart with longing. She needed to break free of the bonds chaining her feet to the solid ground.

Ariel closed her eyes and leaned over the balcony's

railing, straining to better feel the bracing rush of the wind.

The desires beckoning her weren't normal—weren't quite human, a part of her knew this and recognized the longings as impossible. But the pounding of her heart, the ache of her soul begged her to ignore the logical, to instead listen to the cry of the imaginings, to leave logic and reasoning behind.

She curled her fingers tighter around the icy-cold metal railing, ensuring her hold on the tangible. And yet, in the same moment, felt the wind embrace her, pulling her from the earthly confines to soar freely toward the glittering stars.

Chapter 12

Cam whipped his sword through the musty air of the basement wishing he had something more solid to fight than his imagination.

There was nothing like a curse to give one's life meaning. It did, however, explain why his dragon had cared so little for Carol that it had let her be killed.

Since there were no others like them, the beast had known they would never find a mate, never know love. Their hunger and thirst were for Learned blood, not home and hearth.

So, what made Ariel so different? Why this mind-robbing physical attraction when they would never have a life together? It made no sense. But then, when it came to his beast's desire for Ariel, nothing made any sense.

The knowledge of his destiny took away not only his breath, it hammered at his will. What was the point of living alone—without a mate, without love, without making memories of a life shared? Without even knowing what it would be like to have a home and a family.

He threw his sword back into the storage chest. Battling nothing but air did little good. He wanted to rage out loud—scream his human frustration to the wind.

Cam clenched his jaw, fighting to ignore his beast's dire need to hurt something—to shed blood, to transfer this pain to another.

He raced up the stairs, out a back entrance and into the blackness of the forest. He had to get away, needed to find a way to breathe, to think.

From the tightening of his chest, he was certain his dragon needed freedom as much as he did, Cam took one quick glance over his shoulder before stepping off the side of the mountain.

The bite of the cold breeze settled beneath his wings, lifting him toward the blinking stars. He craned his neck, stretching out the kinks from the sudden shift from man to beast.

Aelthed bit the inside of his cheeks to keep from laughing out loud. Doing so would risk detection. And that was the last thing he wanted right now.

So, while the dragon twin had been unsuccessfully venting his frustration, he'd sat in the corner of his cube sensing the twin's anguish.

He knew the changeling had left, but he could still feel the anger, the confusion and the heartrending longing swirling about the area.

It was obvious from the tumultuous conflict that the man had managed to get the woman to help him with the grimoire. Good. It was past time the changeling knew about the curse.

Now, if he could just learn to accept the beast, give

it full rein on its emotions, perhaps the curse could be broken.

It was impossible to tell if this woman would ever be the dragon's true mate. But from the scent of lust fulfilled hanging heavy in the air, Aelthed knew the beast was already convinced.

Would the man come to accept or recognize that conviction? It was hard to be certain. There was little else Aelthed could do except to keep forcing the two of them together, whether the changeling liked it or not.

Satisfied that he'd done all he could today, he leaned back against the wall and closed his eyes. He needed rest to gather strength for the spell casting yet to come.

The stars brightly dotted the sky. The air, crisp and clear, glided beneath his wings. A measure of quiet calm settled his frustration and eased his confusion.

And yet, in the peacefulness of the night, Cam sensed that he wasn't alone.

Someone—or something—else had invaded his territory.

Startled out of his momentary tranquillity by an instinctual response to protect what was his, he dipped low and circled back defensively toward the Lair. A shadowy form glided just above the tops of the trees surrounding the resort.

Head low, wings folded compactly against his body, Cam's beast aimed for the intruder. Moving in closer, he uncurled his talons, intent on grasping the still-unsuspecting prey in order to break its neck and end the looming threat.

Nostrils flared, lips slightly parted, he chuffed the air, seeking a scent of the unfamiliar beast.

No.

Cam pulled up short.

Impossible.

His great beast pumped its wings backward to stop the assault and tipped its head one way, then the other, in confusion. He ascended and settled into lazy circles above the half-formed beast.

This was no intruder threatening his home and family. This shadowy beast was a new changeling, still not capable of complete transformation, let alone danger, doing nothing more than testing its wings.

Cam felt the changeling's excitement, its awe at the feel of air beneath its wings and wonderment at the open heavens above. He remembered those emotions, those first few moments of absolute freedom and unadulterated joy.

But neither the emotions nor the memories had pulled him up short and confused his beast—it had been the scent. The all-too-familiar scent of…Ariel.

Again he recognized that fact for what it was—*impossible.*

She was human. Of that he was certain. Ariel Johnson possessed no magic outside of what a normal, ordinary woman possessed in relationship to a man. He found her desirable. She aroused his passions with nothing more than the slightest touch, or a look.

While that ability might be considered magical, it wasn't true magic.

His beast grunted, reminding him that he could think whatever he wished, could gather whatever reasoning he wanted and hold it as close to his heart as he wanted, but the proof was before them. How could he deny what he and his beast saw or what they sensed?

Still—it wasn't possible. For so long he'd wished not to be alone that now he was imagining this. He and his beast only recognized the changeling as Ariel because of their unwarranted attachment to the woman.

His beast's long-drawn-out sigh was like a heavy weight against his chest.

Determined to put an end to this nonsensical argument, Cam prepared to descend, to make contact with this changeling. But just as his beast angled its wings, the shadowy form looked up at them.

Before Cam could stop the other beast from leaving, the misty, shadowy form disappeared.

He knew from experience that it would be impossible to follow or track the changeling. How many times in the beginning had he been startled from his misty dragon form by one thing or another only to find himself back in his apartment shaken and confused as to what had happened.

It had taken months and many transformations before he'd been able to admit what he was, what he'd become. He doubted if it would be any different for this changeling.

And in the meantime, it would be impossible to know for certain who the changeling was in human form. The one thing he did know for certain was that it was not a member of his family. The changeling's magic was far too weak for it to be of Drake blood.

He ignored his beast's repeated grunts. It wasn't Ariel. And even if it was, what difference did it make? The woman worked for the Learneds.

Cam and his beast shivered at the sudden implication of that uninviting thought.

To prove to himself that he had no worry on that front—that the changeling wasn't Ariel and that she wasn't now a greater threat to him and his family—he headed back to the Lair.

Landing on the balcony outside her bedroom, Cam shook off the lingering buzz common after changing back into human form and then stepped inside.

He nearly laughed with relief at finding her sound asleep on her bed. If his memories served him correctly, she wouldn't be this relaxed or peaceful after an outing as a dragon—at least not the first few times.

His beast groaned softly in longing and regret, chasing away Cam's relief.

He crossed the room and stared down at Ariel. He longed to lie beside her, to gather her into his arms and lose himself in passion and lust.

She rolled over and looked up at him through half-opened eyes. "What's wrong?"

Cam sat on the edge of the bed to stroke her cheek. "Nothing." He kept his voice low and gentle to soothe her back into her dreams. "Go back to sleep."

Ariel covered his hand with one of her own. "Come to bed."

It was painfully apparent that he and his beast had already grown more attached to her than was safe. Compounding that attachment wouldn't be wise for either of them. But he had to keep her at the Lair until the Learneds were defeated. And he would have to do so without adding more risk to his physical and emotional safety.

Careful not to waken her further, he eased down onto the bed alongside her. She burrowed against his chest, one hand beneath her cheek, the other absently drawing circles on his back.

Cam swallowed hard. He hated this easy closeness, and despised himself for being such a liar.

With his lips against her cheek, he whispered, "Go to sleep, Ariel. Go to sleep and dream."

As her breathing slowed, her fingertips grazed the mark on his back. The oddly shaped dragon stretched in contentment beneath her touch.

Cameron drew in a long breath, quelling the sudden urge to awaken her with heated caresses. He rested his forehead against hers and fell headlong into her dream.

Startled that he'd once again left reality behind through no plan of his own, Cam groaned. Didn't his beast understand that this was the last place he wanted to be?

Gentle waves lapped upon the sandy white beach. The shimmering sunlight enveloped him with warmth.

He turned to search the beach, knowing exactly where to find Ariel and her dream version of him. They were together in the hammock that was still tied between two palm trees.

A shadow passed overhead. Cam knew without looking up that his dragon was also here. He felt the beast's torment, and recognized it for what it was—jealousy of the man with Ariel.

If it wasn't so pathetic, he'd laugh. But at the moment, he was grateful that this unwarranted anger emanating from his beast existed only in a dream.

Not wanting to be seen, and not wanting to intrude, Cam forced himself out of Ariel's imagined fantasy.

Careful not to awaken her, he inched away from her lax embrace. Once free of the bed, he tucked the covers around her, then crossed the room to sit at the desk, staring at the grimoire.

She must have been looking at the book after he'd left earlier, because it was no longer open to the pages with the curse.

He watched, fascinated, as symbols and colorful drawings slowly spilled their way onto the pages.

When Braeden had explained this process to him, he'd taken the story with a grain of salt. Now he knew that his brother hadn't exaggerated—the grimoire did fill in the pages on its own.

The intricate magic in action shouldn't surprise him. After all, the family volume had been originally created centuries ago by a High Wizard.

And given his family's history, why wouldn't this item be magical, too?

He could only hope that eventually it would see fit to show him how to deal with the Learneds.

Chapter 13

Ariel pulled into a parking spot and turned off the engine. Cam had been right about the smaller vehicles being easier to handle on the twists and curves in the road.

Thankfully, she'd remembered to triple-check for her cell phone before leaving the apartment and once again after getting in the Jeep. This time she wouldn't have to search for a phone or head back to the bar to call Renalde.

Instead, she'd found a small, secluded park at the far end of town, away from the shops and tourists. The only other person here—a fisherman—had just removed his vest and was loading his gear into the back of his truck. While waiting for him to leave, she sat on the top of a picnic table watching the river rush past.

Her dreams last night had been so real, so vivid. Somehow she'd been flying—and not with the assistance of an airplane, but by herself, under the power of her own…wings.

Dreaming of dragons was nothing new; she'd regularly done so as a child. But rarely had she dreamed about actually *being* a dragon. And never had she done so as an adult until last night.

What bothered her wasn't so much the dream. No, what bothered her was the wishing it could be so.

She was obviously more stressed than she'd first thought. She needed to finish this business with Renalde, collect Carl and get the hell out of here before she completely lost her ability to reason.

But getting the hell out of here would mean leaving Cam. Why did that idea fill her heart with an empty sadness?

Cam—she couldn't help wondering, where had he disappeared to last night? After leaving so abruptly upon seeing something in the grimoire, he'd returned. She remembered falling back to sleep in his arms. But when the alarm went off this morning, she'd been alone.

Except for the grimoire. It had still been on the desk, busy filling in its pages for the day.

It was too bad he hadn't taken the damn thing with him. Between the magical pages and the grimoire's lousy timing, it couldn't have picked a better moment to destroy by making its appearance to Cam last night.

There was nothing like savoring the aftermath of great, mind-blowing sex, only to have the book essentially scream its existence from across the room. She'd had her fill of the thing. As far as she was concerned, its complete disappearance wouldn't prove upsetting in the least.

The sound of the fisherman driving off interrupted her musing. She glanced at her watch. There were a few minutes left before she had to contact Renalde. Since her search of the Lair had still proven unsuccessful, she dreaded making the call.

It wasn't that she hadn't tried, she had. Over and over she'd scoured nearly every nook and cranny. The only places left were the desks and cabinets in the Drakes' offices.

Ariel had no clue how she was going to accomplish that feat, but she knew there'd be no getting around it. The biggest trick would be not getting caught.

After once again checking to make certain she was alone, Ariel pulled out her cell to call Renalde.

"So, Ms. Johnson..." His voice was in her head before she could finishing punching in the number. "Are you ready to make an exchange?"

She gripped the edge of the picnic table, knowing her answer wouldn't be well received. "Not yet. I'm still—"

"Silence." He cut her off, then declared, "It's time you focus your search back at Mirabilus."

"I can't." She was not returning to that place. Here at the Lair there existed only hints of dragons—paintings, statues and the like. But at Mirabilus, they were more than inanimate objects—they were real.

"Yes, you will."

Ariel closed her watering eyes, cringing at the rage echoing in her mind. Before she could explain how hard she'd been trying to find what he wanted, and her plans to invade the Drakes' offices, Renalde bellowed, "It's time you start paying for your failure, my dear. Perhaps you need a little lesson to teach you how to do what you're told."

She nearly fell off the picnic table from the force of his departure. *Pay for her failure? A little lesson?* "No. Please, don't hurt Carl."

Brief flashes of growing up with her brother—
Christmases, birthdays, summers at their grandparents'
lake cottage—ripped through her mind.

She'd always thought that one day their children
would grow up in much the same manner—cousins
creating their own memories together.

"Trust me, Ms. Johnson, you'll be far more coopera-
tive after today."

His swift reentry made her head spin. Sick to her
stomach with fear and worry, Ariel stumbled toward
the Jeep. What was she going to do? If Renalde killed
Carl how would she live with herself?

Blinded by tears and the murky fog of terror, she
rooted through her purse, trying to find the keys.

"Stop." A strong hand closed over her wrist.

The warmth of Cam's familiar touch, just the sound
of his steady voice, chased away her ability to reason.
Ariel turned toward him, seeking something stable and
solid—something reassuring to hold on to—and then
buried her face against his shoulder.

Cam stared over Ariel's head at the trees fencing
the picnic area. She'd turned to him for something he
couldn't afford to offer—comfort.

Yes, she was terrified. Her fear seeped into him with
a bone-chilling cold that nearly knocked him off his
feet.

And yes, she was in danger. He'd felt the foreboding
menace at the same moment he'd breathed in her scent.

Cam chased away the brief urge to tighten his arms
around her to draw her close. She'd put herself in this
position.

Still, no matter how much he denied it, there was
a part of him that longed to drag her deeper into his
embrace and willingly give her whatever she needed.

Quelling that part of him was essential. Because giving in would eventually bring about her death.

Careful not to promise anything, Cam said, "Ariel, I can help, but you have to tell me what's going on."

She shook her head. He should have expected her silent response. Why had he hoped for more this time?

Cam grasped her shoulders and moved her aside. "Give me the keys and get in. I'll drive."

She dropped the keys onto his outstretched hand and circled to the other side of the Jeep. Ariel paused, a frown marring her brow as she scanned the park. "What about your car?"

"It's in town. Harold can bring me back later." Years of practice lent a ring of truth to his lie.

Cam ignored the vibration of the phone holstered on his belt. He slid behind the wheel and started the Jeep.

Again, the phone vibrated. And once again, he ignored it. Whatever it was could wait until he got back to the Lair.

Silence loomed heavy between them as he drove through town. Finally, more to break the deafening quiet than anything else, he asked, "Are you hungry?"

Ariel shook her head, keeping her gaze trained out the side window.

"Well, I am."

"Can we just go back to the Lair?"

He ignored her question. "It's a nice day for a drive. You haven't been into the national park yet."

"Please." She took a shuddering breath. "Please, I just want to go back."

Cam relented at the underlying tone of desperation in her plea, and at the next traffic light turned onto the side road that would take them up the mountain.

She apparently had something important she needed

to do back at the Lair. It didn't require a genius to realize it most likely had something to do with her phone call.

Sirens behind him caught his attention. He pulled over to let the police and emergency vehicles fly by him.

When they didn't turn into the complex of condos, he cursed. Either there was an accident ahead, or they'd been called to the Lair.

His phone once again vibrated. Instead of answering it, he hit the gas pedal, cursing.

Ariel gasped as they lunged ahead. She grabbed the safety handle above her head, praying Cameron didn't roll the Jeep in his attempt to keep up with the police and ambulance.

Renalde had said she would start paying for what he called her failures. Had he spared Carl only to harm someone at the Lair instead?

It would make a twisted sort of sense for him to have done so. If he murdered her brother right off, what would he use to force her to continue her search?

The Jeep careened around a curve on two wheels. Ariel shouted, "Slow down!"

When Cam ignored her, she closed her eyes against the blur of trees and rocks as they passed by at a dizzying pace.

Finally, just when she was certain they were going to fly off the road, Cam slowed down enough to pull into the Lair. Ariel's breath escaped with a whoosh. She bailed out of the Jeep, thankful not to have died in a horrific, fiery tumble down the side of the mountain.

"What happened?"

The strained tone of Cam's question to his aunt drew Ariel's attention from the paramedics gathered around Harold. She followed Cam, trying not to shudder at the hate and rage in Danielle Drake's eyes. How could the woman dislike anyone that much?

"It's *her* fault." Danielle pointed at Ariel. "*She* caused this."

Cam edged in front of Ariel, putting himself between the women. "What happened?"

The police officer interviewing Harold glanced toward Cam.

Danielle whispered, "She tried to kill Harold."

"Nonsense. Ariel was with me."

"You'd say anything to protect her."

Cam refrained from rolling his eyes at his aunt's certainty. "She doesn't need protecting." He grasped Dani's elbow and escorted her away from the curious police, then once again asked, "What happened?"

With her glare riveted on Ariel, she explained, "Harold was on a ladder fixing one of her rose trellises when it exploded beneath him."

Cam frowned at the impossible explanation. "Ladders don't explode."

Danielle shrugged. "Not exactly exploded, more like just fell apart while he was on it."

Searching for a logical explanation, Cam offered, "Maybe it was old."

His aunt disagreed. "We don't have any old equipment here."

"Then it was defective."

"More like it was cursed."

Ariel peered around him, her eyes wide. "Cursed?"

"Don't play innocent with me, Ms. Johnson. You might fool my nephew, but my vision isn't clouded with lust. I see you for what you are."

"And that would be…what?"

Before Dani could answer Ariel's half-serious question, he asked, "Is Harold injured?"

He needed to draw his aunt's attention away from Ariel. The last thing he wanted was a catfight in front of the town police. Dani couldn't be trusted not to resort to magic when she felt provoked. And for whatever reason, Ariel provoked his aunt just by breathing.

"He says no, but the paramedics insisted on checking him out."

Cam nodded toward Harold. "Why don't you go make certain. And if he isn't injured, help him convince the authorities that he's fine, and nothing out of the ordinary happened."

"You want me to get rid of the witnesses."

The censure evident in Danielle's voice let Cam know she wasn't pleased with the idea. He didn't care. She wasn't going to get the chance to get rid of Ariel like this, not before he found out what she was up to. "Yes. That's the idea."

Her disapproval of the idea showed plainly on her face. But to his relief, Danielle stomped off toward Harold and the paramedics.

Cam watched as his aunt engaged Harold and the authorities in a conversation. Her animated gestures and show of concern captured the officers' attention, giving him the chance to inspect the area around the trellises.

He didn't sense any magic whatsoever, not even on the broken pieces of the ladder. However, he did pick up an unfamiliar scent. Breathing deeply, he identified it as belonging to a human.

Cam glanced toward Dani, Harold and the others. Certain they were focused on their own conversation, he followed the scent toward the rear of the Lair.

"What are you looking for?"

He raised a hand, silently asking Ariel to be quiet, and paused.

Without saying another word, she closed the distance between them, coming up against his back. Even though she couldn't have realized it, she'd instinctively sought his protection.

Her reaction dragged a rumbling growl of approval from his beast. Cam gritted his teeth. No matter what the dragon thought, or felt, this woman could not become its…his…their mate.

Somehow he was going to have to convince the beast of that before this interest went too far and they put Ariel's life in danger.

Cam followed the scent toward the woods. He stopped at the edge of the tree line, unwilling to let Ariel follow him into the forest.

He turned to her, suggesting, "Why don't you—" The insistent vibration of his phone interrupted him.

Cam pulled it from his holster, flipping it open as he did so. "What, Sean?"

While waiting for his brother to answer, Cam noticed the emergency vehicles leaving the Lair. Dani and Harold must have been able to convince the authorities that nothing out of the ordinary had occurred.

"I've called for the chopper. You need to get ready to leave for Mirabilus."

Even through the phone, Cam could hear the concern in his younger brother's voice. "Why? Is something wrong?"

"It's Brightworthe."

An icy fist slammed into his stomach. He turned to stare at Ariel, asking Sean, "What about him?"

"He's dead."

Ariel took a step away from Cam. From the look on

his face it was obvious that something was seriously wrong. He flipped his phone closed and just stared at her.

When he opened his mouth, the sound of a helicopter clearing the trees drowned out anything he might have said.

Cam grasped Ariel's wrist and tugged her toward the Lair. She stumbled trying to keep up with him.

Once they were inside, he quickened his pace and headed for the elevators. The doors closed behind him and he punched the button for their floor, still hanging on to her wrist.

Ariel tugged in an attempt to free herself. "Let me go."

He turned on her, rage and pain glittering in his eyes. She backed as far away as she could from the hard, frightening mask that turned his features into an unyielding glare of hate.

She swallowed before asking softly, "What's wrong?"

"Shut up, Ariel."

She cringed at the coldness in his tone. This was the same man who had kissed her and caressed her last night? The same one who had followed her to the park and driven her back to the Lair after her conversation with Renalde?

When the elevator stopped and the doors opened, she grabbed the bar on the wall with her free hand. The last thing she wanted was to be alone in his apartment with him.

Without turning around, Cam nearly snarled, "Your well-being doesn't matter to me. Let go of that bar, or you'll wish you had."

He waited for half a heartbeat before he started for the apartment. Ariel clung with one hand to the bar for a split second before she realized he meant what he'd said. He was so much stronger than she was, and her fingernails scraped around the smooth wood as her hold slipped.

Cam didn't pause to unlock the door, he didn't even turn the knob, he simply shoved the door out of his way, walked through and slammed the door closed behind him.

Ariel struggled against his hold, digging at his fingers with her free hand as he dragged her toward the master bedroom. "Damn it, Cameron Drake, let me go."

He did—just long enough to shove her down onto the bed. She quickly scrambled for the other side.

"Get off that bed and I'll chain you there."

She glanced over her shoulder only to see a pair of shackles hanging in the air between them. There was no doubt in her mind that he would make good on his threat.

Wary and more frightened than she'd ever been, she sat down on the bed. "What are you doing?"

He grabbed two duffel bags from his closet. After tossing one at her, he started packing clothes into the other one. "Packing."

"For?"

"We're going to Mirabilus."

She held her breath. Her heart froze in her chest. No. No. She would not go back there. Not for Renalde, not for Cam—she'd even struggle to return to that place for Carl.

Ariel sucked in a deep breath of air, desperate to still the dizziness threatening to overtake her. "No. I am not going to Mirabilus."

Before she completed her statement, she was flat on her back with him straddling her. "Yes, you are. This game of yours is over, Ariel. Done. Finished. I'm not playing with you anymore."

Unable to meet his rage, she closed her eyes and shook her head. "No. I can't. You don't understand."

"Damn you!" He pounded the bed alongside her head. "Look at me."

Mustering all the courage she could find, she opened her eyes and stared mutely up at him.

"Do you think I'm stupid?"

"No. But——" How could she explain her reasons without giving all away?

"Do you think I don't know who you are?"

Her breath caught. Her stomach twisted into knots.

"You broke into the workshop at my family's keep. The only reason you won't go back is because you're afraid of dragons." When she didn't say anything, he added, "You're a would-be thief, following in the footsteps of your brother. Both of you work for the Learneds—my enemy."

Ariel gasped. "How did you—"

He laughed at her. "Don't you listen? I told you before that I've known who you worked for since the minute you walked into my office for your interview. Why do you think I hired you? It sure as hell wasn't for your nearly nonexistent expertise with plants."

The twisting of her stomach turned to agony. She felt as if he'd reached in and torn her heart from her chest. "Then this…this has all been nothing more than a… ploy…a game to get information from me."

"What else did you think it was? Did you really believe you could come in here to play your own game without any retaliation? Didn't your boss tell you that if you play, you pay?"

Shame and betrayal warred in her heart and mind,

one as potent, as hurtful as the other. Ariel turned her face away. "I—"

"You haven't begun to pay—yet. But you will."

Is that what her life would always be from now on? A pawn in someone else's game? Nothing more than an object to use as retribution? She bit her trembling lip.

"Oh, no, you don't." Cam grasped her chin, forcing her to face him. "A beloved family retainer, a friend, a trusted confidant died today because of you." He paused to visibly swallow before asking, "Do you think your tears mean anything to me?"

"You don't understand!" Her voice broke on a cry.

"You have had more than one opportunity to gain my understanding. I would have willingly helped you, had you just once told me the truth." He rose and looked down at her. The disdain on his face was obvious. "Now I don't care."

Ariel sat up on the bed as he walked away to retrieve the duffel bag. She brushed away the despicable tears spilling from her eyes, and forced back the pain tearing at her to shout, "They will kill my brother!"

He threw the bag at the door and stormed back to the side of the bed. "You fool, they still will."

"No." Ariel looked down at her hands. If she believed that, all hope would be lost. The only thing she had to hang on to was the slim promise of Carl's continued safety. "No. He promised."

"Promised?" She flinched at Cam's harsh bark of laughter. "The Learneds don't know the meaning of the word. Get up, you need to get packed." When she hesitated, he ordered without emotion, "Now."

"Please, I can't. I can't go there."

"This isn't a debate." He pulled her from the bed and shoved the empty duffel bag into her arms. "You'll pack, or I'll pack for you. Doesn't matter to me either way. But you are coming with me."

Cam pushed her toward the door. Following behind her he grabbed his bag on the way out of his bedroom. When they walked into her room, he pointed at the grimoire. "Take that along, too."

She tried once more. "Don't make me do this. Don't make me go with you."

His raised eyebrow should have been answer enough. But when she didn't change her mind, he said, "If I leave you here my aunt will kill you with her bare hands. You'd fare better against the dragon than you would her."

Nathan stared at the flashing computer monitor on his desk. The beginnings of a smile eased his scowl. "It worked."

"What worked?" Jeremy sat up straighter on the chair across from his father's desk. The last conversation with Ms. Johnson hadn't gone well. When he'd seen the whip hanging over the back of Nathan's chair, he had feared that this interview with his sire would end as badly as their last one.

Slowly healing gashes from the whip still burned like fire each time he entered this office. Memories of the whistling sound as the whip flew through the air toward him, the stinging pain as it laced across his flesh and the taste of his own blood as he'd bitten his lips to keep from screaming were still fresh in his mind.

Eventually he'd given up trying to hold back his screams and had let the high-pitched wails tear from his throat until he could scream no more. The only reason he lived was because his father believed he could still prove useful.

Until he could devise a way to catch his sire off guard, he would build upon that belief.

"The Drakes' private jet is being fueled. And flight plans to Mirabilus have been filed." Nathan's voice lightened with each spoken word.

Jeremy closed his eyes in relief. As hard as he'd tried to get to the handyman at the Lair, he'd been thwarted at every turn. Refusing to accept failure, he'd turned his attention to Mirabilus.

It had been fairly easy to hire someone to slip beneath the older, weaker security system on the isle and kidnap Brightworthe.

Unfortunately, killing Brightworthe had been child's play. The mercenary's death had been quicker and even less enjoyable.

In truth, the whole episode had proven quite boring. Brightworthe had died far too easily for Jeremy's taste. He'd found no pleasure, no assimilation of power in the man's quick demise.

"What had you expected?"

His father's question instantly jerked him out of his thoughts. "From what?"

"You killed the soldier too fast—leaving nothing for you to gain. And the old man wasn't a wizard, just long-lived. Surely you didn't expect to find anything worth stealing from his departing soul?"

"No." Absently, Jeremy added, "But I had hoped there would be…something of value."

Nathan laughed softly, drawing the end of the whip through his fingers. "Nothing of value can be gained from a mortal's soul. You need to learn how to take pleasure in their suffering."

Jeremy flinched, afraid to even wonder how he could learn such a skill. From the intent look of pure evil shimmering from his father's eyes, he feared the answer would be found at the painful end of the whip.

The older wizard's roar of laughter set Jeremy's heart racing. Nathan let the whip coil onto the floor alongside his chair and then leaned forward. "You are still useful, my dear boy. And at the moment, I find it far too amusing to watch you seek ways to best me. Your death right now, at this time, doesn't suit my interests."

When Jeremy breathed a sigh of relief and eased back into the chair, Nathan added, "At least not today."

Chapter 14

Through half-closed eyes, Cam studied Ariel while she alternately stared out the window of the jet and fell into a fitful sleep. He should feel bad about having been so heartlessly nasty and manhandling her earlier.

But he didn't.

It was a little hard to have much sympathy for her considering how she'd withheld information that might have prevented Brightworthe's death and Harold's fall.

It would have been quicker, and easier, to fly to Mirabilus alone under his own power. But Danielle Drake would have killed Ariel if he'd have left her at the Lair—not figuratively, but literally.

And while he was beyond angry with her and himself for this strange sense of betrayal, he didn't want to see her dead.

Which was the reason he'd made damn certain he

and Ariel had gotten out of the Lair and onto the jet as quickly as possible.

To his chagrin, his beast had spent the past nine hours making him pay for hurting Ariel's feelings and frightening her. Heartburn and indigestion didn't begin to describe the rumbling and twisting of his stomach.

Still, he found the dragon's snit rather fascinating. What did it hope to gain by this spiteful torment? This woman wouldn't be in their future.

After taking care of things at Mirabilus, he would find a way to get her out of this mess with the Learneds. Then he'd send her on her way.

Cam gritted his teeth against the sudden twisting contraction of his stomach. Silently he tried to reason with the beast, *"Look, you know as well as I do that it was just physical. There was never anything between us except lust. She doesn't care for us any more than I do for her."*

In his mind he could see the dragon toss its head and turn away as if refusing to listen. Cam seethed inwardly. Of all the times to be cooped up with an audience.

He didn't argue with the dragon often. Most times it was a losing battle. But until Ariel, they'd never had to argue about a woman. This was a battle Cam knew he couldn't afford to lose.

He tried another tactic. *"Okay, sure, you seem to think she's your mate."* The beast hitched one spiked eyebrow, but still refused to look directly at him. *"We're cursed, you know. If you keep her, she'll die. It's kinder to let her go. Even more so if she believes we don't care."*

Cam waited a moment, then asked, *"Don't you understand that's it always going to be just you and me?"* When the memory of the shadowy changeling they'd seen last night entered his mind, he added, *"You know as well as I do that last night's vision was nothing more than wishful thinking."*

The dragon's mournful sigh sent a shiver down Cam's spine. The beast lowered its head and Cam knew by the sudden heaviness in his chest that it understood.

"Mr. Drake, we'll be landing soon." The pilot's voice over the intercom drew Cam from his internal conversation.

He nudged Ariel's foot with his own. "Put your seat up and buckle your seat belt."

Ariel jumped at the contact. This was the first thing he'd said to her since they'd left her bedroom at the Lair.

After bringing her seat up and securing the seat belt, she stared back out the window toward the island far below. The last time she'd flown over the island it had been night and she'd jumped out of a perfectly working helicopter into the sea.

Her parents had always thought that it was insane to bail out of an aircraft—especially if the thing was in good working order. She'd agreed. And when she'd dropped from Renalde's helicopter, she'd felt insane.

But right now she'd give anything for a good parachute.

It didn't matter that Mirabilus sparkled like an emerald in the sunlight. Nor did she care that from here even the rocky cliffs looked beautiful and exotic jutting out between the green of the land and the brilliant blue of the sea.

If she had a choice, she'd rather bail onto the rocks without a chute rather than step foot on the island again.

Something deep inside her warned that *it* was waiting for her. The dragon-man she'd encountered in the workshop lurked in the shadows, eager to once again make her acquaintance.

"It'll be all right."

She flinched at Cam's touch against her cheek and jerked her face away. "Don't."

"Don't what?"

"Don't be nice, you don't mean it. Don't touch me."

Naturally, he caressed her cheek before turning her head back to face him. "It's not for much longer. Soon we'll be out of each other's lives."

"Good." His soft laugh at her snide reply chafed, so she elaborated, "I'm glad we won't have to deal with each other for much longer."

He stroked the pad of his thumb across her lower lip. "Of course you are. In the meantime, we could pretend to get along."

She smiled, then caught his thumb between her teeth.

"Bite me, Ariel, and I swear I'll drop you naked to the floor of this plane and make you moan until you beg for release."

Surely he was bluffing.

"I don't embarrass easily. An audience wouldn't faze me in the least."

Still uncertain if he'd truly pull such a stunt with a cockpit full of people, she hesitated.

"The pilots and the attendant are all on the payroll. Do you think they'd say or do anything to stop me?"

When she didn't relax her hold, Cam did little more than arch one eyebrow. Instantly her bra disappeared and she felt the silky smoothness of her blouse rub against her naked breasts.

She opened her mouth, freeing his thumb. But instead of withdrawing, he traced across her tongue, then lightly trailed just along the inside of her lip before pulling his hand away.

A tiny jolt of electricity raced through her, she gasped at the sudden and completely unexpected zing.

Cam leaned back against his seat. He propped his elbows on the armrest and steepled his fingers before him. "We'd be liars if we said there was no attraction here."

He might not embarrass easily, but she felt her cheeks flame and looked down at her lap.

"We're only going to be here a few days. Nothing is going to happen to you—nothing you don't want. I'll see to that."

She waited for the punch line, fully expecting it to include something about sex.

"However, I'm not going to have time to play any more games. You need to tell me what it is you're doing for the Learneds. In return, I'll find a way to get them out of your life."

Ariel blinked with surprise at that unexpected offer. She looked up, not trusting him to be telling her the truth. "Why would you help me now?"

"Honestly?"

She nodded.

"Once they're out of your life, they're out of mine and so are you."

She couldn't understand why that statement hurt so much. To keep him from knowing what she really felt, she glared at him. "And if I refuse to tell you?"

"I have every intention of chaining you to a bed naked and driving you wild until you change your mind."

A part of her wanted to laugh at his ludicrous answer. But the serious tone in his voice and his unwavering stare warned her that he might not be kidding.

Unwilling to put him to the test, she said, "If I tell you, he'll know."

Cam's lips twitched, making her aware that no matter how…interesting he found the idea, he had only been teasing her. He asked, "How would he know?"

"He's like your aunt." She spoke without thinking.

This time, he frowned. "When do you have to call him again?"

"In six days."

"Then we have less than a week to find whatever it is you're looking for."

Ariel debated for a minute. The plane banked and she looked out the window at Mirabilus. Her breath hitched. The less time she spent here, the better off she would be. Finally, she gazed back at Cam. "An emerald dragon pendant and a wooden puzzle box."

He shook his head. "You can't have the dragon. It belongs to Alexia and I know that she'd never give it up."

"Is there another one?"

"Doesn't matter, because even if there is, I'm not about to hand it over to a Learned."

Ariel wanted to scream at him in frustration. Why go through this pretense of wanting to help her if he had no intention of doing so? "If I don't find these things, my brother will be killed."

"Then we're going to have to figure something out, aren't we?" His frown deepened as he glanced out the window at the quickly approaching runway. "I know why they want the pendant, but what magic does this puzzle box contain?"

"I have no clue. It's not like Renalde confides in me."

The jet touched down lightly and taxied toward the small airport. Cam flipped his cell phone open and requested a car be sent to the hangar. He undid his seat belt and then rose. "Let's go. Our ride will be here momentarily."

Queasy and not at all anxious to get off the plane, Ariel took her time. Essentially they were here for a murder investigation and a funeral. Neither would be fun for Cam.

"Will the authorities be here?"

"Authorities?"

Ariel shrugged. "To investigate the murder?"

To her dismay, he walked away. Over his shoulder he explained, "In Braeden's absence, *I* am the authority."

She followed him down the steps, shocked to find a limo already waiting. When Cam stepped onto the tarmac, the driver snapped his heels, came to attention and saluted before opening the limo's door.

Ariel had the sinking feeling that Cam hadn't been kidding about the lord-king thing. She climbed into the car, taking a seat across from him. "Mirabilus isn't just an island, is it?"

He kept his focus on the papers he'd retrieved from the briefcase on the seat, answering absently, "Of course it's an island. It's land surrounded by water."

She closed her eyes for a moment, attempting to rein in a flash of anger. "It's not part of any other country, is it?"

"No."

"So, your brother is…the king?"

"In a sense." He paused to shuffle through the pages in his hands. Finding the one he wanted, he put the rest down, adding, "His official title is High Dragon Lord of Mirabilus."

Of course. "And you are…what?"

"Tired of your questions."

She jerked back as if slapped. "Excuse me, your lord-ship."

"That's 'my lord.'"

"What?"

He glanced at her over the page he was studying. "You address me as 'my lord' or 'my liege' if you pre-fer. But in this case, a simple 'sir' will suffice."

Before she could summon the ability to speak, he went back to his reading. She batted the page with the back of her hand. "Excuse me?"

He lifted his head and stared at her. Ariel couldn't be-lieve she was involved in this conversation. "How about if I *address* you as Cam, or maybe even Cameron?"

"In private that'll be fine."

"In private? You're kidding me, right?"

"Unfortunately, I'm not. This is an official visit, not a vacation. I'm in charge when Braeden isn't in resi-dence. This is my island. Small as it is, it's my country."

"I'm not a citizen of your country."

"Neither are you my wife. If you want to call me by name when we're alone, that's fine. But in public, if you can't bring yourself to show a little respect for the cus-toms of Mirabilus Isle, you can either keep your mouth shut, or stay in your room. We're not in the States. This isn't Tennessee."

"And I didn't ask to come here."

He tapped the tinted window between them and the driver. The limo came to a stop. Cam pulled out his cell and offered it to her. "Would you like to listen to Danielle's voice message? I'm sure then you'll under-stand why you're here. She'd have no problem killing you. And with her talents, trust me when I tell you that she'd get away with it."

He had a point. She waved away the phone. "Fine. So I have to be here. But that doesn't mean I'm suddenly going to act like I've stepped into some medieval court."

"I'm not asking you to." He dropped the phone, reached across the distance separating them to hook a warm hand around her neck and drew her closer. With his lips nearly against hers, he whispered, "Although, the idea of being your absolute lord and master has merits."

Ariel forced herself to ignore the flare of heat threatening to steal her mind. She pushed him away. "Stop it."

"I haven't done anything."

"Oh, no, except try to drive me insane. You can just forget it, *my lord,* you are not sharing this lowly peasant's bed."

He chuckled, then tapped on the divider again before leaning back against his seat. He picked up his papers, asking, "Can I go back to work now?"

The man was infuriating. "Please do."

Aelthed breathed a deep sigh of relief as a welcome wave of homecoming washed over him. Finally, he was back on Mirabilus Isle.

He'd been listening, eavesdropping on the changeling and his mate when they'd argued in the apartment. That's how he'd learned about the jaunt to Mirabilus.

Nothing could have stopped him from slipping unseen into the woman's luggage. He wasn't about to miss what might be his only opportunity to return to the land of his birth—and death.

Granted, it wasn't as if he could walk the grounds, or pace the beach, but just to know he was home was enough to make him weep with gratitude.

* * *

Cameron stared out the tall window of his bedroom, watching as the solitary figure, carrying a duffel bag, crossed the open distance to the workshop.

Did she really think she'd be given complete freedom to come and go as she pleased? Little did Ariel know that two of his staff followed closely behind her at all times.

He moved away from the window and into the sitting room. He didn't need to see where she was going, he already knew. She was going snooping for the pendant and box that she'd finally admitted the Learneds wanted.

At the moment, he didn't care. It wasn't as if she would find anything, or be in any danger. The men were under strict orders to call him if anything unusual happened. He didn't care if the wind changed direction—they were to call immediately.

Nor did he worry about her snooping around on her own. He'd expected it and would have been disappointed had she not taken the opportunity to go out on her hunting expedition.

She wasn't going to discover anything in the workshop. After he'd searched for the items himself, he'd had the circular chamber cleared of everything. Ariel would be lucky if she found so much as a speck of dust, let alone a pendant or a puzzle cube.

Cam poured a snifter of brandy and sat in the overstuffed armchair before the fireplace. Raising his glass, he spoke to the empty air, "To you, Brightworthe. You'll be sorely missed around here."

He'd known the caretaker for his entire life. The man had been ancient when Cam and Braeden were born, so there was no telling how old he actually was in human years.

Like Harold, Brightworthe wasn't quite wizard, but neither was he quite human. They'd both been from the clan of long-lived folks of Mirabilus.

Harold would be devastated to learn of Brightworthe's death. The men had been close, more like brothers than friends. And for that reason Cam had put the funeral off for a couple days. He wouldn't dishonor his own friendship with either man by not giving Harold a chance to attend the ceremony.

The jet would return to the Lair tomorrow. The next day they would bring Harold, Danielle and Sean to Mirabilus. With any luck, his aunt would have had enough time to cool off before coming face-to-face with Ariel.

Cam frowned and set down his brandy. He realized that Braeden deserved and needed this vacation with his wife, but it might be best if he at least made an appearance.

"I'll be there." Braeden's voice raced through Cam's mind, easing his concerns on that score.

"Any idea what happened?"

He had a few ideas, but none he wanted to share until he checked them out fully. "Not yet. I've questioned the men who found the body on the beach, but they had no answers for me. Still working on it. Go pester your wife."

Sensing his brother's departure, Cam leaned his head back against the chair, propped his feet up on the cushioned ottoman and closed his eyes. After being up for over two days, he was exhausted.

Hopefully, Ariel would return to the keep soon so they could all get a good night's sleep. The buzz of his pager drew a ragged sigh from him. So much for a good night's sleep.

He glanced at the backlit screen, then lunged from the chair. Something was wrong in the workshop, otherwise the men wouldn't have contacted him.

Cam slipped into his shoes and grabbed a jacket as he headed out the door of his bedroom. He waved off the men standing guard in the hallway. They were only doing their job, protecting the current ruler in residence, but he didn't want any babysitters around when he confronted Ariel.

Racing across the grounds, he came to a skidding halt outside the old shed that disguised the entrance to the workroom. The two men assigned to Ariel met him at the door. The taller, older man said, "Sorry, sir. There was a strange light."

The other man added, "Then something whizzed past our heads and went inside the shed."

"Did you see if it followed her in?"

Both men shook their heads. "It was there, then just—gone."

Cameron sensed no presence of magic, no Learneds, nothing that gave him reason to believe Ariel was in any danger.

After dismissing the men, he entered the shed. It took a minute for him to locate the panel that would slide open, giving him entrance to the corridor leading to the workroom.

Thankfully, his beast was awake and alert, so he didn't need a flashlight to see his way down the blackness of the hallway.

His mind flipped back to the last time he'd followed her in here. He'd been in dragon form then, intentionally wanting to frighten her enough to keep her from returning.

Apparently, it hadn't worked.

So, this time, he would approach silently and then use attitude and threats to scare the hell out of her.

With any luck, that might work.

He stopped at the arched doorway into the workroom and peered around the bricks. The chamber was ablaze with light from at least a dozen flashlights. Did she really think the light would keep the dragon at bay?

She was using a metal file to dig at the foundation near the old coal brazier. Was she planning to excavate the entire room?

Ariel paused, she had the odd feeling that she was no longer by herself. Had the men following her come inside? She'd closed the secret panel behind her, so unless they knew the trick to opening it, she doubted they had entered the corridor.

Besides, these men obviously weren't skilled at secrecy—she'd spotted them on her tail almost the minute she'd walked out of the keep. If they had figured out how to open the sliding panel, she was certain she'd have heard their approach.

It had taken every ounce of bravery she possessed to make herself come back here. But she'd been able to think of no other way. She had to find that puzzle box for Renalde.

Since Cam had been so certain that his sister-in-law would never give up her emerald pendant, Ariel knew she had to make certain she located that box. Maybe in the process, she'd find another pendant. Hopefully, the significance was in the pendant itself and the color wouldn't make any difference.

She'd vowed never to return to Mirabilus, but since

she was here through no volition of her own, she knew that she might as well make use of her time. After all, Carl's life depended on her success.

A quick glance over her shoulder showed her that she was still alone. Her pulse settled back to a more normal tempo.

No. If someone had opened the panel, she'd have heard it. The thing had screeched so loud when she'd slid it open, she was surprised the entire castle hadn't rushed out to see what all the noise was about.

Besides, she'd brought along her stun gun, so if someone was unwise enough to sneak up on her, they'd be in for a shock—literally.

She resumed picking at the foundation. A closer examination of the wall had shown what appeared to be a separate square, much like the panel in the shed's wall. It was a long shot, but she hoped that her efforts would turn up something of—

Ariel froze at the sound of a footstep behind her. Slowly, with her free hand, she reached inside her jacket to slide her hand through the wrist strap of the gun, then pulled it from the holster.

Before she could change her mind, she spun around, closed her eyes, reached out until the gun pressed against something semisolid, and then hit the button.

Chapter 15

"**D**amn!" Over the ratcheting noise of the gun, Cam's strangled curse took her breath away.

Ariel opened her eyes and backed against the wall behind her for support. Whatever she'd jolted was, yet at the same time it wasn't, Cameron Drake.

It was a—thing—a man writhing on the floor and changing, transforming into a...*dragon*.

An extremely angry, spitting, snarling dragon.

Unable to back away, and too frightened to convince her suddenly paralyzed legs to run, she covered her face with her hands and screamed.

It seemed as if seconds turned to hours, heartbeats evolved into years. Finally, when she was hoarse from screaming, and nearly deaf from the beast's roars, Ariel spread her fingers enough to peer out between them.

Staring back at her was the most magnificent animal she'd ever seen.

Magnificent?

Half afraid she'd lost her mind from fear, Ariel drew in a shaking breath and screamed once again.

The beast jerked its head back and did the same. His roar shook the timber supports.

Desperately trying to think, Ariel knew the only escape route was to find a way around the beast. But it shifted, effectively blocking her path to the door.

She swallowed. *Now what?*

The dragon rumbled, cocked its head to stare intently at the gun still dangling from her wrist.

Ariel fought to clear the haze of fear from her mind. Dragons don't exist—at least not in her world. Hadn't she tried to convince herself of that before?

And hadn't she been wrong then, too?

To keep a grip on what was left of her sanity, she reminded herself that this was somehow Cam. While that didn't help much, it did permit her to breathe.

Besides, if the beast had wanted to kill her, wouldn't it have done so by now? Unless it was like a cat and wanted to toy with its food first.

Ariel forced that fleeting thought from her mind. She untangled the strap around her wrist and tossed the stun gun across the workroom. Then, with her heart in her throat, Ariel stepped forward to stroke the dragon's…chest.

To her surprise, its scales felt more like a soft, supple leather against her fingertips than anything resembling a reptile. Ever-changing, iridescent greens, blues and purples shimmered as his skin rippled beneath her touch. He looked just like the dragon drawing in the grimoire.

But where that was nothing more than a painting, this was a living, breathing beast.

She stood her ground as he lowered his head, but closed her eyes when his breath blew hot against her cheek.

Like a dog chuffing for a scent, the beast slowly nosed her cheek, neck and head. The heavy inhale and warm exhale of his breath blew her hair back and forth against her face.

Whose actions were more insane? The beast's or her own?

Ariel couldn't understand why she hadn't fainted. Then the reason suddenly came to her—this was the beast she'd been dreaming about all along. She had lost her fear of this dragon weeks ago when she'd realized that it wasn't in her dreams to hurt her, but to protect her.

She reached up to grasp the dragon's head between her hands and pull it down so she could gaze into his deep sapphire eyes. "Enough, big guy. You know damn well who I am."

The rumbling in his chest sounded suspiciously like a growl. *Had she gone too far?* Ariel quickly lowered her arms, stepped back and with her eyes closed prayed she hadn't inadvertently turned herself into an evening dragon snack.

"You are seriously a fool. That's who you are."

The voice whispering against her ear wasn't coming from a mythical beast. She relaxed with a shudder of relief.

"Don't get too comfortable." He pushed her aside to inspect the area on the wall that she'd been chipping away at earlier. "What were you looking for?"

"Shouldn't you be asking if I'll live instead of what I was looking for?"

Cam glanced over his shoulder for a split second. "You look fine to me."

"The dragon—thing. That's how you knew I'd been here before."

"Yes."

Ariel frowned. Now that her whirling thoughts had slowed and she'd had a chance to catch her breath, questions flooded her mind. "You are the dragon from my dreams."

"You dream about beasts?"

She approached, hoping to see his face as he talked. Her thoughts now ran in never-ending circles. "On occasion. In fact, more so since coming to the Lair." She narrowed her eyes, asking, "You had something to do with that, didn't you?"

Cam realized that she wouldn't like his answers, so he opted to keep his mouth shut as he picked at the stone block.

"Could you at least look at me?"

He brushed away another crumbling piece of block before turning around. Ariel had crossed her arms against her chest. Her anger swirled around him, hotter and more intrusive than her fear had been.

"So, tell me something, *Sir Wizard*. Can you influence my dreams?"

"A little."

Her eyes widened for a split second before resuming the familiar glare. "A little? Meaning, you have the ability to know what I dream about?"

"Of course."

"Of course?" Ariel stepped back, her shock evident on her face. "And can you participate in them, too?"

He knew exactly where she was headed with this

line of questioning. His first impulse was to lie through his teeth.

But she'd just stood toe to toe with a beast. She'd stroked a dragon, had the audacity to treat it like a pet dog. It was debatable if she'd done so out of bravery or momentary insanity. Nevertheless, she had.

If nothing else, he owed her the truth—or as much of it as he dared give her. "Yes."

Her glare deepened. "Can you make me dream?"

He held her stare, answering, "Yes."

Cam watched as the meaning of that answer sunk in. Ariel blushed with embarrassment, then paled as she whispered, "Oh. My. God."

She uncrossed her arms, and holding them out in front of her, stumbled away from him. "You used me. Then passed it off as nothing more than a dream."

"No, Ariel, I didn't." He didn't know what had happened in her dreams after he'd departed, but he certainly hadn't used her. He'd left her on the hammock untouched, although not unwanted by any means.

"You changed the upholstery on my sofa because I didn't like suede, then accused me of doing it. When I tried to hide from you in my bedroom, you used magic to get inside, then forced yourself on me."

Forced himself on her? "Your memory is a little faulty there."

"Oh, really? What part is faulty?"

"For one thing, *I* didn't change your upholstery." Although he was fairly certain his dragon had. Cam stepped toward her, trying to keep from shouting. "And I certainly didn't force myself on you." He raised his eyebrows and looked down at her. "Not even after you begged me."

"I never—"

"Oh, didn't you?" She really wanted to debate this? From the smug look on her face, she obviously thought she was right. Fine, he'd remind her of the event.

Before she could guess his next move, Cam reached out and grabbed her. He jerked her hard against his chest. "You did beg me, Ariel." He ran one hand through her hair until he cupped the back of her head. Threading her hair through his fingers, he tugged her head back and stared down at her. "Remember?"

Her overbright gaze faded and a frown replaced her glare. Certain he could convince her to think back to that day, he said, "You thought I'd be handy on house-cleaning day. When I claimed to be handy with other things, you asked me to show you what things."

Her cheeks flushed with color. She whispered an unintelligible curse.

"Yeah, you remember now, don't you? Then you should also remember that I didn't just jump to the occasion even after you begged me to."

"Fine. You're right, you didn't." Her flush darkened further. She shook her head out of his hold. "But afterward, you did something to make me think the entire episode, the furniture, the wizardry, the kissing, that all of it was a dream. Why?"

"You were the enemy. I didn't want you to remember that I'd admitted to being a wizard. Why would I let you remember information you might use against me?"

"What did you do?"

"Made you go to sleep and dream to forget."

"Of dragons, flying and making love on a beach."

"No. That was *your* dream." To his regret, he hadn't been there for the making-love part. What he had done was set the stage and nothing more. "I just supplied the beach and opportunity."

She cleared her throat, then asked, "Am I still the enemy?"

Cam released her with a sigh before answering her question with a question of his own. "What were you doing sneaking around the workroom, alone, at night?"

"So, this dragon thing…" She made no pretense of avoiding his question. "How does it work?"

"What do you mean?"

"Do you just decide to be a dragon at whim?"

"Sometimes. Not often." He crossed the room to retrieve her weapon. Handing it to her, he added, "Usually the change is under my control. Unless I somehow get zapped with a stun gun."

At least she had the decency to look away. "Sorry about that."

"Yeah. I'm sure you are."

"It's not like you could have died. There isn't enough juice for that."

"Maybe not, but you could have been killed."

"Good point." She shrugged. "But I wasn't."

"Nor did you answer my question. What are you doing out here alone?"

"I wasn't alone, your goons were with me."

"My *goons* didn't come into the workroom. What if one of the Learneds had been in here, waiting?"

"I thought they couldn't come on your property without you knowing about it."

"They can't. However, Brightworthe's body was found on the beach. And if you remember correctly, it's fairly easy for the Learneds to get one or more of their minions on the property."

Ariel groaned. "I hadn't thought of that."

"Obviously." He wanted to lock her in a room back at the keep, but knew she'd throw enough of a fit to start tongues wagging. Too bad Mirabilus didn't have an equipped dungeon.

"So what now?"

"Now that you know my secret, I'll have to toss you from a cliff into the ocean."

"But…"

He couldn't believe it—she frowned as if she was trying to determine if he was serious or not. Cam rolled his eyes as he walked by her on his way toward the corridor. "Not tonight though. I'm too tired."

She fell in step behind him. "From your point of view you'd probably be justified. I am technically working for your enemy."

When he didn't reply, she added, "And I did lie to get hired at the Lair."

Without stopping, Cam asked, "What are you doing? Trying to convince me to murder you?"

"No, I just…I don't know."

He stopped at the entrance panel and turned toward her. Reaching out in the dark, Cam grasped her shoulders. "Look, Ariel, if killing you had been my intention, don't you think I'd have done so by now?"

"I suppose. But I've never been quite certain what your intentions are."

Unfortunately, neither was he. The more he was around her, the more undecided he became.

She shivered and he brushed a hand down her arm before taking off his jacket to wrap it around her. "My intentions have always been the same—to find a way to get to the Learneds. You seemed the most direct route."

She pulled the jacket tighter around her shoulders. "And now?"

Cam slid the panel open, asking, "And now what? What are you thinking, or trying to figure out?"

Ariel buried her face in the collar of his jacket and breathed in the woodsy scent of his aftershave. She didn't exactly know what she was thinking.

He'd told her before that there was no "us" and he'd been right, they weren't a couple. And they'd both claimed more than once that they were essentially enemies. Again, the claim was correct—regardless of the reason, in the end her job was to rob him and naturally, his was to prevent the theft.

Then why did his touch say otherwise? Why did the lingering memory of his kisses leave her thinking of a future together?

"Ariel?" His breath rushed warm across her temple. "There is no *us*. You understand that, right?"

His nearness, the gentleness of his voice made her brave enough to ask, "How can you be so certain?"

Cam jerked away and walked through the panel door into the old shed. "Certain? I'm positive. It would never work between us."

She hadn't the slightest clue what drove her. Temporary insanity perhaps? Maybe she was overly tired, or more fed up with this entire situation than she'd realized. Or maybe she just felt the need to be contrary. The only thing she knew for certain was that she had to ask, "How can you be positive if we don't at least try?"

Ariel followed him out of the shed and squinted against the brightness of the perimeter light as it swept across them.

"No."

"So, what then? It was just a brief roll in the hay with an employee?" If his intent had been to make her feel cheap and used, he'd succeeded. "And now you'll just send me on my way?"

He still kept walking toward the keep without turning around. "If that explanation works for you, feel free to use it."

"What about Renalde and my brother?"

"I said I'd help. I won't change my mind."

"And once that's all settled I'll be out of your life for good, right?"

"That is the goal."

Ariel's head pounded. This was the reason she'd avoided involvement with men to begin with. She liked her life ordered, uncluttered, compartmentalized.

She'd known that she wouldn't be able to deal with the conflicting emotions a relationship and subsequent breakup would bring.

"It would have been easier if I'd never met you to begin with."

"Probably." He opened the door and held it for her. As she strode past him, he suggested, "Just pretend nothing ever happened."

"I wish I could just forget."

"That is an option."

She came to a dead stop in the foyer. "You're right. It is, isn't it?"

He was directly behind her. "Yes, Ariel, it is."

His voice sounded choked. She turned around and looked up at him. "Will I forget the taste of your kisses? The feel of your caresses? Will I go to sleep at night and not dream of you—or dragons?"

"If that's what you want, yes."

She grabbed his hand and tugged him toward the stairs. "Then do it."

Cam's dragon broke out in a fit of rage that nearly dropped him to his knees. The mark on his shoulder blade felt as if it was trying to pull free of his flesh. He stiffened his spine, clenched his jaw and followed her up the stairs.

As crazy as the idea sounded, it would be easier for both of them if she believed they'd never shared a kiss, or a bed.

Since she seemed to want to forget so badly, he was certain that he could convince her that the grimoire, the dragon—everything—was nothing more than strange dreams and nightmares she'd had while working at the Lair.

They would become employer and employee in every sense. At least until he found the items she needed for Renalde. He'd find a way to sneak them under her nose for her to discover. Then she'd be gone.

It would all be so easy.

And far too much of a coward's choice for him to live with.

Ariel shoved the door to her bedroom open so hard that it crashed against the wall. She tossed his jacket onto an occasional chair, then sat down on the bed. "Okay, I'm ready. Get it over with."

He sauntered in behind her, deliberately taking his time. "Get it over with?"

"Just do whatever you have to do."

Cam glanced at the desk. He swore he heard the grimoire laughing at him. Intentionally ignoring the imagined laughter, he sat down next to her. "You're sure?"

"Yes!" She grabbed his hand and held his palm against the side of her head. "Do it."

Cam nearly choked on his own laugh. She watched far too much television—specifically science-fiction movies—if she believed he could perform this magic with some type of alien mind meld.

He gently pulled his hand free and waved toward the pillows on the bed. "Lie down. Get comfortable."

She didn't need to know that he wasn't going to do anything more than put her to sleep. Tomorrow morning would be soon enough to have this argument.

"I'm ready."

Cam stretched out alongside her and pulled her into his embrace. It felt as if he held an unyielding piece of lumber against his chest. "What are you ready for, Ariel?"

"For all this to go away."

He traced lazy circles on her back, hoping she'd relax beneath his touch. "Really? There's nothing of the last few weeks you'd like to remember?"

"No. Nothing."

The hot wetness seeping through his shirt claimed her a very bad liar. He reached up to brush the telltale tears from her cheek. "Nothing?"

She shook her head against his chest.

For some reason, knowing that there was nothing she wished to remember cut like a razor against his heart. He closed his eyes against the emotions tugging at him, fighting to not act upon the hurt that her revelation caused his beast—and him.

He would get over this temporary pain, but what about his beast? How could she so carelessly, callously touch the dragon's soul only to leave him wanting in vain?

Cam gritted his teeth. This wasn't her fault. She didn't know. How could she know when he'd said nothing to make her believe he truly cared?

Forcing himself to ignore everything whirling inside, he calmed the tumult with a slow, deep breath, and then tipped his head to rest his forehead against hers.

His beast roared, rearing up in stunned amazement. Cam froze at the sudden certainty that he'd been wrong. So very wrong.

This creature, this person now resting comfortably in his arms, was far from human. At her core, at the very depths of her soul lived a shadowy beast.

He probed deeper, needing to know if this beast had been sent to him for some nefarious purpose by the Learneds. What he found was a dragon newly born. It was taking shape, fighting to be free, to be given the chance to fully form.

Relief flowed through him like a mountain stream, sweeping away his hurt in its path and giving him a glimmer of hope that he was not alone. Even though she had yet to realize it herself, she was as much a changeling as he.

"What are you doing?"

Her question startled him from his thoughts. "Nothing, go to sleep."

She halfheartedly pushed against him, complaining, "You aren't going to make me forget anything, are you?"

"No, Ariel. I'm not. Go to sleep."

His mind was too busy to deal with her anger or disappointment. "Just go to sleep. The next two days will be busy. You won't have time to go searching for pendants or boxes, so don't waste your time making any plans."

"And what if I'm not tired?"

A thousand different ways of killing time until she was tired flooded his mind. Each idea more erotic than the last. But the slowness of her words said she'd fall asleep the moment she closed her eyes. "Just go to sleep, Ariel."

She tried to shrug off his arm and push him away. "Go away, Cameron. I'd like to be alone."

And he'd like to be on a deserted tropical island without a care in the world. He kicked off his shoes, letting them fall to the floor. There was one way to make sure he'd get some sleep tonight.

He lifted an eyebrow at her curses as their clothing joined his shoes.

She lifted her head to glare at him through sleepy, bloodshot eyes. "This isn't your room. Leave."

"In case you haven't noticed, that isn't going to happen, so stop arguing."

The quilt at the end of the bed unfurled over them. Cam slid his arm from beneath her, flipped over onto his stomach and then draped an arm securely across her. "Now, either go to sleep on your own, or I'll see to it myself."

She pounded a fist on the mattress. "God, I despise you."

"I wouldn't have it any other way."

Chapter 16

Ariel watched from her seat in the far corner of the ballroom as the inhabitants of Mirabilus poured into the room. She was out of place in this crowd of mourners.

Brightworthe had been nothing more to her than a name she'd heard once or twice. From the number of people at his funeral, it appeared she was the only person on this entire island who hadn't known him.

Young or old didn't matter, everyone she talked to had had a story to tell her about the man. If just half the stories were true, Brightworthe had been a good person—one who shouldn't have died because of her.

Knowledge that she was responsible for Brightworthe's death and the pain these mourners were suffering fueled her guilt. Renalde had taken care of two objectives with this one horrendous move. He'd made good his threat of making her pay by killing Brightworthe, and that move had guaranteed she'd end up back at Mirabilus.

Although, how she was supposed to find anything here was beyond her comprehension. Between Cam and his goons this was the first time since yesterday morning when she felt as if eyeballs weren't boring into her back.

They'd watched her every move. Going so far as to stand outside her bedroom door while she'd changed clothes for the funeral service.

When confronted, Cam had claimed the guards were posted for her own safety. She only partly believed that explanation. The only danger to her physical safety was Danielle Drake.

Sean and Harold had seen to it that Ms. Drake was never within striking distance. Cam was keeping close tabs on her for some other reason, too. Her guess was that he didn't want her snooping around the keep.

A woman nearly tripped over her, snapping Ariel's attention back to the crowd. She pushed her chair farther back into the corner.

"Ariel?"

She didn't need to look up to recognize Cam's voice. What was he bugging her for now? Didn't he have other things to keep him busy?

Without taking her focus from the pink-hued veins crisscrossing the marble floor, she said, "I'm not doing anything. I'm just sitting here like an obedient little serf."

She gasped at the strangled chuckle that met her response. Quickly jumping to her feet, she stared up and frowned. This wasn't Cam. From his identical looks, this must be his twin, Braeden Drake. "I apologize. I am really sorry. I—"

"Stop." He touched her shoulder. "It's a common mistake people make the first time they see both of us."

A common mistake? Granted, Cam and Braeden were nearly identical twins—if one didn't take in the different eye color. However, it was a little hard to mistake Braeden's mesmerizing amethyst gaze for Cam's sapphire one. He must think she was a complete idiot.

"No. Misguided on some things perhaps. But not a complete idiot."

Ariel groaned. Another one like Danielle. "Please, don't do that."

"I forgot. Cam doesn't like to drop into people's minds, so you probably aren't used to it."

She wasn't about to tell him how far off the mark he was on that assumption. "No, he doesn't intrude on my thoughts. But he has other talents."

Braeden clenched his jaw and swallowed visibly. "Unfortunately, it'd be inappropriate for me to laugh right now."

She didn't know what to say to her faux pas, she hadn't meant his talents in the bedroom, but it was obvious that's what Braeden thought.

"Braeden, don't harass the guests." His wife, Alexia, linked her hand around his arm. "Whatever you do, Ariel, do not let him bully you."

Swallowing a moment of embarrassment, Ariel tore her stare from Alexia's stomach. She knew Braeden's wife was pregnant. But she didn't know how many babies the woman carried. From the looks of it, there had to be more than one—maybe three?

Cameron joined them. "Private discussion, or can anyone participate?"

The sight of the twins standing next to each other

was breathtaking. Even Alexia's eyes widened briefly as she moved to stand next to Ariel.

Both were decked out in black tuxes—including the shirts and ties. The only spot of color were the sashes at their waists. Braeden's in purple. Cam's in sapphire. Even the scabbards of their dress swords were etched with identical dragons.

Braeden winked at the women before answering his brother. "We were just talking about you. Feel free to leave."

Before Cam could respond, a commotion broke out across the room. Ariel watched in shock as a plume of red smoke curled up toward the vaulted ceiling.

Both brothers turned toward the ruckus at the same time. Braeden said, "It's just a group of rowdy kids showing off. I'll deal with it."

Cam hung back. He pulled a chair forward. "Alexia, here, get off your feet."

"No, but thank you." She shook her head, sighing with apparent exasperation. "His *lordship* just ordered me to go take a nap, so if you'll excuse me, I'll be heading upstairs like a good wife."

Ariel had to smile at Alexia's good-natured sarcasm. It seemed the brothers had at least one other thing in common besides their looks—they shared a commanding arrogance that wore rather thin at times.

"I don't have to be a mind reader to know exactly what you're thinking."

"Oh, really?" She turned toward Cam. "And what might that be?"

"You're wondering how Braeden trained her so well."

The man was obtuse at times. She tapped his chest. "You really need to practice that mind-reading thing a little more."

He grasped her wrist before she could lower her arm. "I was just teasing you, Ariel."

"Isn't such familiarity normally reserved for family and friends?" Easily pulling free, she added, "As your enemy I don't fit either category. So, I would appreciate it if you would drop the bantering."

"Alexia complies because she knows that Braeden would never force her to do anything she really didn't want to do." Cam totally ignored anything she'd just said. His unblinking gaze never left hers, and Ariel found herself concentrating solely on the way his hair fell across his forehead as he looked down at her.

"I would go so far as to say that Alexia most likely asked him to get her out of here because she really was tired." His voice was so deep, so steady, yet it sent shivers down her spine.

"That's the way the two of them work together most of the time."

A cool, mist-laden breeze rushed against her neck. Ariel tore her attention away from Cam long enough to see that he'd somehow led her outside.

"You did that on purpose."

"I wanted to show you something."

"And you couldn't have done so inside?"

The ends of his sash flapped behind him in the wind like some sapphire tail as he walked toward the workshop. The sight would have been comical had she not known the color of his scales.

"Coming?"

As much as she wanted to turn around and go back inside Mirabilus, her curiosity got the better of her. Ariel followed him into the shed.

"We're going to get filthy in there…"

Before she could complete the sentence, a brief flash

of cool air rushed against her suddenly naked limbs. "Cameron!"

"Nice." He touched the lace trimming her bra, his knuckles grazed the curve of her breast. "Lace bra and matching thong." He moved closer. "Standard attire for funerals?"

She had to tear her stare away from his heated gaze—otherwise the warmth already chasing away the chill from her arms would spread like wildfire. "Next time I'll be sure to get your approval first."

Instantly, jeans and a sweatshirt—clothing more appropriate to rooting around in an ancient workshop, not to mention protect her from herself, covered her body. He, however, was still attired in his tux.

Nervously, she asked, "Aren't you coming in, too?"

"You'll be fine. Nobody will bother you." In a much deeper, raspier tone he added, "Not even a dragon." His eyes shimmered, his pupils elongated for a moment before settling back into a more human shape. "I'll be standing guard."

She pitied anyone who decided to visit the workshop uninvited. "So, what am I supposed to see?"

"I finished chipping away at your block. You guessed right, it was a hiding place. I thought you might want to retrieve what's inside."

Could it be? Had he found the box, or another dragon pendant?

He slid the panel open and pushed her into the corridor. "Go, Ariel."

"But, why—"

"We can discuss why, what, and how, later. Go see what's there first."

It was all she could do not to run the length of the

corridor. But she didn't want to risk a tumble on the uneven floor.

Finally, her heart racing with renewed hope, she stepped into the chamber. The chandelier and half a dozen candelabras were lit, setting the room aglow.

True to his word, the mortar around the block had been chipped away. But there wasn't enough room for her fingers to simply pull the block free.

A metal file tapped against wall alongside her head. Ariel silently thanked Cam, then used the tool to pry the block from the wall.

After dropping the block and the file to the floor, she reached inside the opening and pulled out a small leather pouch.

Ariel moved into the brighter light at the center of the chamber. Her fingers shook as she flicked the rotted tie from the pouch and emptied the contents into her palm.

She gasped, clutching a dragon pendant to her chest. Surely he wasn't going to let her give this to Renalde?

This had to be a trick. He was torturing her by giving her hope that she really could save Carl's life. In the end, he would just take the pendant from her and laugh.

Ariel frowned. While that might be something she would expect Renalde to do, Cam wasn't like that.

She held the pendant up to study it in the light. Instead of emerald, it was sapphirelike. A shimmering, near-iridescent mix of blue, green and purple.

Just like Cam's beast.

She stroked a finger gently over its head, down the back and traced the length of the curled tail before running the tip of a fingernail up the scaled belly.

She would have expected the gemstone to be cold, but surprisingly, the pendant was warm beneath her touch—again, just like Cam's beast.

And when she held it up, the light twinkled off the eyes as if it looked back at her.

Giving something this intricate to Renalde would hurt, but not as much as Carl's death.

Ariel slipped the pendant back into the pouch and turned to leave the chamber.

She jumped in surprise at finding Cam in the doorway.

"I thought you were going to stand guard."

He leaned against the doorway. "I sealed the door shut. Nobody is getting in."

She blinked at the deep huskiness of his voice. "Is something wrong?"

Slowly he came toward her. "Wrong? What could possibly be wrong?"

He stalked over to her. Steady, unwavering. Muscles clenched. Jaw tight. Nostrils flared. His piercing gaze riveted solely on her. Ariel suddenly felt like small helpless prey.

"Cam?" She backed away until she slammed against the far wall.

But he kept moving steadily forward until the hard plane of his chest pinned her to the solid wall. "You found the pendant."

"Yes, I did." She swallowed, hoping to chase away the shakiness from her voice.

He reached down and uncurled her fingers from around the pouch. "And you…inspected it?"

"Of course."

Cam pulled the pendant from the bag and held it up by the chain. The small dragon twirled in the air before her. "Touch it."

"What?"

His breaths were a little more stable than they had

been a moment ago. "I said, touch it." He grasped her wrist to lift her hand and placed the pendant in her palm. "With a fingertip, touch it."

Confused, but oddly afraid not to do as he asked, she kept her stare on him as she once again gently stroked her finger along the gem.

Cam shivered. He could physically feel the warmth of her touch as it trailed down his back. The same thing had happened while he had been standing guard. But he'd brushed it off as some strange fantasy.

Until he'd felt one manicured fingernail trace slowly up his stomach, driving him wild with desire, leaving him near panting with lust. Then he'd realized that the sapphire dragon pendant he'd found last night was more like a spelled voodoo doll than a piece of jewelry.

Ariel's eyes widened. She curled her finger and grazed the tip of her nail along the belly. When he gasped, she asked, "Do you *feel* that?"

He clamped his hand around hers, stopping her from tormenting him further. "Yes. And if you don't want to be ravished right here, right now, I suggest you stop."

He leaned closer. With his lips brushing the soft skin beneath her ear, he invited, "Unless the idea turns you on as much as it does me."

Ariel wasn't certain what possessed her—but something had. She couldn't have stopped herself had she wanted to. She turned her head and lifted the pendant to her lips, whispering, "Tell me, do you feel this, too?"

She exhaled on the pendant, then ever so slowly drew the tip of her tongue along the beast's spine.

Her touch drew a guttural roar from Cameron. In the back of her logical mind, Ariel knew it would be wiser to back down, to be afraid.

But it wasn't fear coursing through her veins. And

it most certainly wasn't anything logical that uncoiled deep in her belly.

Even if she had decided to pull back, to change her mind, it was too late. Need, hunger, near-wild desire drove her body to find the fulfillment it required. Her mind had no say.

Cam pulled her roughly into his arms and lifted her from the floor. Instantly the barrier of clothing fell away, flesh pressed against heated flesh. The hard plane of his chest in perfect opposition to the softness of her breasts.

When he claimed her lips it wasn't with the gentleness of passion. He was as hungry for her as she was for him, if not more so. She gladly met his demanding kiss with her own. Drowning in the need swirling around them, Ariel tightened her legs around him and curled her fingers in his hair.

A throaty growl was her only warning before he pushed her against the wall of the workroom. She ignored the roughness against her back and clung to him moaning, begging for more than a kiss.

Cam lowered his arms, hooking his hands beneath her as he caressed his way along the sensitive flesh until his teasing touch found her heat.

She gasped, melting into his touch. Their kiss broken, he nuzzled the soft spot beneath her ear, drawing another moan from her lips.

His touch, his lips were driving her toward the edge, but it wasn't enough. Ariel drew in a ragged breath and grazed his scalp with her fingernails. She still wanted more.

Ariel jumped at the jolt of wild desire within her as he sunk his teeth into the tender skin where her neck met her shoulder. She closed her eyes at the dizzying, near-frantic pace of her heartbeat while twisting hard against him, trying to get closer, needing him to end this torment.

Suddenly, her mind filled with nothing but lust, she sensed the beast within him. The powerful strength of the dragon, his own great need, was laced with torment and longing. Her heart ached for what this beast thought he could never have.

Tears stung behind her eyelids at her inability to comfort him. She couldn't give him what he sought—regardless of what the dragon wanted, the man wanted no part of her heart.

Not knowing what else to do, she forced herself to relax in his hold. Gently stroking the side of his face with a trembling hand, she whispered hoarsely, "Cam, please, I need you."

He released her shoulder and drew his lips back to hers as he entered her. The hard length of his erection filled her. She met his thrusts, knowing by the tensing of his shoulders and arms that he was as close to the edge as she.

Ariel curled her arms tightly around his neck, tearing her mouth from his to cry out as their shared climax left her shuddering against his chest.

Breathing hard, Cam tilted his head to rest his forehead against the wall. His arms trembled beneath her.

Ariel reluctantly unhooked her feet and let her legs slide down the length of his body. But she kept her arms wrapped around his neck, fearing her legs wouldn't yet be able to hold her upright.

She wanted to ask him about his beast, but knew he wouldn't talk to her. No matter what passed between them physically, in the end, they were still and always would be enemies.

It didn't matter that neither of them had other choices. She had to protect her brother. He had to protect his family.

Cam leaned away and gently stroked a finger along her cheek. "We need to get back."

Once they were both dressed, and after placing a gentle kiss on her lips, he turned around. "He's like a teenager in love for the first time, Ariel. Leave him be. He'll be fine."

She blinked in shock at his rough dismissal of his beast's feelings. How could he be so callous?

"The subject is closed."

She knew by the tone of his voice that she would only be wasting her time and energy arguing with him. Ariel drew in a slow breath as she picked up the pendant and put it back inside the pouch.

She frowned. If she could cause such physical havoc by simply touching the stone dragon, what damage could Renalde cause? Her heart skipped and her throat tightened at the thought of Cam's death. "I can't give this to Renalde."

Unsure if he was relieved or disappointed that she'd put the dragon away, he answered, "You don't have a choice."

"What if he can do this, too? He could kill you without warning."

"True. But I don't think it works that way."

The reason the Learneds wanted Alexia's pendant, was because it turned into a living breathing dragon. What they didn't realize was that it only transformed for her. He and Braeden had put that to the test numerous times—always with the same result.

Considering his beast's unquenchable lust for Ariel, he suspected that this extremely tactile magic worked only for Ariel, too. He would test that theory and if it proved true, he'd gladly suggest she hand the pendant over to the Learneds. At least then it'd be out of her hands—away from her exotically magical touch.

"Is there anyone you could ask?"

"No."

"Nobody?"

"Look, Ariel, outside of Brightworthe, no one else knows about my ability to change into a dragon except you. I'd prefer to keep it that way."

"Your brothers and your aunt don't know?"

"Thankfully, no. It's not like I was born like this. It just started happening one day."

He felt her body tense as she gasped. "It just happened? Without any warning?"

"Other than some odd dreams, intuition, and a birthmark that started to burn, there wasn't any warning."

He watched the color drain from her face. "Odd dreams?"

Uncertain how to answer in a manner that wouldn't frighten her, Cam only nodded in response.

"Intuition?"

He knew exactly what she was wondering without having to delve into her mind. Reaching out to offer a measure of his strength, he said, "Ariel, it will be all right."

She pushed his hand away and slid down the wall until she sat on the floor. "No. It isn't possible. I can't do this."

This wasn't the time or the place to have this conversation. But who else, besides him, could help her understand what would eventually happen to her? Who else could explain that it was a gift, not a curse? "You can't do what, Ariel?"

"I can't be like you. I'm a human. I'm not a…thing."

Unable, unwilling to believe what he was hearing, Cam grabbed the front of her sweatshirt and hauled her to her feet. "*Thing?* Is that what I am to you? A *thing?* A freak of nature?"

"No, no." She shook her head. "That's not what I meant. This can't be happening. It can't be real. It's just a dream, that's all. It has to be. If not, I don't know what to do, how to stop it."

"You can't stop it." He released her. "Don't worry, you won't be alone.

"Won't be alone?" Her bark of laughter bounced off the stone walls. "Yes, I will. Once this is all over with, I'm going home."

She'd be aghast to realize that he and his beast had just made a decision on that score. "How about if we worry about this when it becomes necessary?"

"That will be easier said than done."

Since his mind had been spinning around all the possibilities, he agreed. "True. But right now, I need you to relax. There's someplace else we need to be."

"Relax?" She stared up at the ceiling. The flickering light twinkled off her tears. "How?"

Cam quickly pulled her against him and lowered his lips to hers. "Let me help."

Her tears were salty against his tongue, but her kiss was the sweetest thing he'd ever tasted. He wanted more than just her lips beneath his, but for now it would have to do.

She relaxed against him, her fear and worry slipping away. He reluctantly broke their kiss to ask, "Ready?"

At her nod, he escorted her out of the chamber, through the corridor, pausing at the hidden door only long enough to switch her sweatshirt and jeans for her dress. Then they exited the shed, heading back to the castle.

Walking alongside Cam, Ariel held up the pendant to ask, "Are you sure you want me to hang on to this?"

"I need to test a theory or two, but after that, yes, it's yours."

She let the pendant dangle. With a soft, seductive laugh, she briefly trailed a finger down the dragon's back before letting it fall into her palm.

Cam and his beast shivered in unison. "You just don't know when to give up, do you?"

"No, not when I know what the outcome will be." She slipped the chain over her head, letting the pendant disappear behind the front of her dress. "There, I'll save us both some embarrassment."

From the fire suddenly teasing his back, warming his blood, and making his dragon rumble once again with need, he feared embarrassment was the least of their concerns.

"That's her!" Danielle Drake screamed from a balcony.

She pointed a finger toward Ariel. "She's the one who should pay. Brightworthe's death was her fault."

From the gathering of people beneath the balcony, Cam knew this had been planned. Determined to get rid of Ariel one way or another, Danielle had craftily staged this show.

His aunt stared directly at him, stating loudly, "I demand that thieving murderess be punished."

Chapter 17

Cam groaned at his aunt's strident accusation. From the looks on the faces of those gathered, his aunt's showdown could turn ugly fast.

He couldn't determine what the people of Mirabilus might do if they believed Ariel was at fault for the death of one of their own.

The people of this isle were closemouthed out of necessity. They didn't want strangers—outsiders—nosing around any more than he or his family did.

But more threatening was their closeness. Each and every one of them heralded from tribes long thought extinct. And following the ways of their ancestors, they were clannish when it came to protecting or defending their own.

Ariel was not one of them. As the Drakes' enemy, she was theirs also. Worse, if they thought she threatened Braeden in any way, she'd be lucky to get off this island alive.

Naturally, even though he had no idea the reasoning behind her drastic decision, Danielle would do everything—and anything—in her power to make certain that Ariel was seen as a threat. Once she made up her mind on something it was almost impossible to reason with her.

Determined to protect Ariel, Cam draped his arm across Ariel's trembling shoulders. "Don't engage her. Let me and Braeden deal with this."

"I'm trembling with rage, not fear. I'm not afraid of her."

That's what worried him. "You should be. Ariel, no one here will be shocked or surprised by any use of magic—good or bad. She could set you on fire with the flick of a finger and none of these people would come to your aid, or find fault with her action."

She looked up at him, frowning. "I haven't done anything to them, why would all of them stand by idly while another person was killed?"

"Simple. You aren't one of them." He nodded toward his aunt. "And because her word carries a lot of weight here."

"More than you or your brother carry?"

"Depends."

"On?"

"On whether Braeden sides with me or her."

Ariel pulled away. "This isn't your fight."

Like hell it wasn't. Did she really think that he was going to stand by while she put herself in danger? Did she truly believe his beast would allow another of its kind to be harmed? "I said, don't—"

Before he could finish his command, she rushed forward to stand beneath the balcony. "I've stolen nothing. And I was with your nephew when Brightworthe was killed."

Danielle leaned over the railing. "You may not have killed him with your own hands, but you are still responsible."

From the corner of her eye, Ariel saw the people closing ranks around her. She gritted her teeth. Why hadn't she expected that?

A flash of light was her only warning that something deadly was headed straight toward her. Ariel ducked, cringing as a jagged blade whizzed past her head.

At almost the same heartbeat, a ring of fire surrounded her. Ariel closed her eyes against the heat of the dancing flames. She knew Danielle Drake disliked her intensely. But since she'd missed with the blade, did the woman hate her enough to actually burn her alive?

It took more than a few minutes for Ariel to calm her pulse enough to breathe, and a few more to realize the fire wasn't getting any closer to her. She opened her eyes.

In fact, it seemed to act more as a protective ring than a threat. She turned her attention back to Cam's aunt. From the surprise on Danielle's face, the fiery protection was about the last thing she'd expected.

Ariel knew that reasoning with the woman would prove useless. But without knowing how to use any magical powers she might possess, if any, words were the only thing she had to defend herself with, so she had to try. "Ms. Drake, you're upset. That's understandable. Everyone here has suffered a great loss. But I've taken nothing from you or your family and I did nothing to harm anyone."

"Oh, really?" Danielle reached behind her and held

up the grimoire. "Then what was this doing in your room?"

The crowd gasped as one before turning their hard stares on Ariel.

"Enough!" Braeden pushed his way through the gathering. He waved a hand toward the fire, dousing the flames, then did nothing more than glance up at his aunt and hold out his hand. When the book ripped itself from Danielle's grasp to come to Braeden, he held it up, claiming, "I gave her this book to study."

Ariel tried not to show her surprise at his easy control of the crowd and outright lie.

Cam joined Braeden. "We've all looked for a way to defeat the Learneds. The answer might be in these pages."

A man in the crowd stepped forward, asking, "Then why not let one of us look for the answer?"

Cam shook his head. "Why don't you come up here and read a page or two. Then you'll have your answer."

The man boldly strode to the brothers. When he shot Ariel an angry glare, Cam pushed her safely behind him.

Braeden handed the man the grimoire. "Go ahead. Pick a page. Any page."

With a grunt of disdain directed toward Ariel, the man opened the book. He stared hard at the blank pages before him, then flipped to another set of blank pages, then another and another, before saying, "It's a trick."

"Oh, really?" Alexia walked out of the castle to stand at her husband's side. "I entreat any, or all, of you to give it a shot. See for yourself if it's a trick, or if it's more Mirabilus magic at work."

Ariel watched in mute surprise as one by one about half the crowd lined up to see for themselves. Visions of men and boys taking turns to try pulling a sword from a boulder flitted through her mind. The problem with that fanciful image was that she was not a young King Arthur.

And one by one the people of Mirabilus were disappointed to discover nothing but blank pages in the grimoire.

After the last person flipped through the book, Alexia took it from Braeden. "Ariel, come here."

Startled by Alexia's commanding tone, Ariel edged around Cam to do as the woman bid.

"When I read the pages, I needed to have Braeden in the room." She handed the book off to Ariel, asking, "Do you need anyone present?"

Ariel shook her head. "No, not for the pages to appear." She separated the cover, letting the grimoire flip to the page it wanted. "They just fill in by themselves."

As it had done before, images and symbols painted themselves on the page.

Alexia suggested, "Hold it up so they can see."

With the open book held up over her head, Ariel took a step back from the gasps rippling through the crowd.

"What does it say?" a woman from the back asked.

Ariel lowered the book. "I don't know the history or lore of Mirabilus, so it's hard for me to decipher."

She glanced at Cam. Even though his expression remained placid, she could nearly feel his anger. He hesitated long enough to set her heart racing. Finally, he stood beside her and said, "That's why I've been helping."

Relief that he hadn't decided to feed her to the wolves made her sway. He slipped his arm behind her, whispering, "Not now." Then turned back to the gathering to explain, "Ariel turns the pages so they fill in and I try to figure out what's written."

"Does that satisfy everyone?" Braeden's voice boomed over the crowd. "Are there any complaints? If so, voice them now."

Other than some mutters and whispers, nobody stepped forward with a challenge.

Braeden stated, "The existence of this grimoire is a threat to all of us at Mirabilus. If the outside world knew it was real, we would be hounded night and day. Thieves who merely suspect the grimoire exists already haunt our land seeking to steal it from us. They have caused damage to our island and brought death to our people."

Ariel heard Alexia's soft groan of dismay and wondered if anything was wrong. She looked up at Cam, but he only said, "Later."

Continuing, Braeden pulled his sword from the scabbard hanging at his side. "Do you swear to keep this secret safe? To protect our lives and the lives of our children?"

Everyone answered in the positive.

"Do you believe it is imperative this incident, and this grimoire, remain sacred and hidden?"

Once again, they all agreed. Ariel suspected magic was in play.

He lifted his sword, ordering, "Then so swear it."

As one the crowd swore to protect the secret. Then, without another word, they dispersed to either go back inside the castle or take their leave.

When there was no one except her and the Drakes in the yard, Ariel asked, "It's just that easy? You order, they swear and nobody says a word?"

Both men looked at her as if she'd lost her mind. Braeden asked, "What else would you suggest doing?"

"I don't know, but this doesn't seem right."

Cam added, "They won't remember any of this ever happened."

"So, you manipulate them whenever you see fit?" Somehow, that felt…wrong to her. "Isn't that the same as lying to them?"

"Had you listened to me, it wouldn't have been necessary." She flinched at Cam's harsh tone.

"Perhaps to you it does seem wrong." Alexia touched her arm. "But innocent people have died because rumors of that book's existence reached the general public."

"How would anyone have known?"

Braeden drew Alexia to his side. "Because in a fit of spite, my wife saw fit to write a paper about it."

"Estranged wife." Alexia corrected.

"True, you were strange at the time."

Alexia rolled her eyes. "Aren't you the clever fellow."

"Always." Braeden sighed. "What I am right now though is remiss in my duties. I need to get back to work, so to speak. Not to mention deal with Danielle." He stared at Cam. "Meanwhile, you need to get her out of here."

"Agreed."

Braeden started to turn away, then stopped to ask, "Do you want me to call the pilot?"

"No." Cam looked down at Ariel. "I'll deal with it myself."

Ariel grasped his meaning. Her heart and stomach hit her feet. Once Braeden and Alexia were out of earshot, she said, "You can't possibly be serious. Just because you can fly doesn't mean I can."

Aelthed swallowed his shock at what had just happened. The idea that the elder Drake female would threaten or kill the one person who could help the changeling decipher the grimoire and break the curse was outlandish.

He'd been able to throw a ring of protection around the changeling's woman only because he'd been aware of the danger threatening her. What if he hadn't been aware?

The Drakes', and his, enemy was the Learneds. They needed to direct their energy into defeating Nathan and his spawn. It was a terrible waste to focus their powers on one of their own.

He needed to find a way to communicate with the Drake woman. She was telepathic, maybe she could hear him.

In the meantime, since he wasn't certain he could levitate himself across the ocean, he needed to make certain his cube was safely hidden in the luggage that would be headed back to Dragon's Lair.

He could deal with this Danielle Drake soon enough.

Cam lowered his arm from Ariel's shoulder and stepped away. "I told you not to engage her."

"I was supposed to just stand there and say nothing in my defense?"

"Since she was right, there was nothing to defend."

"Nothing to defend?" She didn't disagree with being responsible. However, her participation hadn't been direct, nor had it been willing. As far as she was concerned, her defense had been justified.

"What part of this don't you suddenly understand?" He swung around to glare at her. "Have you forgotten that Brightworthe is dead because of you? Granted, your hands didn't deal the blow that killed him, but you did something to push the Learneds to this extreme."

"No, I didn't forget anything." How could she? Her guilty conscience ate at her. Only the desperate need to gain Carl's freedom and save his life kept her walking straight through the guilt.

"I'm not shifting the blame to anyone else. But how could I *not* defend myself when she made it sound like I killed Brightworthe with my own hands?"

"What difference would it have made? Neither Braeden, nor I would have let anything happen to you. We would have gotten you off the island before anyone could harm you."

"So, I should just let the entire island think I'm a murderess?"

"It's not like they're your family. Since you won't be coming back here, why would you care what they might think?"

She couldn't refute anything he'd said, because it was true. So, why did it sting? Ariel glanced at the castle, then she gazed out toward the shoreline.

She hadn't wanted to come back here to begin with. She shouldn't want to ever return. But the idea of never seeing this island again felt like a loss. A loss of what?

Before she completely lost her mind, she agreed with him. "You're right. I don't have any family here." She couldn't agree with the rest of his comment though. "But I don't want anyone—not even strangers—to think I'm a murderess."

"It would have hurt no one."

"And correcting the assumption hurt no one, either."

"No?"

"Not from what I could see, no." But Ariel had the feeling she was missing something. "Your brother seemed to have the crowd under complete control."

"If that was true, he wouldn't have suggested getting you off the island so fast."

"Are you saying your magic doesn't always work?"

"Of course not. But it didn't do anything to sway Danielle."

"Nothing would change her opinion."

"Your death would."

Ariel shivered as Cam's meaning sunk in. Warranted or not, now Danielle Drake would be even more determined to hand out her own brand of justice—this time without any warning.

Everything she'd already done could be for nothing—she could end up dead before saving her brother. Ariel swallowed a curse, then whispered, "What have I done?"

Cam threaded his fingers through hers and tugged her away from the castle. "You can't take her on, Ariel. You have nothing in your arsenal that comes close to what's in hers."

Numb from her own lack of forethought, she followed, knowing that Braeden had been right, she had to get off this island. While leaving here was the best, and the only sane, option, Cam's intended method of departure gave her cause for concern.

Ariel tugged on his hand, slowing his stride. "Is something wrong with your jet?"

Stopping, he turned to look at her. "Scared?"

That would be putting it mildly. These dreams and feelings inside her claimed her to be like Cam. She prayed that wasn't true, but even if it was, she had no experience at flying. How was she supposed to cross an entire ocean under her own power?

And even if he carried her part of the way, what was to stop him from dropping her into the water? While she doubted his dragon would do so willingly, she had no idea how much control Cam had over the beast. Dropping her would solve all his troubles. She wasn't about to voice that fear, it might give him ideas. "No. Not really. I just think it's a waste of a—"

Quicker than her eyes could follow, the dragon—Cam—loomed over her. Ariel gasped at his rapid shift. There was no slow transformation, no display of limbs and flesh turning into wings and scales. It was nearly instantaneous. Her breath caught when he scooped her up and took flight.

The ground spun away beneath them at a dizzying rate. She wrapped her arms tightly around one smooth talon and closed her eyes, suddenly certain this was a very bad idea.

Even in his current form, Cam was aware of the terror charging through the woman securely imprisoned inside his curved talons. The scent was too familiar for him to mistake as anything else.

Before soaring out across the seemingly endless water, he circled the isle, slowly gliding, easily adjusting his wings to ride the wind. When her death grip lessened and the tang of fear warmed to a more spice-filled aroma, he spread his wings against the wind to land gently on the beach.

Ariel slid off his now-opened foot, and backed away enough to gaze up at him. "Is this a choice?"

Cam stayed in dragon form, lowering his head to chuff a breath against her hair. Yes, it was a choice—of sorts. She could choose to come willingly, or he could snatch her up again.

She walked around him, reaching out now and then to touch, to stroke a wing or his scales before coming to a stop before him. "Apparently you don't intend to drop me to my death."

Insulted, he turned his head and snorted. Sand puffed up around them. Drop her? If he had any intention of killing her, he wouldn't resort to something as clumsy as dropping her.

Her soft laugh sent tremors shivering the length of his spine. Had she, or her own beast, somehow understood?

She closed her eyes and he could sense her shadowy dragon fighting for its freedom. Unable to help her make the transformation, he could only watch and wait.

Finally, either frustrated or too inexperienced, she gave up with a sigh and asked, "Are you certain you can carry me all the way back to the Lair?"

Cam dragged a talon through the sand, then picked up a tiny pebble. He held it out to her.

"Okay, I get the gist. But I think I might weigh a little more than a pebble."

He dropped the stone and reached toward a car-size boulder.

"Oh!" Ariel shrieked and swatted at his chest. "Funny."

Pleased he could humor her so easily, he relented and held out a forefoot.

A gust of wind rushed across the water onto the beach. Ariel shivered. "I'm going to freeze to death, aren't I?"

He stared down at her. She wanted a nest? A bed? He studied the beach, looking for something that might suit the woman. Finding nothing, he shook his head, then tapped a talon to his chest. The warmth of his body would keep her from freezing.

A questioning frown marred her features, creases lined her forehead. "Can we try it first?"

He wiggled his talons, beckoning her to climb aboard.

Ariel scrambled onto his foot, gasping when he closed his talons around her like a cage, then lifted her against his chest.

She reached between his hooked claws to place her palm against his chest. Cam willed his body heat to flow into her, knowing full well the effect would do more than just warm her flesh.

With a trembling sigh, she sat down, circled one arm around a talon and asked hoarsely, "How long is this going to take?"

While Cam fought the urge to change back into human form and satisfy the lust wafting thick around them, the beast growled softly, content to do nothing more than hold the woman close.

Chapter 18

She wanted to push away the nagging voice whispering in her ear. It rudely interrupted her dream. The wind whipping through her hair as she flew across both sea and land had made for a wonderful dream. Stars dotted the night sky, blinking like twinkle lights against the darkness.

"Ariel."

No. Angrily brushing away the hand shaking her shoulder, she groaned with regret at being forced to leave her dreams behind.

"Come on, we're home."

Home? She opened her eyes and looked around. "This isn't home, it's the Lair—"

Dragon's Lair? The last thing she remembered was falling asleep against Cam's—his beast's—chest. Although how she fell asleep was beyond her knowing. The warmth emanating from the dragon had been the most erotically intoxicating sensation she'd ever experienced.

"Are you awake?"

She quickly closed her eyes, hoping to avoid having to look at him. While she knew she wouldn't die from embarrassment, she'd rest easier if he didn't know what she'd felt.

"From that blush I'd say you're awake." The mattress dipped then shifted as he rose from the bed. "It's still early, get a couple more hours of sleep."

She rolled onto her side and glanced at him. "Where are you going?"

"To my own bed." He paused at her bedroom door. Without turning around, he said, "Christmas."

Ariel rose up on an elbow, waiting for an explanation to his strange comment spoken in such a surprised tone of voice.

"Your lust smells like Christmas—exotically spiced Orientals laced with cinnamon and cloves."

She fell back down onto the bed with a groan. Before she could think of anything to say in reply, the door slammed closed behind him.

Relief flowed through her—followed by desperate need. Ariel sighed. This was all wrong.

Her gut feeling told her that no matter what her logical reasoning believed, she was just like him, but he was the enemy. He and his family would be victim to her thievery.

Dismayed, Ariel groaned. Cameron Drake and his accursed dragon was the last person she should care about.

Yet, if it was so wrong, why did she want him so badly? Why did just the memory of his fingertips graz-

ing her naked flesh make her bite her lip to keep from
crying out for his touch?

If this wasn't right, if this wasn't meant to be, why
did she so willingly, so eagerly, go into his arms each
time he beckoned?

If this wasn't right, why did his easy acceptance of
what she might be matter so much to her? Why did his
understanding and his willingness to help calm the fears
tearing through her mind?

And if this was wrong, why did the thought of leaving Dragon's Lair create such an aching hole in the pit
of her stomach?

"Why can't you want me as much as I do you?" she
whispered into the empty darkness of the bedroom.

Cam rested his forehead against the cool wood of
her bedroom door. It did nothing to temper the need
urging him to open the door and satiate the lust raging
through both of them.

While he'd been merely surprised that she'd trusted
him enough to carry her across a vast ocean with nothing separating her from the icy-cold water except his
talons curved around her, his beast had been touched—
deeply.

More so than he'd ever imagined possible.

Added to that was the fact that she'd sensed his
beast while they'd made love in the workroom. Not
only sensed him, but ached for the dragon's pain and
longed to comfort him.

Comfort. This mortal, this enemy of his, had been
upset that she didn't know how to comfort a cursed,
magical beast.

And most of all, this enemy sent to defeat him and
his family was more like him than any other person in
the world. With her, he was no longer alone.

He needed to get her out of here, away from Dragon's Lair, away from him before he was unable to let her go.

Already the dragon mourned what would soon be an end to Ariel's stay at the Lair. Thankfully, the beast understood what had to be done to keep her alive. But that understanding did little to quell the hurt ripping through his chest.

He turned away from the door with a ragged sigh. Time had eventually healed the hurt of losing Carol. But the beast hadn't been involved then, what sort of time would accepting this loss require? Would a lifetime be enough?

It would have to be, since that's all he had to give.

He slid a hand into the pocket of his jeans, curling his fingers around the dragon pendant that would soon find its way into the Learneds' hands. A shame since Ariel seemed to be the only one who possessed the ability to transfer her touch on the pendant to his beast. It was too bad she couldn't keep it with her when she left.

Right now, he needed to find the last item that would send Ariel from the Lair, and place her out of danger's way. A wooden puzzle box. Unfortunately, he hadn't the slightest clue of where to begin his search.

"You what?"

Jeremy cowered from the heated anger, the pure rage spewing from his father's shouted question. "I don't know how it happened. One minute he was there—and the next...he was just...gone."

Nathan slammed a fisted hand on the top of his credenza, sending candles and dragon statues flying as the ancient piece of furniture cracked in two. His curses filled the room, forcing Jeremy to press even tighter against the locked door at his back.

He clawed at the door, frantically chanting and mumbling in his haste, seeking the right spell to break the lock and set him free.

"Jeremy, my child, are you thinking of leaving me?"

He froze, terrified by his sire's cold, even tone of voice. Slowly, he turned to face his father. "No, I would never…"

His words trailed off as Nathan raised a hand and pointed one boney finger toward Jeremy. "Be still, boy."

The older wizard waved abruptly toward a chair, laughing as his son's body was flung, arms flailing and legs kicking, across the room to land unceremoniously atop the seat.

"We need to fix this."

How were they going to fix dead? The Johnson boy was dead. Nothing he nor his gifted father did could change that.

"Oh, but there is a way to fool people into believing he is still alive. At least until I get what I want."

Jeremy silently cursed his wayward thoughts. Apparently he'd given his sire an idea—one that most likely wouldn't bode well for him.

"Come, come now, boy. You got us into this mess, surely you feel the need to do your part to make it right."

Since it hadn't been posed as a question, Jeremy knew the choice had already been made. He shrunk, folding himself into the chair, trying to forestall the inevitable.

His father's hand against his neck was cold enough to freeze his flesh. Jeremy trembled as the older wizard chanted, his warm breath forming ice crystals that hung like clouds in the air.

"Relax, my son. It will only hurt for a moment."

Frozen in place, Jeremy was unable to escape his

father's stroking touch along his cheek. Unbearable pain forced a scream from his throat.

The instant he parted his lips to cry out his torment, his father swallowed the scream with his own mouth.

Nathan smiled at the warmth flowing through his body as he drew in his son's soul. He hadn't felt this alive, this vital, in more months than he could remember. Not since the Drakes' dragon had carted him off.

Before he drained too much of his son's spirit, he released the boy. Eventually, Jeremy would regain strength, but until then he would be nothing more than a breathing shell.

He needed Jeremy to have enough soul to at least be able to speak on command. Thinking wasn't necessary—in fact, it was giving the boy the opportunity to think that had caused this mess to begin with.

Nathan didn't want to risk the Johnson woman's co-operation, so for now at least, it served him better to let her speak with Jeremy. That way she wouldn't become overly suspicious.

Although, it was truly a pity he couldn't retain this energy for himself. Not just yet. First he wanted that pendant and his box returned. For that, he needed Jeremy alive—more or less.

Nathan straighten his spine, enjoying the feel of not being hunched over for a change. He thrust out his arms, turning and twisting in ways he'd been unable to do for so long now, before heading toward the door.

He paused to glance back at the half-lifeless body of his only remaining child. Perhaps being childless wouldn't be so bad after all.

It was something he'd have to consider seriously, once the items were in his possession.

* * *

Ariel grasped the edge of the picnic table for support. "Why would you do that?"

Renalde's exasperated sigh made her fear he'd changed his mind. "I'm not going to keep repeating myself, Ms. Johnson. Do you want Carl with you, at the Lair or not?"

"Of course I do. But I don't have the puzzle cube, just the pendant." She didn't mention that it wasn't the emerald one he'd ordered her to find. She'd deal with that issue when the time came.

"I have every confidence that you'll find it. I'm sure Brightworthe's death is still ingrained in your mind. So you know just what I'm capable of doing."

"Yes, but—"

"There are no buts. I tire of seeing to your brother's care. Let his continued life, or eventual death, be on your hands."

"What's to stop me from leaving the Lair with Carl?"

Renalde's laugh sent shivers down her spine. "Go ahead and try. I'll have my hands on the both of you before you reach the edge of town. Do I need to explain what will happen then?"

"No." She knew without a doubt that he would make her suffer and pay dearly for trying to thwart him. "When do you want to make the exchange?"

"I'll be at the gates in front of the Lair in about fifteen minutes."

Ariel scrambled from the picnic table and raced toward the Jeep. "I'll meet you there."

"I won't wait."

Before she could assure him that he wouldn't have to, the call went dead.

She tossed the phone onto the passenger seat as she

climbed behind the wheel and started the Jeep. She pulled into traffic briefly before turning off onto the back road along the river that would dump her out onto the main road leading up to the Lair.

The sun glinted off the sapphire dragon pendant swinging on a chain that was looped around the rearview mirror. She hated to give it up, and still couldn't believe Cam had given his blessing for her to do so.

Actually, he seemed sort of relieved that it would soon be out of her possession. She shot the inanimate piece of jewelry an evil grin, then leaned forward to drop a kiss on top of its shiny head.

In her mind's eye she could see Cam flinch at the contact. He'd know it was her, how could he not? Which is probably why he was so anxious for her to hand it over to Renalde.

That knowledge made her sad. These past few days had been the most pleasant of her stay at the Lair. For the most part they hadn't argued. To be honest, other than the three new pages she'd uncovered for him in the grimoire, they hadn't spent enough time together to argue.

If she wasn't working in the gardens, or the workshop, she was hiding from Danielle Drake. Either Cam, Sean or Harold saw to it that she and Ms. Drake were never alone together.

Never. Not even for a minute.

In fact, the men made it a point to physically place themselves between the two of them at all times. Which she supposed was for the best, considering the deathray looks Ms. Drake shot toward her.

She'd intentionally worked hard all day long so that at night she'd fall into bed exhausted, passing out almost before her head hit the pillow. As far as she knew, Cam had spent his nights in his own bedroom.

Still, that hadn't prevented her from dreaming about him. Some of the dreams had been so real that she'd sworn she'd caught the scent of his aftershave on the pillow beside her in the morning.

And sometimes she'd awaken exhausted, as if she'd spent the night flying, working muscles she didn't know existed.

Since Cam was a dream wizard of sorts, she realized that a portion of those dreams might have been true. But she couldn't bring herself to question him. She didn't want to know if he'd actually taught her how to soar, glide or land. And she didn't want to know if he'd held her while she slept, or kissed away her tears.

The knowing would only make things worse when it came time for her to leave. She'd have her hands full with Carl, and wouldn't have the time to grieve for something that never was, or might have been.

It would be easier to leave just a job than it would be to leave a lover.

Who was she trying to fool? It would be easier for whom? Certainly not for her.

Ariel drew in a shuddering breath. She knew damn well that as soon as she pulled her packed van through the gates for the last time, she'd be a wreck.

While it was true, she could keep her distance now, making it easier to pretend Cam was nothing more than an employer. She would always long for just one more kiss, one more touch, one more night spent in his arms.

Dragging her wayward thoughts back to the task at hand, Ariel slowed the Jeep around the last curve, then came to a stop outside the gates to Dragon's Lair.

She glanced at her watch to make certain she hadn't

missed Renalde, relieved to find she had at least two minutes to spare.

A long panel van pulled up alongside of her. Renalde's goon Bennett got out of the van and walked to the rear of the vehicle. When she didn't get out of the Jeep immediately, he shouted, "You want this or not?"

She rolled down her window. "Is Mr. Renalde with you?"

"Nope. Just me and Mr. Talkative here." He jerked a meaty thumb toward Carl's prone body.

"Where am I supposed to put a stretcher?" If Renalde wasn't in the van, surely that meant it would be all right for Bennett to drive onto the property. There was one way to find out. "Why don't you just follow me up to the Lair."

Unintelligible curses rained down on her, but the thug slammed the back doors closed, climbed into his van and waved her forward.

Luckily her assumption had been right—no one rushed out of the Lair as they approached the entrance doors. No one except Harold.

He opened her door, asking, "He with you?"

"Yes, he is." Regretfully, she pulled the dragon pendant from the mirror. "Could you give me a hand?"

Harold followed her to the back of the van. His bushy eyebrows rose at the sight of Carl, but he didn't say a word. Instead, he helped Bennett pull the stretcher out of the van, hiked down the wheels and then nodded toward Ariel. "You lead, I'll follow."

She handed the pendant to Bennett, who pocketed the jewelry without a glance, jumped back into the van and left.

It wasn't until she stepped into the maintenance hall off the side of the lobby before she realized that she probably should have called Cameron. She'd rather he hear about the new *visitor* from her instead of Harold.

Once in the elevator, Harold hit the button for the family floor, asking, "Which apartment?"

Ariel paused. She didn't want to impose on Cam any more than she already had. Even if moving into his apartment hadn't been her idea, she hadn't done much about moving out.

"Mine." Her cheeks burned at Harold's questioning look. She hastily added, "My old apartment."

Thankfully, he only nodded in response.

Once they had Carl tucked between the sheets in the guest bedroom, Ariel walked with Harold to the door. "I haven't talked to Cam yet. Could you…" She wasn't sure how to ask him to withhold information from his employer. "I mean, would you let me…"

"It's not my place." Harold let her off the hook. "I don't know a thing, Ms. Johnson. I'm just a lowly handyman."

Yeah, he was just a handyman who'd lived a few hundred years or so. "I don't agree with you on that, but thank you."

When he left, she pulled out her cell phone as she walked back to check on Carl. After trying Cam's number for the third time, without leaving a message, she gave up. Sooner or later, he'd come barging into her apartment demanding an explanation. She could talk to him then.

For now, however, she was content to sit next to her brother and watch him sleep.

She pushed his overlong bangs from his face, her fingers brushing against his oddly cold flesh. Ariel frowned. Was that normal? She knew nothing about comas, other than what she'd seen on television or the big screen. She'd assumed it would be as if he slept.

She laid the back of her hand against his cheek, checking for a fever. He was so cold, yet not one shiver raced the length of his body.

Ariel pulled the down-filled comforter from the quilt stand and draped it over him, tucking the edges around him. She needed to call a doctor. If nothing else, she wanted reassurance that what seemed odd to her was in fact normal for someone in his condition.

Another shiver of unknown dread raced down his spine. Cam paused, the papers in his hands momentarily forgotten. Something was wrong.

He could sense it in the air—something evil, vile and extremely dangerous lurked inside the Lair. Even his restless beast sensed the danger at hand.

Cam pushed back from his desk and turned to stare out the windows. His careful study of the area turned up nothing that should unsettle him, or the dragon, in this manner.

His computer screen flickered off just as the door to his office slammed against the wall. "What has she done?"

He faced his aunt, realizing that fear and worry added to the shriek to her voice. Seeking to distract her, he shuffled the papers on his desk, and casually asked, "Who?"

"That—that woman you're sleeping with."

Cam raised one eyebrow in silent warning. He wasn't about to listen to any more tirades about Ariel.

Danielle flung herself into one of the chairs. "Something has broken through security."

"I know."

"You know?" She leaned forward, her cheeks flushed, eyes blazing. "Yet you just sit here doing nothing?"

"You might think it wise to race off half-cocked after God knows what, but I don't. I'd rather wait and discover exactly what danger we face first."

Sean strolled into his office. "You'll have to do it without the systems."

Danielle gasped. "They took over the computer?"

There were times when Cam wanted nothing more than to bang his head on his desk—this was quickly turning into one of them.

But before he could say anything, Sean laughed. "They? You mean your hocus-pocus friends?" He folded his lean form into the other chair. "No."

He turned to Cam. "Your freak meter went nuts right before the security warnings on the system flashed. Since a breach threatened, I shut the whole system down."

When he and Braeden had designed what Sean called the freak meter, they'd all discussed what to do with the system during a breach. Since he and Braeden didn't need the cameras to sense an intruder, it was more logical to shut the system down. If nothing else, it would at least save the data from destruction.

"Did either of you invite anyone here?"

Sean rolled his eyes. "Don't look at me."

Danielle tensed her jaw and glared at him. "You know we didn't. It was her."

"She's not family. You know how this works. Nobody with any powers could have come onto our property even with her invitation."

Unless she was either pregnant by, or soul-mated to, one of us.

His dragon rumbled, surprise resonated in the beast's soft roar. Cam instantly slammed a steel wall between his mind and his aunt.

"What are you hiding?" Danielle leaned forward. "You know something."

He knew something all right, but he wasn't about to share it with his aunt. Cam rose. "Go to your apartments, lock the door and stay there. Don't let anyone in until I let you know it's safe." Anxious to find Ariel, he spared them both little more than a glance before racing from his office.

Chapter 19

Aelthed shook from the effort it took to levitate his cloaked puzzle cube through the Drake woman's door before she slammed it closed behind her and threw the locks in place.

He rested the cube atop a small table in the entryway, then stumbled to the hard floor of his prison gasping for breath. While his powers had been getting stronger, it required more energy to remain invisible than anything else.

And it didn't seem to matter how strong his powers became, he was still unable to free himself from this cube that was his cell.

Thankfully, what he was about to do didn't require a great deal of energy. He made himself comfortable in a corner and cleared his mind before bringing a mental vision of the apartment, and the woman, into view.

He paused at the sight before him. For some reason

he hadn't expected her to be so enticing. She pulled a clasp from her hair, letting her long raven tresses cascade freely down her back.

It was a shame she kept her hair bound in such a severe manner. Did she not realize how a man would long to run his hands through such silken beauty?

He was taken aback by her youth. She couldn't possibly be more than sixty years old. From her serious nature, her constant concern for her family, he'd expected her to be older—much more ancient than the woman he watched go about mundane chores.

She paused while washing a mug and turned to stare directly at him. Aelthed let his cloak fall away. He wanted her to see his cube. To touch it.

"Come to me, woman. Come chat a while."

Danielle—he hated that name, it was far too masculine for such a feminine creature—tipped her head and gazed around the empty apartment. "Who's there?"

"I, Aelthed, High Lord of Mirabilus."

"My nephew is the High Lord."

Aelthed cursed silently. He'd momentarily forgotten that little fact. "He is now. But once, long ago, I was the High Lord."

"Where are you?"

He felt the warmth of her thoughts as she searched the apartment for him. She was strong and could prove a worthy adversary. But he had no interests in becoming her foe, he wanted to offer support, in whatever manner might be most helpful to her and the Drake family.

After not reaching out for centuries, Aelthed found the idea daunting. He took a deep breath, then gently rocked the puzzle cube atop the table.

Danielle's curiosity drew her toward him. She stared down at the still-rocking box, asking, "Is this some kind of joke?"

Aelthed steadied his cube and stroked his beard. Joke? She thought this nothing more than an attempt at humor?

"Woman, I am no joke."

She picked the puzzle box up and Aelthed groaned from the heated promise of her touch. Yes, this woman could help him, just as he could help her.

"Is someone in here?" She shook the box, flinging the wizard to the floor.

"Egads, woman, stop it before you kill me yet again." Certain she would still be able to hear him, he transformed back into the misty form of his essence.

"Sorry." Danielle held the cube steady, stroking the smoothness of the ancient wood. "Who cursed you in such a manner?"

"My nephew, Nathan the Learned."

"It must have been long ago, because now it's rumored that he sucks the souls from the dying into his own body."

"It was long ago. And yes, the rumors of his recent atrocities are true."

Danielle crossed the room and stood before the blazing fireplace. "Did you teach him that trick?"

"No." Aelthed wondered idly if the cube would burn, and if it did, would the fire set him free?

"Is that what you want? To be free?"

He'd been right, she was strong. "Isn't that what we all want?"

"Right now I'd settle for being free of Nathan."

Marshaling every iota of power he could muster,

Aelthed sent a caress to press against the woman's cheek. "Then let me help you, Danielle Drake. Let me help you to help me."

Ariel paced the floor alongside her brother's bed. The receptionist had finally found a doctor who would come to the Lair, but due to an emergency, he couldn't make it until tomorrow morning.

After a rather long, sketchy conversation over the phone, he had tried to assure her that as long as Carl was breathing normally, he would be fine. She need not worry overmuch.

Easier said than done since his breathing was hard to detect.

"When had you planned on telling me?"

She jumped at Cam's question and stopped pacing to stand protectively over Carl. "He's my brother, what else was I going to do?"

Cam moved away from the door, coming to a stop behind her. "There wasn't any other choice you could make, but that's not what I meant."

His breath raced warm against her neck. "I thought it best to move him here rather than your apartment."

"You thought wrong, but we can discuss that later, but that's not what I meant, either."

The low, raspy tone of his voice captured her complete attention. His face was expressionless, making it impossible to gauge his mood. She couldn't tell if he was tired, angry and holding back his temper, or if lust was deepening his tone.

But right now, she didn't care. To her astonishment, just his presence was enough. She turned to rest her cheek against his chest. "Then what are you asking?"

His hands covered her shoulders. "When were you

planning to tell me that your beast had chosen mine as a mate?"

Time seemed to come to a screeching halt. Ariel blinked, trying to convince herself that he hadn't spoken in some strange language she couldn't understand.

Finally, she asked, "That I what?"

He leaned back to look down at her. "Don't tell me you didn't know."

To her surprise, when she pushed away he let her go. "No, I didn't. And since I have no clue what you're talking about, how can you be so certain anyone chose you?"

The last thing she needed right now was a mate. Ariel glanced at Carl. She already had one male to care for, how would she manage another?

Cam clenched his jaw. Obviously she wasn't yet as in tune with her inner beast as she should be. He studied the body on the bed and silently groaned. Regardless of what she knew, or didn't know, that's how the intruder had tricked her into inviting him inside the Lair.

If the news that she'd unwittingly chosen a mate wasn't well received, how would she react when he told her that the form on the bed wasn't her brother?

"Sit down."

To his amazement, she did. Although, he would have been less concerned had she not sat on the bed.

He didn't like the idea of her being so close to the threatening danger. But he realized that making an issue of it would get him nowhere, not until he convinced her of the truth. Without alerting her to his actions, he threw an invisible shield between her and the body.

Again, she asked, "What makes you think I've somehow chosen you?"

"Since we're most likely the only two in existence, surely you had to have wondered if it was a possibility."

"No, actually it hadn't crossed my mind."

Her darting glance landed everywhere except on him. "You may be able to lie to anyone else, but not to me, Ariel. Never to me." Cam paused before continuing, "Do you remember when I explained about the added security here at the Lair?"

"The one you use to keep out other wizards?"

"The only way someone with abilities who isn't related to us can physically gain entrance onto the property is if a Drake invites them."

She nodded. "Right, I remember you telling me that before."

Cam motioned toward the body on her bed. "You invited that in, didn't you?"

"That?" She visibly bristled. *"That* is my brother."

"Answer my question."

"Yes, I invited him in. Where else was I going to put him?"

The answer at the tip of his tongue was crude and uncalled for in this situation. She'd be putting Carl's body in a grave soon enough.

Cam held out his hand. "Come here."

She looked up at him, then turned her face away again and crossed her arms against her chest.

He'd known this wasn't going to be easy. He'd known she would fight his explanation every step of the way. She believed that body on the bed to be her brother. A sibling she loved more than she did herself at times. A loved one she would do anything to protect.

It would hurt her terribly when she learned and accepted the truth. But she had to know, had to face what would most likely be the worst pain in her life.

Dragon's Lair was his family's home. Knowingly or not, she'd brought evil here. Not only was his brother and aunt in grave danger, so was his mate.

And nothing on this earth—mortal or otherwise— was going to stop him from protecting what was his.

Cam gave up any attempt at reining in his anger and shouted, "Get up and come here."

Her eyes widened, but she didn't move.

So, once again he took matters into his own hands. The look she shot him as he magically forced her body to him was thunderous. She was beyond angry and he didn't care.

"Let me go." She swatted a hand at him when she was within his reach.

He pulled her into his arms. "You really don't think that's going to stop me, do you?"

"From what?" She pushed uselessly against his chest. "Stop you from doing what?"

"From keeping my mate out of danger."

"Cameron Drake, you've lost your mind. Get your hands off me."

He turned her around so she faced the bed. With one arm snuggly wrapped around her waist, he held her imprisoned tightly against his chest, then grasped her chin with his other hand. "You're going to listen to me."

"You're hurting me, let me go."

He laughed at her bald-faced lie. "Nobody is hurting you."

Yet. Nobody is hurting you yet. Cameron kept the thought to himself. He was going to hurt her in a moment in a way that she might never forgive.

But his feelings didn't matter, neither did his desire for any sliver of forgiveness. The only thing that really mattered was that she know the truth. He had no choice but to force her to clearly see what was before her and then be there for her when despair threatened to swallow her whole.

Ariel tried to tug her head free of his hold. "Cameron, I swear—"

"If you want to swear at anyone, it should be at that thing on the bed."

"Thing?" She kicked back at him. "That's my brother."

"No, Ariel." He easily dodged her foot. "I'm sorry, but it isn't. Your brother is gone."

He held her close enough to feel the tensing of disbelief flow through her. But he knew from the shudder of her indrawn breath that she'd yet to accept the truth.

"No. He's right there. Don't you think I'd know my own brother?"

"You're right, that is his body." In an attempt to lessen the blow, he tipped his head, and with his lips against her ear whispered softly, "Ariel, I'm so sorry, but his soul isn't there. What you see is nothing more than his flesh and bones."

With a strength he didn't know she possessed, she tore free of his hold, shouting, "No! You're wrong." Her voice rose along with her hysteria. "He's just in a coma."

"Ariel, stop." Cam reached out to grab her before she returned to the body, but she quickly dodged his grasp.

Why was Cameron doing this to her? Ariel knelt on the floor beside the bed. This *was* her brother. She watched the shallow rise and fall of his chest. "See? He's still breathing."

Cam was wrong. He had to be. She couldn't lose her brother. He was her life. He was the reason she got up in the mornings and went to work, the reason she forced herself to keep going after their parents died.

She had so much to make up for. They still had things they needed to do together.

He was *not* dead.

Cam silently shook his head and slowly approached the bed.

Ariel reached out to touch Carl's cheek.

"No!" Cam lunged toward her. "Don't."

Before she could reach her brother's face, her hand hit an invisible barrier that prevented her from touching him. She glared at Cam. "What did you do?"

She tried to touch Carl again, and was just as unsuccessful as before. But this time, when her fingers made contact with the unseen shield, her stomach lurched enough to draw a gasp from her lips.

Cam studied her closely. "What's wrong?"

Ariel shrugged off her sudden bout of twisting unease as nothing more than overwrought nerves. "Nothing, I'm fine."

"No, you aren't. You're pale and shaking." He grasped her arm, forcing her to her feet. "I want you out of here. Now."

"I'm not leaving my brother's side."

"And I'm not giving you the choice." He waved a hand toward her.

Ariel closed her eyes, knowing that he was yet again going to physically, magically, propel her from the room. Her heart raced as her stomach once again lurched. But this time, instead of making her ill, the movement fed warmth and strength into her veins.

In her mind's eye, she saw the dragon inside her stretch and unfurl its wings as it came to life on its own.

She opened her eyes, surprised to find herself still standing next to Carl's bed. Ariel smiled before saying,

"I guess you were right all along. It is more than just a dream. I do have a beast of my own."

"More obviously, the beast is as stubbornly foolish as it is human."

"Foolish?" He had no idea of the emotions coursing through her. No inkling of the instinctive need to protect the only family she had left. Nor could he know the strength of her resolve.

Instead of answering her, he caught her off guard and snaked one arm around her waist to draw her close. Ignoring her squirming, Cam pulled her tightly into his embrace.

Ariel relaxed as his warmth radiated through her. She recognized the distinctive heat of Cam's dragon as it sought to bond with the beast inside her.

Unsteady from the emotions whipping through her, she leaned her forehead against his chest. "That isn't fair, you know."

She felt him shrug, before he replied, "Both of you must trust me in this. You have to obey me."

She chuckled to hide her shock. "Obey you?"

Cam slid his arms from around her to grasp her shoulders and hold her slightly away from him. "Ariel, I am not playing some cruel hoax on you. I would never do that. Carl is gone. The Learneds used his body to slip inside the Lair."

The man standing before her was so solemn, so sure of himself. But he was wrong. Dead wrong. "That isn't possible."

"And dragons don't exist, do they?"

Well, he had her on that one, but still, what he was suggesting was ludicrous. She glanced over her shoulder at Carl. "He's still breathing."

"It's nothing but an illusion. The Learneds want you to believe he's alive."

She stared up at Cam. "Since you can't prove otherwise, I do believe he's alive."

He frowned. "I can't protect you well enough in my current form."

"Then let the dragon do it."

"But he doesn't know any magic."

She laughed, not even bothering to hide her amusement at his ridiculous statement. "Oh, Cameron. For the love of God, your dragon *is* magic. How do I know that but you don't?"

His fierce expression deepened for a moment before he gently pushed her aside. "Go stand by the door."

By the time she reached the door and turned around, Cam was gone. But an iridescent dragon loomed over her brother.

She watched, transfixed, while the beast waved away the shield and then with his hand…forefoot… held barely above Carl's face crooned some strangely melodious tune.

Her brother's body vibrated on the bed. The dragon extended one talon and gently drew the tip down Carl's forehead, nose, across his lips and finally to his chin without leaving a trace of blood behind.

A fog swirled around her brother. Ariel's breath caught in her throat as the thick fog gathered speed, darkening with every passing turn.

It rose from around Carl's body like a tornado, spinning into alternating forms of Carl and Jeremy Renalde.

Certain he'd done this on purpose, Ariel screamed at Cam. "What have you done?"

Without waiting for a response, she turned and ran from the room. Ariel raced out of the apartment not sure where to go, but knowing she had to get away from Cam.

Carl had been fine until now. What reason had Cam had to kill him in such a manner before her eyes? Why would he do such a thing?

Didn't he know how much she loved her brother? Didn't he realize that everything she'd done had been for Carl? Didn't he care?

Her breath hitched as a sickening heaviness settled over her heart.

What if her enemy wasn't Renalde? What if the enemy who threatened her more was Cameron Drake?

Frantic, she slammed her palm against the elevator buttons, not caring which floor she ended up on.

"...and that's how I ended up here at the Lair." Aelthed fell silent. He'd not spoken this much in centuries. Now he would wait to hear what Danielle Drake thought of all he'd told her.

"My nephew is a dragon changeling?"

That's all she got out of his overlong explanation? "You didn't know this before?"

"No."

There was a sadness in her voice that he couldn't quite pinpoint. "Maybe he wanted it to be his secret."

"I suppose. But what are we going to do about Nathan and that woman's brother?"

"*That woman* is your nephew's mate."

"No need to remind me." Danielle's long sigh was audible even inside his cube. "I should have expected as much."

"If she dies, he will not get another chance at happiness or love."

"Perhaps, but according to the curse you mentioned, he isn't going to get a chance even if she lives."

"I do not think you quite understand."

"And what don't I understand?"

Her voice came from farther away. Aelthed opened a mental view of the apartment to find that Danielle had gone into the kitchen for something to drink. She returned with a steaming cup in her hand.

"The woman is not just his soul's mate, she too is a changeling."

"Impossible." She took a sip from the cup then set it on the table. "I think you're mistaken."

"Not in the least."

Danielle laughed softly. "Of course not."

Aelthed bristled at the haughty tone of her voice. She thought he was speaking in jest? "Since your nephew is getting ready to do battle with the younger Learned, and the woman has run away to hide in the basement, what are you doing here?"

"How do you suggest I help Cameron?"

"He doesn't need your help. You'd only be in his way."

"Wonderful, I get to go find his gardener."

"Ariel." Aelthed shook his head. "Her name is Ariel."

He sensed, rather than saw, Danielle rise from the sofa and head toward the door. "Where are you going?"

Her footsteps paused. "To the basement?"

"Don't leave my cube here." The last thing he wanted to do was risk ending up back in Nathan's hands.

Danielle returned to grab the cube and drop it into the pocket of her jacket. She patted the pocket. "Happy now?"

"Woman, go do your job."

Chapter 20

Ariel rested her head against the cool brick wall at her back. The basement was shrouded in darkness, yet she'd still chosen to squeeze into the small space between the ancient chest and the wall in the far corner.

With her knees bent beneath her chin and her arms wrapped tightly around them, she wondered what would happen to her now. She had to find a way out of the Lair. If she waited long enough it would be nighttime.

And while she realized that Cam—or his dragon—would sense her every move, she might have a shot at escaping if she could only hold out until he fell asleep. But how was she going to know if he slept or not?

She rested her forehead on her bent knees. Harold had helped her get Carl up to her apartment, perhaps he might be willing to help?

The door to the basement creaked open. Ariel stiffened, pressing farther back into the corner, trying to make herself as small as possible.

For a moment, when the lights didn't come on, she feared the visitor was Cam and held her breath, too afraid to breathe lest he hear the slightest sound.

Footsteps drew nearer, stopping directly in front of her. Ariel bit the inside of her lip to keep from crying out.

"Ariel?"

Her breath escaped on a gasp of shock and fear of another threat to her life. If anyone wanted her dead more than Danielle Drake she didn't know who it might be.

"Ariel, I'm not here to hurt you. I swear it." The woman flicked a lighter and held it to the wick of a candle. She set the candle on top of the chest and sat down on the floor. "I came to help."

"Help?" It was all Ariel could do not to laugh. "Then get me out of here."

"Out of where? The Lair?"

"Yes."

Danielle shook her head. "No, that I won't do. I fear my nephew needs you."

A flash of panic raced down her spine. "Is Cam hurt?"

"No. Not as far as I know."

"Then he doesn't need me for anything."

"Yes, he does." Danielle pulled a wooden puzzle cube from her pocket and set it next to the candle. "Listen carefully. Tell me if you can hear him."

Ariel stared at the cube, certain it was the one Renalde had ordered her to find. Danielle had had it all this time?

"Can you?"

"I don't hear anything."

Danielle sighed. "I know it's hard, but relax, clear your mind of as much clutter as you can and just listen."

Clear her mind? That would be like trying to sweep away a roiling windstorm with a flyswatter. But she closed her eyes and tried her best.

"Ariel, are you listening? Can you hear me?" A strange man's voice seemed to reach out of the darkness toward her.

She jumped. "Yes. Who are you?"

"Aelthed."

She frowned. Why did that name seem familiar? Suddenly it clicked. "You wrote the grimoire."

"Yes."

"And you're related to the Learneds."

"So are the Drakes. We're all related."

Danielle added, "Just one big happy family."

Ariel agreed with the overt sarcasm in Danielle's tone. "So, tell me, what am I supposed to do to help Cam and why should I?"

"You should help him because he's your mate."

The seriousness of Aelthed's tone took her by surprise. "My mate? Why does everyone keep saying that?"

"Because it's true. Are you not as he is? Do you deny the connection of your beasts?"

Ariel ignored Danielle's gasp and subsequent mumbling. "He killed my brother."

"Who?"

"The dragon."

"That's doubtful, my dear. Highly unlikely since his single-minded goal is to protect you."

"You weren't there." Ariel swallowed against the sharp pain in her throat as the scene of her brother's death passed through her mind over and over. "He killed Carl right in front of me."

"No. Listen to me, hear me, Ariel. Cameron has had more than ample opportunity to kill you. But neither the wizard, nor the dragon, have ever harmed you. Am I right?"

It was so hard to think clearly. Her mind was such a jumbled mass of confusion that she had to force her thoughts into some semblance of order. Finally, she answered, "Yes."

"I have no way of knowing what did or didn't happen to your brother. But I sense no lingering, unidentified spirit here at Dragon's Lair. 'Tis doubtful the lad died here. If he had, I would know it."

"How? How would you know?"

"Because, my dear, I too have already passed beyond this life."

Ariel swallowed the sudden lump in her throat. She heard the sincerity in his words. Oh, God, she was alone, there was no one but her. What would she do now?

"I'm sorry. I don't know what you will do besides carry on. You have to, because you aren't alone. You have a dragon lord as a mate. Like it or not, Ariel, if you don't help the man and the dragon become one, there will be no future for either."

Recent images from the grimoire raced across her mind. A man and a dragon fought or a half man and a half dragon fought each other. The participants in the battle were different each time, but cowering in the background was a woman, who was always left alone and unprotected.

She'd wondered at the meaning of the drawings, but Cam had abruptly brushed her off, so she hadn't grilled him again. The thought that formed in her mind was insane. But what aspect of her entire stay at the Lair hadn't been insane in some way?

"He's the one who is cursed, isn't he?"

"Yes, but you can help break that curse. Just as you can now help him defeat your common enemy."

She laughed weakly, more from mental exhaustion than humor. "I don't know how to use my powers. I can't help him."

"Ah, but you can." Danielle broke into the conversation. She leaned forward and touched Ariel's shoulder. "You currently possess more power than anyone else at the Lair, including Cameron."

Ariel stared at her in the flickering candlelight. "I don't know what you're talking…" She paused as a warmth filled her, spreading up through her chest, making her heart pound and lending strength to her overtired mind and body. "What is this?"

Danielle explained, "It's unfettered power. Since you have no experience, you don't yet know what you *can't* do. So everything, anything, is still possible."

"That doesn't make any sense. Why would that happen?"

"There isn't time to teach you what is or isn't possible. All you need to know, what you need to believe, is that your mind has no limitations. You are capable of anything you can imagine."

Ariel looked back at the puzzle cube. "Where are they now?"

"In the gardens behind the Lair."

Marvelous. All her work would have been for nothing. She rose. "You'll see to each other?"

Danielle picked up the cube as she, too, rose and dropped it back into her pocket. "We'll be waiting in my apartment."

* * *

Another fireball flew past Cam's head. He dipped his long neck, easily dodging the flames as he once again circled the unfamiliar wizard. So far he'd been unable to break through the barrier the man had cast around himself.

At this point, it was a standoff that would last until one of them tired and made a costly mistake. As far as Cam was concerned, that would be fine, because he wasn't going to be the one paying the cost.

This wizard, this spawn of the Learned, wasn't leaving the Lair alive.

"Come on, Drake. Come down here and fight like a man instead of an animal. Do you always hide behind a dragon's mask like a coward?"

Cam knew the man was taunting him, trying to get him to let go of dragon form and face him on a more level field of battle. He would have to be an idiot to do something that stupid.

This wasn't a battle he could lose. To keep his family and his mate safe, he had to win.

The only sure way to do that was to use every weapon at his disposal. His thicker hide, wings and ability to breathe fire wasn't something he planned to toss into a closet. That would be like going into a gunfight without bullets.

"Or are you afraid? Do you fear that I'll drain the life from you like my father did that idiot boy?" The Learned tossed back his head and laughed. "I'm sure your little gardener will be just as concerned for your lifeless body as she was for his."

Unheralded, from out of nowhere, another dragon dropped from the sky. In all its iridescent glory, it dived straight for the Learned.

Cam's beast roared as the other dragon jetted past him without a glance. Ariel. She'd only just learned how to take on a dragon's form, and had only flown in a half-altered dream state.

And now she planned to take on the Learned?

He didn't know whether to be merely angry or insanely outraged. So he chose both.

This was *his* kill and she wasn't going to cheat him out of it. If she wanted to play in his world, then she'd do so by the rules.

His rules.

Quickly overtaking her, he soared beneath her, forcing her to break her dive. Once she headed back up toward the clouds, he spun above her and grasped her shoulder between his teeth and shook her.

Frantically beating her wings, she tried to break free, but Cam grabbed her with his talons, forcing her to submit.

Her screams of pain and anger softening to a mewling cry, she slowed the frantic pace of her wings and fell lax in his hold.

He released her instantly, and butting her away with his head, turned back to the stunned wizard. Without wasting another precious second, he dived full force into the now-weaker barrier and broke through.

Talons easily broke through flesh and bone, the man's piercing scream split the air for less than a heartbeat. Cam felt the life force fade away, and within moments, the wizard's body disintegrated into a pile of ashes on the ground.

Certain the immediate danger was gone, Cam turned to face Ariel. She hovered in the air at the tree line, meekly meeting his stare.

To his astonishment, the dragon was as angry at her

as he was. He would have thought the lovesick beast would be willing to cave.

Instead, he wanted to shake his mate until her teeth rattled and she realized what a stupid foolish move it had been to put herself in such danger.

His mate.

Cam lowered his head and closed his eyes as he changed back into human form. He didn't look to see what Ariel was doing.

Right now, he needed to get as far away from her as possible.

He needed to think. To figure out what was different, because something was very different. For the first time in ages, he felt as if there could be a future with someone, with Ariel.

He felt it. His dragon felt it. The curse had suddenly become meaningless.

He should be overjoyed. Elated. Relieved.

Instead, he was uncertain of what sharing a future with another changeling would bring. He'd been the only one for so many years now that being alone was normal.

Having another changeling around—a female one, to boot—would be added responsibility, someone else to worry about. Was he ready for that? At just this second, no. He needed a little time to sort things through.

"Cam!"

He heard her shout, but kept walking toward the door.

"Cam, please. I'm sorry."

Pausing at the side door, he asked, "For what?"

"For accusing you of killing Carl. I should have known better."

Since he hadn't thought she'd actually meant it to

begin with, he'd almost forgotten the incident. "That's not what you should be sorry for."

When she didn't say anything, he left her standing in the night air alone.

Ariel sat on the edge of her bed staring at her packed bags. Harold would be up around six in the morning to take them down to her van. The police and a local doctor had declared Carl's death as related to his prior accident, so the funeral home had just picked up Carl's body. Tomorrow she would make the final arrangements to transport him home for burial.

She fell sideways onto the bed. None of this was supposed to happen. She'd only had to find the pendant, the box, free Carl and then they would go home, together—alive and well.

Instead, Carl was dead, and the only man who would ever understand her, ever accept her for what she was had walked away from her.

Oh, wouldn't her parents be so proud? Actually, she doubted they could have been any more disgusted or disappointed with her than she was herself.

She wanted to cry, needed to sob herself to sleep. But inexplicably, the tears wouldn't come. Finally, she gave up and stood outside on the balcony watching as two owls hunted by moonlight.

What was wrong with Cam? She needed desperately to apologize before she left, but she didn't know what to apologize for.

The idea of leaving the Lair without seeing or speaking to him again made her ill. Physically queasy ill. Her head pounded and her stomach twisted and turned so much that she hadn't bothered to find something to eat for dinner.

Ariel's wandering attention fell briefly on the two owls again. One landed just clear of the woods, while the other seemed to be hunting.

Even if she did get up the nerve to go apologize to him, what would she say then? Sorry? He'd respond with a nod, or maybe even a one- or two-word answer and then what?

In her current state, Ariel knew that even though she could summon the tears now, they would do a free fall if he was around.

The hunting owl returned with what appeared to be some kind of rodent, and dropped it at the other owl's feet.

She frowned. Straightening from her position leaning on the railing, Ariel swore softly.

She shook her head. That was it. She should have realized what she'd done earlier.

Back inside the apartment, she ran a comb through her hair, freshened up her makeup a little and headed for Cam's apartment.

When he didn't answer the door after her third knock, Ariel drew in a deep breath and crossed her fingers before willing herself inside his apartment.

She felt the air around her move and when she opened her eyes, nearly cheered to see she'd actually gone through a solid object.

"You weren't invited in here."

She spun around to face him. "There are rules about that, too?"

"Do you just walk into someone's house uninvited back where you live?"

"No."

"Then don't do it here, either." He turned away. "You can get out the same way you got in."

"Cameron, I'm sorry." Ariel followed him down the hall toward the master bedroom.

He didn't stop, but asked, "For what?"

"For not knowing my place in your world. For not being a proper submissive female dragon."

"Figured that out all by yourself?"

"Actually, no." She saw no reason to lie. "A couple of lovebirds showed me."

He stopped outside his bedroom door and turned to face her. "You and I might be equal here, in human form."

"Might be?" She snapped her mouth shut.

"Fine. You and I are equal here, but not there, Ariel. A beast is a beast. It doesn't matter how civilized I might be as a man, that falls away when I take another form. My human logic can't always control a dragon."

Hesitantly, she reached up and touched his cheek. "I'm sorry."

"Apology accepted." He grabbed her wrist. "Now will you go away?"

Ariel shook her head. "No. Don't you think there's a few things we need to talk about?"

"Like what?"

"Us perhaps?"

"We can discuss it tomorrow."

"No, we can't. I'm leaving in the morning, Cam." She pulled her wrist free and turned to leave. "I just wanted to let you know how sorry I am. And say goodbye."

Ariel swallowed, then gritted her teeth. Just as she had expected, her eyes filled with tears.

"Goodbye? Just like that?"

Knowing she wouldn't be able to speak without making a fool of herself, Ariel nodded.

"You aren't going anywhere, Ariel."

She spun around and shouted at him, "I can't stay here, not like this, not where I'm not wanted."

"You aren't a fool, so don't act like one now." He swept her into his arms, carried her to his room and kicked the door closed behind them. After depositing her on the bed, he warned, "I can find you wherever you go, so don't even think of disappearing."

"I'm not going to disappear. All I want to do is go back to my apartment, finish packing and cry myself to sleep."

"You should cry. You've lost so much today."

The enormity of her brother's death settled around her like a mountain-size boulder. She gasped for breath beneath the weight.

Cam sat next to her and pulled her onto his lap. Holding her tightly against his chest, he urged softly, "Let it go, Ariel. Let it go."

She shook her head, fearing that if she let the tears fall they would never stop. "No. I'm fine."

But he ignored her. Without exchanging another word, Ariel felt his beast reach out to comfort hers. It was as if a great wing pulled her grieving beast closer against the warmth of a steady heartbeat.

She didn't know if the gentle crooning against her ear came from Cam or his beast, nor did she care. The only thing she knew for certain was that she was protected, she was safe and that she was held by someone who cared for her deeply.

A sob tore from between her teeth and she curled her fingers tightly into his shirt, seeking a solid anchor in the coming storm.

He rocked her, whispering over and over, "It's okay, let it go."

Chapter 21

When Ariel awoke, darkness still blanketed the room. She sat up on the bed and took a deep, shuddering breath. She scanned the room wondering how long she'd been asleep.

The door to the bedroom opened, letting in a sliver of light along with Cam. "Here, drink this." He handed her a glass of water.

She took the glass, muttering, "I'm sorry."

While unbuttoning his shirt, he said, "You've nothing to be sorry for, Ariel. Nothing."

"What are you doing?" She eyed him suspiciously.

"Getting ready for bed." He winged one eyebrow in her direction. "You should be doing the same."

"Oh, no, you don't." She nearly leaped from the bed. He wasn't going to trick her into making love. Right now, with her defenses down and no strength to resist him, this would be the most unwise and dangerous mistake she could make.

If he touched her, or kissed her again, how would she ever spend the rest of her life without him?

Ariel tugged on the bedroom door. It wouldn't budge beneath her hand. She closed her eyes and wished herself anywhere but here, but to her chagrin her wishes went unanswered.

"Ariel." He breathed her name against the back of her neck. "Ariel, we're not letting you go. We can't."

She clung to the doorknob for support. "Don't do this, please, don't do this."

"What? Don't do what?" He brushed her hair aside and placed his lips against her heated flesh. "This?" He moved up her neck, angling over to the sensitive spot beneath her ear. "Or this?"

She needed it to be something more than just sex and desire. "Don't try to confuse me by using lust against me."

He stepped away. "Lust?"

"Yes, lust. Desire. Passion. Call it what you will. But isn't that all we share?"

When he didn't respond, she turned around. Cameron stood fully clothed across the room with his arms crossed against his chest, glaring at her.

"Cam?"

The bedroom door swung open. "If that's all this is to you, feel free to leave."

Something in the tone of his voice checked her exit. He sounded unbelievably hurt—disappointed. She took a step toward him, feeling her way with her heart instead of her head.

The longing and pain swirling around her were familiar. She'd sensed them in the dragon, without realizing the man shared the same emotions. Her need to comfort both of them drove her forward.

Ariel swallowed hard, trying to convince herself that she wasn't making a grave mistake. She squared her shoulders and met his hooded gaze. "It's always been more than just lust for me. Always."

She took another step toward him. "I thought that's all it was to you. A way to gain what you wanted from the enemy, until you and your dragon made love to me." She took a deep breath to steady her faltering voice. "I love you, Cameron Drake. I love both the wizard and the dragon, dearly."

He met her halfway across the room. "I won't lie. I desired you the moment I caught you in the workshop at Mirabilus."

He took her hands in his and lifted them to his lips. Placing a kiss on her fingertips, he said, "And I've been madly in love with you since you shot me with your stun gun. Then, to make matters worse, you went and petted the dragon, making him fall head over heels goofy for you, too." He lowered his voice. "And you heard his need for love and answered it by caring."

He shot her that all-too-familiar half smile that took her breath away. "If that wasn't enough, you laughed at me when I claimed my dragon had no abilities. You, a mere mortal, with one sentence, made it clear that just being a dragon was all the magic needed to end an ancient curse. It wounds my ego deeply to admit you were right."

Cam dropped down to one knee. "Ariel, I love you. You are my angel of healing, my harbinger of rebirth. Stay with me. Marry me and I swear that I will prove how much I love you each and every day we share together."

She knew that crying again would make him feel guilty and that if she started, it would be hard to stop. So, to keep from falling into a weeping puddle, she tossed her head and quipped, "I suppose I still have to be a submissive female dragon to your dominant male?"

He laughed softly and before she knew what he was planning, found herself naked on the bed, with him next to her.

Cam handed her a silk scarf. "I'll make you a deal. You be the submissive dragon and I'll be the submissive lover in bed if you want."

Ariel dropped the scarf to the floor, rolled over onto his chest and gazed down at him. "I'll have to think about that one. But I do know one thing."

He wrapped his arms around her and kissed the end of her nose. "What?"

"That I love you more than I can say. But if you don't kiss me quick, I'm going to turn into a blubbering nit."

Cameron pressed his lips against hers, whispering, "We can't have that, now, can we?"

* * * * *

REQUEST YOUR FREE BOOKS!

2 FREE NOVELS FROM THE PARANORMAL ROMANCE COLLECTION PLUS 2 FREE GIFTS!

YES! Please send me 2 FREE novels from the Paranormal Romance Collection and my 2 FREE gifts (gifts are worth about $10). After receiving them, if I don't wish to receive any more books, I can return the shipping statement marked "cancel." If I don't cancel, I will receive 4 brand-new novels every month and be billed just $21.42 in the U.S. or $23.46 in Canada. That's a saving of at least 21% off the cover price of all 4 books. It's quite a bargain! Shipping and handling is just 50¢ per book in the U.S. and 75¢ per book in Canada.* I understand that accepting the 2 free books and gifts places me under no obligation to buy anything. I can always return a shipment and cancel at any time. Even if I never buy another book, the two free books and gifts are mine to keep forever.

237/337 HDN FEL2

Name	(PLEASE PRINT)

Address	Apt. #

City	State/Prov.	Zip/Postal Code

Signature (if under 18, a parent or guardian must sign)

Mail to the **Reader Service**:
IN U.S.A.: P.O. Box 1867, Buffalo, NY 14240-1867
IN CANADA: P.O. Box 609, Fort Erie, Ontario L2A 5X3

Not valid for current subscribers to the Paranormal Romance Collection or Harlequin® Nocturne™ books.

**Want to try two free books from another line?
Call 1-800-873-8635 or visit www.ReaderService.com.**

* Terms and prices subject to change without notice. Prices do not include applicable taxes. Sales tax applicable in N.Y. Canadian residents will be charged applicable taxes. Offer not valid in Quebec. This offer is limited to one order per household. All orders subject to credit approval. Credit or debit balances in a customer's account(s) may be offset by any other outstanding balance owed by or to the customer. Please allow 4 to 6 weeks for delivery. Offer available while quantities last.

Your Privacy—The Reader Service is committed to protecting your privacy. Our Privacy Policy is available online at www.ReaderService.com or upon request from the Reader Service.

We make a portion of our mailing list available to reputable third parties that offer products we believe may interest you. If you prefer that we not exchange your name with third parties, or if you wish to clarify or modify your communication preferences, please visit us at www.ReaderService.com/consumerschoice or write to us at Reader Service Preference Service, P.O. Box 9062, Buffalo, NY 14269. Include your complete name and address.

Harlequin®

ROMANTIC
SUSPENSE

CINDY DEES

takes you on a wild journey to find the truth
in her new miniseries

Code X

Aiden McKay is more than just an ordinary man. As part of
an elite secret organization, Aiden was genetically enhanced
to increase his lung capacity and spend extended time under
water. He is a committed soldier, focused and dedicated
to his job. But when Aiden saves impulsive free spirit
Sunny Jordan from drowning she promptly overturns his
entire orderly, solitary world.

As the danger creeps closer, Adien soon realizes Sunny is the
target…but can he save her in time?

Breathless Encounter

Find out this August!

plus
**BONUS
STORY
INSIDE!**

Look out for a reader-favorite bonus story included in each
Harlequin Romantic Suspense book this August!

Werewolf and elite U.S. Navy SEAL, Matt Parker, must set aside his prejudices and partner with beautiful Fae Sienna McClare to find a magic orb that threatens to expose the secret nature of his entire team.

Harlequin® Nocturne presents the debut of beloved author Bonnie Vanak's new miniseries, PHOENIX FORCE.

Enjoy a sneak preview of THE COVERT WOLF, available August 2012 from Harlequin® Nocturne.

Sienna McClare was Fae, accustomed to open air and fields. Not this boxy subway car.

As the oily smell of fear clogged her nostrils, she inhaled deeply, tried thinking of tall pines waving in the wind, the chatter of birds and a deer cropping grass. A wolf watching a deer, waiting. Prey. Images of fangs flashing, tearing, wet sounds…

No!

She fought the panic freezing her blood. And was gradually able to push the fear down into a dark spot deep inside her. The stench of Draicon werewolf clung to her like cheap perfume.

Sienna hated glamouring herself as a Draicon werewolf, but it was necessary if she was going to find the Orb of Light. Someone had stolen the Orb from her colony, the Los Lobos Fae. A Draicon who'd previously been seen in the area was suspected. Sienna had eagerly seized the chance to help when asked because finding it meant she would no longer be an outcast. The Fae had cast her out when she turned twenty-one because she was the bastard child of a sweet-faced Fae and a Draicon killer. But if she found the Orb, Sienna could return to the only home she'd known. It also meant she could recover her lost memories.

Every time she tried searching for her past, she met with a closed door. Who was she? Which side ruled her?

Fae or Draicon?

Draicon, no way in hell.

Sensing someone staring, she glanced up, saw a man across the aisle. He was heavily muscled and radiated power and confidence. Yet he also had the face of a gentle warrior. Sienna's breath caught. She felt a stir of sexual chemistry.

He was as lonely and grief stricken as she was. Her heart twisted. Who had hurt this man? She wanted to go to him, comfort him and ease his sorrow. Sienna smiled.

An odd connection flared between them. Sienna locked her gaze to his, desperately needing someone who understood.

Then her nostrils flared as she caught his scent. Hatred boiled to the surface. Not a man. Draicon.

The enemy.

Find out what happens next in THE COVERT WOLF by Bonnie Vanak.

Available August 2012 from Harlequin® Nocturne wherever books are sold.

red-hot reads

He was looking for adventure...and he found her.

Kate Hoffmann

brings you another scorching tale

With just a bus ticket and $100 in his pocket, Dermot Quinn
sets out to experience life as his Irish immigrant grandfather
had—penniless, unemployed and living in the moment.
So when he takes a job as a farmhand, Dermot expects he'll
work for a while, then be on his way. The last thing he expects
is to find passion with country girl Rachel Howe, and his
wanderlust turning into a lust of another kind.

THE MIGHTY QUINNS:
DERMOT

Available August 2012 wherever books are sold!